"Oh Carly, Carly, what are you doing?"

Carly suddenly felt very cold. "I'm looking for my father, Millie. That's all."

"No, Carly. That's not all." Millie turned toward her, her dark eyes huge and sorrowful. "I'm sure you don't mean to hurt anyone. The problem is, you don't understand the harm you're doing."

Carly gestured impatiently. "Then explain it to me."

Millie smiled and reached out, gently touching Carly's hair. "You don't understand anything, Carly," she said, her voice dreamy. "You don't understand how I feel about you. How much I care."

Carly blinked. The woman was acting in a very puzzling way and Carly wasn't sure she liked it. Taking a deep breath, she said, "If you care so much about me, why don't you tell me the truth?" She turned to keep Millie from avoiding her gaze. "What is it that you know about my father?"

ABOUT THE AUTHOR

"I've lived in Holland and Guam, Hawaii and Washington, D.C.," writes Helen Conrad, "but I'm a native born Californian and I must admit the Golden State is my favorite setting. Right now I'm living in the Los Angeles area, raising four boys." A popular author of children's books and short stories as well as romance novels, Helen Conrad has published more than forty love stories. "I love the spark that ignites between a man and a woman," she writes, "and happy endings are the only kind I want to hear about. After all, isn't that what life is all about?"

Books by Helen Conrad

HARLEQUIN SUPERROMANCE
322–DESPERADO

HARLEQUIN TEMPTATION
3–EVERLASTING
118–DIAMOND IN THE ROUGH

HARLEQUIN ROMANCE
2731–TEARS OF GOLD

JOE'S MIRACLE

Helen Conrad

Harlequin Books

TORONTO • NEW YORK • LONDON
AMSTERDAM • PARIS • SYDNEY • HAMBURG
STOCKHOLM • ATHENS • TOKYO • MILAN
MADRID • WARSAW • BUDAPEST • AUCKLAND

Published April 1993

ISBN 0-373-70544-1

JOE'S MIRACLE

To Marie,
who survived her cattle
dying in the halls and ended up
owning the ranch after all

CHAPTER ONE

"I NEED A REAL WOMAN, Doris. Not some slick little refugee from the fast lane."

The rugged man in the denims and cowboy boots pushed his wide-brimmed hat back on his head, his handsome face a picture of stubborn resistance.

Doris sighed, rolled her brown eyes and leaned across the Formica café table so that she wouldn't be heard by all the eavesdroppers at the other tables.

"Joe Matthews, you've got some nerve. It's not like you've got people lining up to take this job of yours, you know. Those two little kids are cute as the dickens, but they aren't angels, and everybody knows it. You've gone through all the local talent. There's not a woman left in this town who would tackle taking care of Jeremy and Beth, much less you and that big old house of yours. I'm offering you someone decent who will do for you for a while. You won't find anybody better, and you know it."

"'Decent,'" Joe echoed, his voice, usually edged with humor, just this side of bitter this time. He raised his dark, cloudy eyes and gazed at her with self-deprecating amusement. "Is that what it's all come down to, Doris? Do I have to settle for 'decent'?"

Doris leaned back, her plump hand smoothing the apron of her waitress uniform. She was pleased, thinking she was finally getting through to him.

"My cousin Carly is more than decent, honey. Come on. You can see that for yourself."

Reluctantly, he turned and looked at the woman Doris was talking about. She was perched on a stool at the counter, her long, silver-blond hair hanging like a banner of silk down her back. The dark panes of her sunglasses stared back at him. Even though her eyes were obscured, he could see she was pretty. Too skinny. But pretty. Her long, slender legs were made for the designer jeans she wore. The plaid shirt was rayon rather than cotton. And the short suede jacket was cut for fashion rather than utility. Expensive clothes. City clothes. This woman was no more a farm housekeeper than he was a stockbroker.

He thought of his two kids, Beth and Jeremy, and that awful empty feeling in the pit of his stomach was back again. He felt like a man in a shipwreck trying to save his kids, trying to get each one something to cling to while he searched for the life raft, and all the time the water was swirling harder and harder around them, and he was beginning to wonder if he was really going to save them after all.

He needed help. That was certain. But this little piece of city driftwood wasn't a life preserver.

"Give me a break, Doris," he growled, turning back. "When it comes to feeding a family, the only thing she'll know how to make is reservations. I need someone better than that."

Doris set her round shoulders and glared at him. "What you need, Joe, is a miracle. You haven't had anyone who lasted more than four weeks with those kids in two years of trying." She sighed and shook her head of soft brown curls. "Well, Carly ain't no miracle. But she's about the only chance you've got of having your kids looked after any time soon. You'd be a fool to turn her down."

He looked back at her and his wide mouth twisted into a grin that held as much pain as humor. "Call me crazy," he drawled. "But I'm not ready to take in tourists yet, just because the Dewdrop Inn went and burned down just when you needed it." His dark eyes sharpened. "Say, why can't she stay with you, anyway?"

"I..." Doris hesitated. This was something of a sore spot with her and she almost blushed. "Well, you see, Brian's been sort of staying with me for a while now, and he's lookin' to be just on this side of proposing. Carly is my cousin and all, but...well, darn it, look at her. She's just too...too good-looking."

His grin was affectionate but teasing. "And you don't want Brian to lose his focus before he gets that big question out of the way. Is that it?"

She slapped at his hand and he threw back his head and laughed. "Even you can see that the woman is bad news," Joe told her when he sobered, glancing back across the room. "So why the hell would I want her?"

CARLY WATCHED the two of them nervously. Her slender hand reached automatically for her purse, going for a cigarette. Stopping herself, she sighed softly. No more smoking. That had been one of the conditions she'd laid down for herself. She was going to be clean out here in the country. Organic foods. Lots of sleep. She needed space to think, and clean living was going to be her way of finding it.

She'd already quit smoking, actually. She'd thrown away her last pack just before her bus had left Washington, D.C. The funny thing was, she hadn't really missed it. There had been so much to see and think about on that bus trip, she hadn't had time to miss it.

The bus. It made her smile to think of that trip. She'd decided to take the bus to California because she knew Mark would search the airports. And the private limousine companies. And maybe even the luxury shipping lines for cruises around the Gulf. But he would never think to check the bus lines. The concept of his little Carly taking a bus with the other plebeians would be beyond his comprehension.

But she'd done exactly that and she'd been pretty darned proud of herself. She'd had plenty of time to calm down and begin to get her head together on the long trip. And the bus had brought her right into town, straight to where her cousin Doris worked as a waitress in this little corner café.

The only problem was, Doris didn't seem to have room for her.

"Why don't you go on down to L.A.?" Doris had suggested. "You must have old friends there from your high school years."

"No." Carly had been glad for the dark glasses at that point. Without them, Doris would surely have seen the emotion in her eyes. Going to L.A. would be no better than staying in Washington. She had to get away from that sort of life, those sorts of people. She'd come all the way across country looking for Amberville, the little town she remembered as a piece of slow, simple heaven in the Central California farm belt—the heartland.

"No, Doris, I don't want to go to L.A. I want to be here, to remember my childhood, to learn to breathe again."

Her cousin's kindly face had softened. "How old were you when your mama dragged you off to Hollywood to try to make you a movie star? Let's see. I was about eighteen, so you must have been . . ."

"Ten. I was just ten."

"And you never did become a movie star, did you?"

It wasn't said in a malicious way, but there was a certain satisfaction in Doris's tone. *And why not?* Carly thought to herself. *Why not?*

"No, I never did become a movie star, or even anything close," she admitted with a smile. "That was my mother's dream, not mine."

"But you've done pretty well for yourself in the East, haven't you? Didn't you say you were a secretary . . . ?"

"Administrative assistant," Carly corrected her quickly, then frowned, impatient with herself. As if that really made any difference. It had seemed an important distinction once, but the farther away from Washington she got, the more those lines seemed to blur.

"Whatever," Doris said. "But you work for somebody in government or something, don't you? A good job in the big city. So what do you want to come back here for?"

Carly hesitated. There was no way she was going to be able to explain such a complicated set of reasons to her cousin right here in the café between customers.

"I...I needed a rest," she said simply. "I wanted to go back to my roots and remember who I really am."

Doris looked at her as though she'd suggested worshiping pyramids and having her body frozen for posterity. "Roots," she muttered rather scornfully. "Well, I never had no time to think about my roots. I've been too busy making a living all these years to worry about things like that."

Carly knew there would be no percentage in trying to explain, so she ignored her cousin's remark. "I just wanted to come back, Doris. I wanted to see the town where I lived my first ten years."

Doris pursed her lips and leaned closer, saying in a low voice, "Are you sure that's all? You haven't come back looking for your father, have you? Because I can tell you right now he hasn't been seen in this town for years and years. Let sleeping dogs lie, I always say. You shouldn't go hunting for things that might end up hurting you in the long run."

Carly's heart skipped a beat and suddenly she was short of breath. "No, I didn't come back to find my father."

At least, she hadn't thought that was why she'd been so obsessed with coming back here. Now that Doris had put it in words, she wasn't so sure. "Did you...did you know him very well?" she ventured.

Doris shook her head emphatically. "My mama didn't have no truck with that man. You probably don't remember, but she wouldn't even let me go over and visit with you and your family the last year you were in town. That next year, I went away and lived in the Bay Area for a while, and when I came back, he had left."

"Oh." It was just as well. Something in her had shied away from even thinking about her father for years. In planning to come back, she had never once considered that he might be here. But now that Doris had brought the subject up, thoughts began to tease her. She had always said that she didn't miss her father, that her mother was all she needed. The memories of that last year she knew him were full of arguments and hurt silences. She'd loved him, of course, and he had never been unkind to her. But he'd never tried to contact her either, in all these years since her mother had taken her away. That, and loyalty to her mother, had kept her from wanting to see him.

But her mother was gone now. Meeting her father might be interesting. What if she found him? Would that help take care of this emptiness she felt inside? She shrugged those thoughts away and turned back to her cousin.

"If you don't have room for me," she said, "maybe you know someone with a room to rent out for a few weeks. I would certainly be willing to pay. And to help with housework, or whatever, if that would make a difference."

It was at that moment that a little light had appeared in Doris's eyes and she had looked over at the table where Joe Matthews was having a late afternoon snack of biscuits and gravy.

"I wonder..." she said softly, speculatively. Her brown eyes studied Joe, then shifted and gazed at Carly for a moment with a frown.

"All I need is a place to sleep," Carly was saying. "I plan to spend most of my days sitting out in the sun and smelling the good clean earth."

"Smelling what?" Now Doris was pretty sure her cousin really was tetched. She made a face and shook her head. "Roots," she muttered. She looked back at Joe and a faint smile tickled her lips into a mischievous curl. "Oh well," she said with a short laugh. And then she turned back to Carly, all business.

"What would you think about staying on a citrus ranch with two cute little kids to look after?" she said.

"Kids?" Carly looked around and noted the man Doris was staring at. He looked big and attractive. The last thing in the world she needed was another man in her life. "I don't know about kids. I've never—"

"There's nothing to it. The kids are adorable. And they haven't had a good woman to look after them for almost two years now. That's when they lost their mom. And it wouldn't be awkward or anything, because Joe's mother lives with them, too. She's kind of an invalid, but..."

A widower with two little motherless children. Carly frowned, pretty sure this was a situation she wasn't experienced enough to cope with. "I don't know, Doris—"

"Don't be ridiculous! It'll be a piece of cake." She reached for a slice of pie and thrust it in front of her cousin. "You just sit here and eat this. I'll go on over and ask Joe if he wants you."

"Doris!"

But Doris was gone and Carly could only stare after her and wonder what it was she was getting herself into. Little kids. A man who had lost his wife. This was a far cry from scheduling briefings with analysts and taking constituents out to lunch. She didn't have the slightest idea how she would manage it.

But wait a minute. How hard could it be? Other women did this sort of thing all the time. Nurturing was supposed to be intuitive, wasn't it? She was a woman; therefore, it should all come naturally.

She glanced down at the piece of pie, tempted. For years now she had trained herself to be so careful of what she ate, knowing her tendency to gain weight easily. Rice cakes, fruit juices and thin slices of cold-water fish—that was what she lived on. Just one bite of that cherry pie and she was sure she would gain fifteen pounds. Pushing it away, she turned back to look at Doris and the man she was talking to.

Things were not going well. She saw him shaking his head, his face slightly amused, as though he couldn't imagine Carly doing a real day's work. He glanced her way, saying something to Doris, and the scorn in his gaze stung, making her sit up straighter, making her fingers begin reaching for that nonexistent cigarette again. He was going to turn her down. Her pride rose, and she swung her legs around and slid off the stool. A moment before she hadn't been sure she wanted this job. Now it was a challenge she couldn't ignore. Maybe it was time to plead her own case.

JOE WATCHED HER coming toward the table and he knew his first instincts had been right. This woman wouldn't last a week in the country. She'd break a nail and be on the phone to the paramedics. It wouldn't be worth the effort.

He had to admit she was attractive, in an angular sort of way. She walked nice, all smooth and gliding. He might have said she moved like a cat, if only she weren't so darned bony.

"Hi." She stopped and looked down at him, slipping off the dark glasses to reveal eyes as crystal blue as winter frost on a mountain pond. "I'm Carly Stevens."

She held out her hand and he took it, noting the perfect, crimson nails, just as he'd thought.

"I'm Joe Matthews," he said slowly, looking her over, his eyes cynically hooded. "Nice to meet you, Carly."

"I can tell you've got your doubts about me," she said bluntly, moving her hands to her hips. "You're turning me down, aren't you?"

Doris gasped. "Now, Carly, Joe doesn't know—"

She glanced down at Doris and put her hand on her cousin's shoulder, pressing gently. "Doris, why don't you go on back to work? Let me talk to the man."

Doris looked from Carly to Joe and back again, then slid out of the booth, shaking her head. Carly slid in to take her place, her long, silvery hair fluttering in behind to settle around her shoulders.

Joe watched her hair come to rest and noted how her hands reached up automatically to straighten her collar with a little tug. She looked good and she knew how to look even better. She was just a little too sure of herself for him. A little too self-aware. So she thought she could use her feminine charms to talk him into this, did she? He felt the muscles in his neck tighten. What did she think he was, some hayseed she could manipulate at will? His eyelids drooped and he waited for her to speak first.

She flattened her hands on the shiny red surface of the table and took a deep breath. Staring straight across the table, her smile was friendly but reserved. "I understand you need someone to stay at your house and take care of your two children," she said coolly. "I need a place to stay, and I'm willing to do the work." She shrugged and her porcelain chin rose slightly. "It seems to me there is a logical connection here. Don't you agree?"

Her smooth, no-nonsense tone usually worked just fine with congressional aides and pages, but Joe Matthews seemed to be made of sterner stuff. Instead of answering, he merely grinned, slow and sassy.

"Are you one of those big-city feminists?" he asked. "What do you want to hang around our little backwater town for?" His eyes narrowed as a thought occurred to him. "Unless you're hiding out. Is that it? Are you running from something?"

Carly blinked, stunned. Was that really how she came across? That hurt, and some of her reaction was evident in her voice when she replied. "I was born in this town, Mr. Matthews. I think I have as much right to be here as anyone."

He frowned. Either she was playacting, or she wasn't really as hard as he'd thought. "Hey, look, I'm sorry. I..."

Looking up, she met his eyes and caught something strange there as he studied her, some sort of shock of connection. She looked away quickly. She wasn't sure if she were going to get this job or not, but just in case, she wanted to make sure he didn't make any mistakes about her intentions.

"Well, you can see that I'm from the city. And you can see that I'm not usually looking for this kind of work." She paused, wondering why she was trying so hard to get a job she wasn't even sure she wanted, why she was trying to convince a man who was definitely getting on her nerves to let her into his life.

"I'll be perfectly straight with you. I'm not going to be here forever. I've taken an indefinite leave of absence from a career position in the city, a position I have every intention of returning to eventually. And yes, I'm running from something, hiding from something." This impulse to be so open made her heart beat just a little faster. She was usually a very controlled person, and she didn't confide in strangers. "But it's not the law or anything like that. It's purely personal, nothing that could hurt your kids in any way. Still, it does mean I won't be offering any references. If you can't take Doris's word for my honesty, I guess we might as well hang it up right now. But I do need a place to stay, and I would like the job." She spread her hands on the table again and looked at him hopefully. After all, what was she going to do if he turned her down?

She looked damned appealing, gazing up at him like that. He frowned, just to make sure she realized he wasn't a pushover, and thought it over. What would it hurt to have her come out for a couple of weeks? The kids needed someone desperately, and he . . .

His jaw tightened and he swore silently at himself. What the hell was he thinking? He didn't need anybody.

"What do you know about raising kids?" he asked her softly.

She lifted her chin even higher. "Not a thing."

He sat back as though that settled it, but she wasn't ready to give up yet. "That doesn't mean I couldn't learn. After all, I was a kid once myself. And it wasn't all that long ago."

He couldn't tell her age. She could have been forty, or fourteen, with those long, slim lines and that flaxen hair. Her blue eyes had a weathered look, as though they'd seen too much, and yet her mouth was soft, the lips full and tender-looking. She was like no woman he had ever met before. But that didn't mean she would be good at looking after his kids.

"How old are you?" he asked.

She drew back just a little, hesitating, as if the question was almost too personal for some reason.

"I'm twenty-seven," she said at last.

"Ever been married?"

"No."

A cynical impulse twisted his wide mouth. "Ever want to be?" he flashed at her, one eyebrow raised.

She opened her mouth but didn't know what to say. "I . . . I don't know," she finally said.

"You don't know? Twenty-seven and you still haven't decided if you ever want to marry and have kids of your own?"

But that was just the question, she thought, the reason behind all the other reasons that she had come all this way. She looked into his eyes and wondered if she could tell him that. Years of image-making, of being careful of every syllable she uttered, stood in the way.

She'd told him her age, but that had been simple compared to this. She glanced around the room as though looking for help. She saw Doris, leaning on the counter and talking to an elderly man in overalls, his face tanned and lined from years in the sun. The huge old ceiling fan was spinning, making a slight chugging noise. A young mother was feeding her toddler ice cream in a corner booth, and he was laughing, ice cream running down his chin. The jukebox was playing soft and low, a fifties tune about the sea of love. A teenage boy walked in, his shoulders hunched slightly, apologetically, as though he weren't yet used to his new body. This could have been a scene from her childhood. Hardly a thing had changed. The sounds were right. The smells were right. She felt at home here in some irrational way she couldn't explain. A wave of grateful affection swept over her and she looked back at the man across the table.

"I don't know," she told him. "If you want to know the truth, that is what I came here to figure out for myself. Getting married is a big step."

His brown eyes darkened and a line appeared between his brows. "But a natural step for most people."

"Yes, but—"

"You've got a career to consider," he said.

Carly hesitated. "Sort of," she allowed. "But it's more than that. I..."

His voice hardened. "You left some poor jerk behind waiting for your answer while you came out to the country to 'find yourself.' Is that it?"

Not quite. But close. "That's not important," she said, waving the concept away with a flick of her hand. She was trying to be honest here, trying to get it right. "I did come back here to think and try to get my head together—"

"Not important?" He cut in with the words, using them like weapons. There was something smoldering in his eyes and Carly frowned, surprised by it, not sure what to make of it. "Not important?" he said again. She had a feeling he was taking what she'd said the wrong way. She was trying hard to be honest, but it wasn't working the way it should.

A place to stay was slipping out of her grasp. What was she going to do if she was left with nothing? There was always the Rodeside Inn in neighboring Stampton, but that wasn't what she wanted. She had to stay in Amberville, to breathe it in, to be a part of it again. She was just going to have to try harder to convince this stubborn man.

"What does it matter to you why I came?" she asked him earnestly. "I'm here. I'll be here long enough to help you out, but not long enough to do any damage." Sitting back, she gazed into his dark eyes with all her conviction. "I'd like to stay at your place. Why don't we just try it for one night? Then, if you still can't stand me..."

Despite himself, he was smiling. "Who said I can't stand you?" he asked gruffly. What the hell—why was he torturing her this way? She was certainly a damned sight better than the other women he had hired to take care of his children. He could see that right away. Maybe it would work. "Who knows? Maybe I was wrong. It might just do you a world of good to come on out to my place and 'find yourself.' "

She blinked, not sure how to take this turnaround, not sure she liked his new mood. "Do you mean I can have the job?"

He didn't answer for a long moment, his gaze sliding over her face as though he were searching for something, some identity or some remembered feature.

"I'll give you a chance at it," he said at last. "Let's call it a probationary period."

"Great." She looked at him expectantly, wondering why he didn't look at all pleased. "When do I start?"

He shrugged. "No time like the present." He started to slide out of the booth. "You got bags someplace?"

"By the door."

"Let's go. My truck's outside."

He went for her bags and she went to the counter to say goodbye to Doris, not sure if she were elated or apprehensive. "I guess I'm off," she told her cousin, giving her a hug.

"Give me a call and let me know how you're doing." Doris wrote down her number on a slip of paper and pressed it into Carly's hand. "You'll be okay out there. The kids—well, they've had their problems, but then they haven't had a mother for almost two years now. I'm sure you'll be great for them."

Carly looked at her uncertainly, wondering if she shouldn't take this opportunity to back quickly out of this deal. A horn sounded and she looked outside.

"That's Joe," Doris said. "You'd best be going."

Carly looked at her and nodded. "I guess so." She squeezed her hand. "Thanks." And then she was off, running for the door.

"She going out to Joe's place?" the elderly man at the counter asked Doris.

"That's right."

The man shook his head. "A pretty little thing like that? Didn't anybody tell her those kids are hell on wheels?"

Doris shook her head slowly, watching as the truck rode out of sight around the corner. "She'll be okay," she said softly, almost to herself. "Don't you think?"

CHAPTER TWO

THE TRUCK WAS A PICKUP, relatively new, not quite clean, but pretty comfortable. Carly clung to the seat, bouncing but determined not to let the man driving know that she couldn't find the seat belt. Looking out the dusty window she examined the town in a way she hadn't been able to coming in on the bus. It was small but bustling, with stores and gas stations and a general feed supply, a city hall that could have used a coat of paint and a park where young mothers took their babies. What she saw didn't look very familiar, but why should it? After all, it had been almost twenty years ago that she had moved away. Things changed in that length of time.

Joe drove slowly. Horns honked and people waved. He seemed to know everyone in town. More than one friend did a double take when they noticed her sitting beside him in the cab. She glanced over to see how he was reacting to that sort of interest, but his face didn't give her a clue, and she looked back out at the town.

It would be fun to see her old house again. If only she could remember where it had been. She knew it was near a little mom-and-pop grocery store, and that there was a church on the corner....

"Oh, could we...would you mind turning here and going down that side street?" she asked him quickly.

There was a small white church that looked familiar. Maybe...

"Just turn left and go to the end of the block. Thanks."

She studied the houses, looking for something she might recognize. But there were only two or three left that might date from her era. Half of the block had been razed and a huge apartment building hovered malevolently over the neighborhood. The other end of the block had been turned into a parking lot for a new supermarket. Carly turned, looking back. Could this have been her street? She would probably never know now.

"What are you looking for?" he asked her, slowing to a crawl.

"I...nothing." She gave him a quick smile. "Sorry. You can go back to the main drag."

He glanced at her. She looked tense, sitting there on the edge of her seat. It was on the tip of his tongue to tell her to use the seat belt, but he held it back. Something about her just plain annoyed him, and he wasn't sure what it was.

"Hey, Joe!"

Joe braked and backed up to where the teenage boy who had called out his name was standing beside his shiny but aging silver Firebird.

"Hey, Trevor. How are you?" He turned to Carly. "Trevor Gordon," he explained quickly as they stopped beside the tall, skinny and very blond young man. "He works for me on afternoons and weekends."

The boy's eyes widened as he caught sight of Carly. "Uh, I'm fine."

"What are you doing here?"

"I, uh, I was just giving Tracy Kramer a ride home from school." He craned his neck a bit, trying to see better around Joe's head. Carly's presence was obviously a source of wonder to him.

Joe smiled, enjoying the boy's interest. No one in this town had seen him with a woman since Ellen. In fact, probably no one could remember him ever with anyone else. He could easily introduce her, let Trevor know she was just someone he was hiring. But what the hell. Let him stew. Let the whole town wonder.

"Hey, did you hear?" The boy gave up trying to see Carly and gazed intently at Joe. "The avocado rustlers hit the Abbott place last night."

"No. I hadn't heard. Did they get much?"

Trevor shrugged. "Darn near his whole crop of Haas, so I hear. I guess he's about wiped out."

Joe nodded slowly, frowning. "We're going to have to go through with the patrol the fellas have been talking about. And we'd better do it soon, before more of us get hit." He put the car back in gear. "Say hi to your mom for me," he said.

"Right. Sure will."

They were on their way again and Joe glanced over at Carly one more time. Something caught in his throat as he looked at her. She'd taken the sunglasses off again and her silver hair was swirling around her in the breeze from the window. She looked almost surreal, otherworldly. He had a pang, wishing he had introduced her to Trevor and explained. No wonder the boy was staring.

Damn it all, he didn't know what he was doing with her anyway. She wasn't going to work out. Anyone with half a brain could see that. Why was he wasting his time? When she'd said she was letting some poor sap who loved her wait while she ran off to figure things out he should have put on the brakes right there. He wasn't running a drop-in center, after all. If he went out and hired all the women who were wandering around trying to "find" themselves, he'd have himself quite a harem.

Well, he'd give her one night to see what taking care of two active youngsters was all about, and then he'd probably be giving her a ride back into town in the morning. There was nothing he could do about it now. He was more or less committed.

The houses fell away and they were on the open road. Carly hadn't realized they would be going so far out of town. But that was what she wanted, wasn't it?—to be as far away from civilization as possible, out in the clean, fresh air. Sitting back, she breathed in the scent of orange blossoms and thought about her situation. Just a week before, she'd been riding in the back of a taxi as it fought heavy traffic to make a few blocks headway in the gridlock that was downtown Washington, D.C. And now, here she was, in a pickup truck, heading for a farm, with the wind in her hair and not another vehicle in sight. Orange blossoms versus exhaust fumes. She had a feeling she was going to like this.

What would Mark think if he could see her now? She almost giggled. He'd take it for granted she'd been kidnapped by a crazed lumberjack and feared for her life. He might even unbend enough to lift his car phone and call the police to come rescue her.

She shrank back against the seat at the thought, because that was exactly why she didn't want anyone to know she was not only Carly Stevens, hometown girl; she was also Carolyn Stevens, supremely competent assistant to Congressman Mark Cameron, a rising star in Washington's power circles. But that was in another life. And she wanted to keep that strictly separate from this.

"Can you cook?" Joe asked abruptly, plunging her back into reality.

"Well, of course." Bagels and cream cheese. TV dinners. A box of macaroni and cheese. Spaghetti. Good old spaghetti. She could do that, as long as the sauce came in a jar. She looked around at the open fields and guessed there wasn't going to be too much opportunity for take-out in this neighborhood.

"I've got a cleaning lady who comes in twice a week. She takes care of washing the clothes, too. So you don't have to worry about things like that. Just be there for the kids, and keep them fed."

She nodded. That didn't sound hard at all. She didn't know much about children. She hadn't had any contact with any since she had been a kid herself.

"They go to school, don't they?" That should mean her days would be mostly free—exactly what she needed.

He nodded, and for just a moment she thought he was actually smiling. "Yeah, they go to school. They leave at about eight in the morning and the bus drops them off at home at about three-thirty. Today they're playing at a neighbor's until four." He glanced at his watch. "Actually, they ought to be home by now."

She noticed he was pressing a bit harder on the accelerator, hurrying home now that he realized the kids were already there. For the first time she saw him as a father rather than just a large, very attractive man who didn't like her much. It was something of a revelation and threatened to soften his edges, if he would let it.

"How old are they?" she asked.

"Beth is seven. Jeremy is six."

So young to be motherless. But they did have a grandmother, didn't they? That ought to help.

"And your mother lives with you?"

His mouth seemed to tighten. "Yes. She stays in her own apartment on the third floor. She's not well. She has a private nurse who drives out to check on her every morning. She won't give you any trouble."

She settled back a little more into the big bucket seat and smiled to herself. This was going to work out beautifully. She could see herself spending her time wandering in the fields, listening to birds and gazing at the sky. She would have so much peace and space to think, she might be able to get things straight in no time.

"And I suppose you leave for work about the same time the kids leave for school," she mused.

He glanced at her as though she were speaking Swahili. "I don't 'leave for work.' I run a citrus orchard, remember? My work is right where I live. I'm in and out of the house all day."

"Oh." Her shoulders sagged. Darn. She'd forgotten that. So she wouldn't have quite as much privacy as she had thought. Still, he would be busy. It couldn't be all that bad.

He turned the truck down a side road lined with a windbreak of tall eucalyptus. Rows of small, neat trees with shiny green leaves and gorgeous orange fruit spread out for what seemed like miles. "Are these yours?" she asked, delighted with the scene.

"Yup."

Bright green against a clear blue sky. She sat forward, pressing her hands to the dashboard. The tranquility was there. She could see it, sense it. Now if only she could absorb it.

"What are those?" She pointed to a hill covered with larger trees. The leaves were more olive-colored and at first she couldn't discern the fruit.

"Avocados." He glanced in the direction she'd indicated. "I've been nursing them along for years and we're about to take our first paying crop off them."

"Avocados." She let the word roll around on her tongue. She was glad she'd come.

They passed through a huge wrought-iron gate that stood open and turned up a long, winding driveway. On one side were sheds; on the other, a barn. They finally stopped before a rather shabby residence.

A small girl sat crying in the dust that must once have been a front lawn. Tears had mixed with dirt and her face was a muddy mess. Joe jerked the truck to a stop and was out the door before Carly had completely taken in what she was looking at.

"Bethy." He knelt beside the little girl. "What is it? What's happened?"

"I...I..." Huge sobs got in the way of the words. "Jeremy...he..."

Joe's hands clenched at his sides and his pulse throbbed at his temple. "What is it? Talk slowly. Tell me, Beth. What is it?"

Carly was out of the truck by now, and coming up beside them. The little girl was trying to point.

"The tractor..." she sobbed. "Jeremy..."

Joe spun and stared at the large irrigation ditch running near the barn. One corner of an overturned tractor could be seen protruding.

"Oh my God!" Joe cried, beginning to run. "Oh please, please God..."

Carly was only just beginning to piece this tragedy together. The little boy must have been in the tractor when it went into the ditch. Her heart leapt into her throat, choking her, and she looked down at Beth, who was sobbing on the ground as though the worst had already been confirmed.

Carly didn't know children, but she knew misery. Reaching down, she scooped the child up into her arms and held her close, turning to look at where Joe was reaching the ditch and vaulting over the side.

"It'll be okay, honey," she said soothingly, patting Beth's back. "Your daddy will fix everything."

She looked down at the matted blond hair, fully aware that she might just be lying through her teeth. But Joe was the sort of man a person could lean on. And if he couldn't fix this, who could?

"Jeremy...he isn't moving and I...I tried to call 911," Beth managed to get out between sobs. "But the door was l-l-ocked. I couldn't g-get in the house."

"It's okay. You did your best."

The little girl turned her huge gray eyes up and stared at her, tears making wavy lines down her dirt-stained face. "Is Jeremy dead?"

Despite everything, the words shocked her and she had to look away for a moment.

"No, no, of course not. Your daddy..." She looked out at the irrigation ditch. Nothing moved where she could see it. Her stomach fell away and she began to breathe a little faster. The little boy couldn't be dead, not this suddenly. It wouldn't be fair; it wouldn't be right. She took a deep breath and said with all the conviction she could muster, "Your daddy will fix everything. Okay?"

Staring up at her, Beth nodded. "Okay," she said and took a deep breath, then put her head against Carly's chest. "Who are you?" she asked simply.

Carly held her close, working on pure intuition. "I'm Carly Stevens. I'm going to be staying with you for a little while."

"Okay." The prospect seemed to be one she was used to. "But Jeremy won't mind you."

That was the least of her worries at the moment. She wanted to go out and see if she could help Joe, but she didn't want to leave Beth alone. She stood there, torn, and then Joe was coming up over the ridge with a boy in his arms, a little body that lay limp and lifeless.

Carly gasped and held Beth more tightly against her chest. Words stuck in her throat and she couldn't call out to ask his condition. Instead, she held her breath and waited, everything suspended.

"He's breathing," Joe said as he came toward them. "There's a cut on his forehead. But nothing's obviously broken."

She let the breath out in a rush and closed her eyes for a few seconds. When she opened them again, she realized he was heading straight for the truck and she turned and ran ahead to open the door for him with one hand while holding Beth with the other. Joe laid Jeremy on the seat, fumbling for the seat belt to strap him down securely, and Carly noticed how tenderly he touched him. The little boy's face was white, his dark lashes long on his rounded cheeks.

"I'm going to take him in to the emergency room," Joe said evenly. "You can handle Beth, can't you?"

Carly looked at him and nodded. He was so calm, so cool, and yet there was a white line around his mouth, a throbbing pulse at his temple, that told her he was anything but calm inside. "Don't worry—about us," she said. "Get him to a doctor."

"Damn it," he muttered, shaking his head. "If only I had been home on time..."

Carly shivered. They both knew what had kept him. But he didn't look at her.

"I'm sorry, Daddy." Beth was crying again. "I tried to call 911. I really tried, but I couldn't."

He barely gave her a glance and didn't answer, swinging up into the truck and gunning the engine to life. Carly stood back as he left in a swirl of dust. Beth clung to her and cried again. Confused, Carly looked down at the little girl. So much had happened so quickly Surely Joe hadn't meant to snub his daughter. It was just that he was so worried about Jeremy, and he'd been in a hurry.

"It's all right, Beth," she said soothingly. "Jeremy is going to be fine and they'll both be back in no time."

The little face was buried against her shirt. A sudden vision of the vast quantity of mud the face had carried when last she'd seen it flashed in Carly's mind, but she dismissed the thought immediately. She wasn't going to be concerned about clothes or fashion, not for one minute, while she was here. She was going to be real and natural. And if that meant taking on a little mud, so be it.

"Let's go in the house, Beth," she said.

The little head came away from her shirt and gray eyes looked up at her. "We can't."

The face began to crumple again, but instead of returning to her hold on Carly, Beth let go and slid to the ground. She blinked rapidly, holding back her tears. "We can't go in," she said again, her voice shaking but strong.

"Why not?" Carly asked, with a sinking feeling.

"The door is still locked. Daddy forgot to let us in before he left."

Carly was beginning to notice a tendency to sag. It had been a long day, beginning in Colorado and ending here in central California. She was tired. She wanted a nice long soak in a tub, maybe a cool drink, some New Age music. What she didn't want was to spend the next few hours in a dusty yard, waiting for Joe to get back, worrying about Jeremy, feeling guilty.

"Well, what about your grandmother?" she asked, a note of desperation edging her voice. "Isn't she home?"

Beth nodded, rubbing her eyes with dirty fists. "She doesn't come down. We're not supposed to bother her."

Carly stared out at the endless sea of orange trees and wondered how long it was going to take her to get sick of the sweet smell of the blossoms. Half an hour ago she would have said they were heavenly. Now she wasn't so sure.

LUCKILY there had been a window left open in the kitchen and Carly was able to hoist Beth up and through. The little girl ran to the door and let Carly in.

The inside of the house was almost as shabby as the outside. Dishes from breakfast had been left out, bowls with cereal hardening like cement clinging to their sides. But then, what could you expect? This was exactly what she had been hired to correct, wasn't it? Although he hadn't said as much, she was sure Joe wanted more than someone to look after the kids. He wanted the house back the way it was when his wife had been there. Carly had understood that from the first.

But if she was going to get things in order, she would have to get the lay of the land. She walked quickly through the ground floor. The living room looked virtually unused, the furniture very nice, the decorations tasteful. Joe's wife's work, Carly imagined. From the looks of it, she had been a traditionalist with a touch of whimsy.

The family room was where they actually lived, she guessed. There was a television and the floor was littered with books and toys and clothing. The den was basically bookshelves and a desk covered with papers.

"Do you know which room I'll be using?" she asked Beth.

The little girl nodded and led her toward the stairs. "I guess you'll have the same room all the ladies get," she said.

Carly hid a smile. "I guess so." Then she frowned. "Have there been lots of them?"

"Ladies?" Beth nodded, her hand on the banister. "They come to take care of me and Jeremy. But they don't like us. So they go away again." Her gray eyes were huge and candid. There was no particular sadness for all those ladies who had marched in and out of their lives. But Carly felt a tug at her heartstrings just the same.

"Did you like any of them?" she asked.

Beth paused and considered for a moment. "No. I don't think so." She looked at Carly, head to the side. "They weren't young and pretty like you." Her eyes widened with sudden wonder. "Are you going to marry Daddy?" she asked.

Carly nearly backed into the wall. "No," she said, laughing. "No, no, nothing like that. I'm here to take care of you, just like the others."

But Beth had hold of an idea and she wasn't going to let go of it that easily. "But you're not like the others. Not like Greta." She shuddered. "She was ugly and her teeth were green and Daddy didn't like her."

Carly smiled. "Well, my teeth aren't green, but I don't think he likes me much either."

Beth's brows came together worriedly. "Did he call you a . . . a blistering id-jet and a cueball?" she asked in her matter-of-fact tone of voice.

Carly hid a grin. "No. Not yet."

Beth nodded, her face clearing. "Then it's all right. He used to call Greta those things all the time." She turned and started up the stairs.

"I see," said Carly, coming along behind her. "If he calls me a blithering idiot and a screwball I'll know my time has come. It's all over."

Beth nodded solemnly. "If he doesn't call you those things, then he really likes you."

Carly smiled. "I'll keep that in mind."

Beth showed off her own bedroom, which was impossibly neat, and Jeremy's, which couldn't have been messier, and the room Carly was to occupy, which was ordinary but comfortable. "And this is Daddy's room," she said, pointing to an open door.

Carly glanced at it with little interest, then turned and looked up the staircase that led from the second floor to the third. The top of the stairway was shrouded in shadows, but if she bent down she could just make out a dark green door at the top.

"Is that your grandmother's apartment?" she asked.

Beth looked up the stairs. "Yes. We mustn't bother her."

Carly hesitated. "Wouldn't she want to know about Jeremy's accident?"

"No!" Beth grabbed her hand and tugged her away. "No, don't bother her! You mustn't."

So she didn't. But she was becoming more and more curious about this lady, locked away in an attic apartment, and she knew there would come a time when she would visit her, "mustn't" or not.

"Let me freshen up and unwind for a minute, Beth," she said, heading back toward the bedroom Beth had designated for her. "I'll come down and fix you some dinner in a moment."

Beth skipped away and Carly went into the bathroom to splash some water on her face and attempt a revival. She was feeling the effects of her eventful day. She looked longingly at the bed before leaving the room. It was odd having someone else she had to do things for. She was used to having no one but herself to consider. It had been a long time since she'd lived with another person.

Hesitating outside the door to Joe's room, she couldn't resist peeking in for a moment. Surely he would have a picture of his wife by his bed, and she was interested in seeing what she had looked like.

The room was clean, neat, with a curiously unlived-in look, like the room in a comfortable motel. And there was not a picture in sight, not even of the children.

"Joe Matthews," she whispered, shaking her head as she examined the room. "You are a deep one."

Maybe he hadn't liked his wife any more than he liked her. She grinned at that. Or maybe he didn't like anyone very much. That was a suspicion to keep in mind, she told herself as she went down the stairs. The man was awfully handsome and this tragic thing with his wife dying tended to play on the sympathies. But there was something very prickly about him, too. And he obviously wasn't looking for a cool hand to soothe his troubled brow.

"Which is just as well," she muttered as she made her way toward the kitchen, looking for Beth. "Because I've never been much of a soother."

She found the child pulling a no-longer-frozen dinner out of the microwave oven. "Beth, I was going to fix you something for dinner!"

"It's okay. Jeremy and me, we have frozen dinners all the time."

Just like she did, all alone in her apartment. She stared at the girl. Beth was too young for this. She should have a big happy family around her, a long table full of freshly prepared food, loving parents. It hardly mattered that Carly couldn't really remember having all those things herself. Suddenly, achingly, she wanted it for this little urchin child

"Well, I'll cook for you tomorrow, okay?" she said quickly.

Beth nodded and gestured toward her plastic-wrapped dinner. "Do you want one?"

"No thanks. I'll just..." What would she do? She looked about quickly. "I'll just munch on one of these apples," she said, taking a bright red fruit from the bowl in the middle of the kitchen table. "You go right ahead."

She sank into a chair across from the girl and watched her eat, her little lips pursed earnestly, her eyes demurely downcast, and suddenly she thought of herself at ten when her mother had told her they would be leaving the Central Valley, leaving her father, and heading for Hollywood to make Carly a star.

What had she felt? Had she been scared? Had she missed her father? Why couldn't she remember? All that came back to her now was the memory of that long car ride over the Grapevine, the sign that said, "Hollywood, next seven exits," the seedy little cottage with an overgrown courtyard that would be their home for the next seven years. Looking back, she could hardly remember her father at all.

But she could surely remember her mother. A reluctant smile curved her lips. She'd hated the business, the auditions, the dancing lessons, the voice training, the endless hours of waiting in line with a hundred other little girls. But she had never hated her mother for putting her through it all. For years, her mother had been the spark to her life. What would she have done without her?

She'd done all right without her father. Would Beth do all right without a mother?

"Do you think Jeremy is at the doctor's yet?" Beth asked suddenly.

"I'm sure of it," Carly returned reassuringly. "The doctor is fixing him up and he'll be coming home very soon."

The gray eyes continued to regard her. "I'm glad you're here," Beth said at last. "I'm glad they didn't leave me alone."

Tears threatened to sting Carly's eyes. Implicit in Beth's statement was the way her mother had left her. Carly thought quickly, wondering if she should draw her out about her mother or ignore it. Reaching out, she took Beth's small hand in her own.

"You miss your mother, don't you?" she asked softly.

Beth hesitated. "Maybe. A little."

That seemed a strangely reluctant answer for a grieving child.

"What was her name?"

"Ellen."

"Do you remember much about her? What was she like?"

Beth blinked twice, then said very calmly, "We don't talk about my mother. Grandma says we must never say her name again. It hurts Daddy too much."

"Oh." Carly withdrew her hand, feeling properly reprimanded. Dealing with children was turning out to be a bit tougher than she'd expected. She watched as Beth put her fork in the tray and carried it to the sink.

"Well, what now?" she said with heartiness too jovial to be real. "Want to watch a little television?"

Beth turned and regarded her coolly. "No, of course not," she said. "You're supposed to make me do my homework. It's a school night."

"Oh. Of course." She pretended to hit her forehead with the flat of her hand, then winked at the girl. "I knew that." She grinned.

It took Beth a moment, but she did smile back. "I'll need help with the fractions," she said, skipping from the room.

"Fractions," Carly muttered, rising from her chair and looking without enthusiasm at the dishes that needed to be washed. "But, of course, ask me anything. I can always take the Fifth."

CHAPTER THREE

EVEN THOUGH IT WAS LATE when he turned up the long drive, the house lights were on the way they used to be and his heart gave a little lurch before he remembered Carly. He pulled the truck to a stop and turned off the engine and sat for a moment, looking at the boy sleeping in the passenger's seat. A white bandage covered half his forehead, just one in a long line of similar badges of honor that had peppered his career as an active boy. He was going to be okay. Scarred maybe, but okay.

Joe wanted to lean over and kiss him, but something held him back, and he looked at the back door, expecting Carly to appear there any second. Frowning, he tried to remember just exactly why he'd agreed to have her come out here to stay. It seemed ridiculous now. She wasn't going to work out. She was hardly the type for farm life. She might as well sleep here for the night, but in the morning he would take her back into town.

Still, he'd been lucky she'd been available to take care of Beth, under the circumstances. There was always something—some crisis, some disaster. It was damned hard raising these two kids by himself. Sometimes he thought it was almost too hard. If only... He closed his eyes. "Oh God, Ellen," he breathed aloud, his voice shaking as much with anger as with agony. Why? Why?

Jeremy stirred and he took him up into his arms, preparing to leave the cab of the truck. He looked down at the little face, the chubby cheeks, the turned-up nose. A wave of love swept through him and he held the boy close, taking in everything about him, his feel, his heat, his smell.

This was his son, the only boy he would ever have. Thank God, he was all right. Thank God.

The back door swung open and he straightened quickly, reaching for the door handle.

"Hi," Carly called from the back porch. She shaded her eyes against the light from the bright, naked bulb. "Is that you?"

"It's me."

Jeremy moved and opened his eyes as Joe came up onto the porch with him.

Carly noticed and smiled. "Thanks for calling us from the hospital and letting us know he was all right," she said softly as she followed Joe into the house. "Beth couldn't go to sleep until after she heard."

He nodded and went on through to the staircase. There was something unsettling about having Carly in the house. He felt uncomfortable, holding Jeremy the way he was—as though he were letting this stranger see into his emotional life in a way he didn't want revealed. So he didn't say anything as he ascended the stairs. But Jeremy's head came up and his dark eyes regarded Carly from over his father's shoulder.

She smiled and waved at him, then sighed as the two of them disappeared from sight. Beth's words, "Jeremy won't mind you," echoed in her head. Just one glance at that stubborn little face told her Beth knew what she was talking about. But that was a bridge she would have to cross in the morning.

As for Joe—he'd looked tired and was probably hungry. Maybe she could fix him something to eat while he tucked Jeremy in. The question was, what? He didn't seem like the frozen-dinner type. She had a vague idea that men like Joe sat down to huge plates of meat and potatoes, but there really wasn't time to fix anything like that, even if she had the slightest idea how to do it. She would have to delve into her very abbreviated repertoire and hope for the best.

She worked on it while he took care of Jeremy and went back out to the truck to get Carly's bags and carry them up to her room. His meal was ready by the time he came back down the stairs. He looked a bit startled as he saw her there waiting for him.

"I've got some dinner for you," she told him. "In the kitchen."

He was surprised, and even a little impressed. She could see it in his eyes. But all he said was, "Thanks," before he turned into the kitchen.

She followed him, feeling pleased with herself. Omelets—she'd had plenty of experience with them at three in the morning after an evening of theater and dancing. This one was lightly browned and perfectly shaped. A nice piece of buttered toast lay beside it on the plate. Joe was staring down at it as well, but he didn't look nearly as pleased as Carly felt. He looked at her.

"This is it?" he asked.

She nodded, the pleasure melting away with his tone. "It's a cheese omelet. Don't you like eggs?"

"Eggs? Sure, I like eggs. For breakfast." He lifted his arm and made a show of reading his watch. "But isn't this a little early?"

If the feelings warring inside her chest were any indication, she was going to have a bit of trouble remembering she was just an employee here. She held her temper in check, but it wasn't easy.

"Listen, mister," she said crisply. "If you're hungry, this is what's available."

He looked from her to the plate on the table and back again, then sank with seeming reluctance to take his place. "It's better than nothing, I guess," he grumbled, picking up his fork and poking at the food as though he thought it might get up and run away if he provoked it enough. "Is this what you call a real man's meal in the city?"

She had expected to give him the food and beat a hasty retreat to her room, but now she found herself pulling out the chair across the table from him and perching on the edge of the seat.

"You know what your problem is?" she announced, not bothering to answer his question. "You're behind the times. Stuck in your ways. I guess out here in the country you haven't heard that we don't have to be locked in by traditions any longer. You can eat what you want, when you want."

She flipped her hair back over her shoulder in a sassy gesture. "And—here's a shocker for you—if a man doesn't like what a woman serves him, he can darn well get up off his duff and fix his own meals." Her sweet smile belied her words. "And that's the way we do it in the city."

"Yeah. I'll just bet you do." To her surprise, his eyes were sparkling and little crinkles were appearing beside them. He took a bite, but he was still watching her, looking her over speculatively.

"So... did you make any headway in finding yourself yet?" he asked.

She knew he was goading her and she considered it for a moment, wondering whether to rise to the bait or ignore it. Funny how a man could be so attractive and so annoying at the same time. "Not yet," she said at last, unable to resist. "I think it's going to take more than a couple of hours cleaning a kitchen to do it."

He glanced around the room, taking in the shiny sink, the uncluttered counters as though he hadn't noticed before, but he didn't comment.

"I don't know why you people all seem to go and get yourselves lost in the first place," he muttered instead, taking a long sip of coffee.

She responded again, even though she knew she shouldn't. "'You people'? What's that supposed to mean?"

Yes, she hadn't been wrong. His eyes were definitely flashing with amusement. He was laughing at her. Strange, though, she didn't seem to feel offended. What she did feel was a slight prickly sensation that she wasn't sure she liked. She sat farther out on the edge of her chair and tried to ignore it.

"'You people,'" he was saying, "means human beings like you—mostly women—who have too much time on their hands and tend to spend it staring at their navels and wondering why they're alive."

He was teasing her, but she had a feeling there was a serious undertone to his words. She wasn't sure she wanted to call him on it, but she wasn't going to let it pass either. She leaned forward across the table.

"Are you saying that you never have any doubts or questions yourself?"

He shook his head, exuding male confidence from every pore. "I don't have time for that kind of garbage." He waved his fork in the air. "I've got work to do, trees to irrigate."

She nodded, head to the side. "And kids to raise," she added for him.

He looked just a bit startled. "Yeah," he said. "Them too." But his face told her that was a concept he hadn't quite come to terms with yet.

Looking up, he met her gaze, and for just a moment she couldn't look away. His eyes were dark and clouded and there was a wariness in them that made her want to reach out and touch him, as though to comfort him for some hurt someone somewhere had inflicted. Her hand even moved, but he noticed and she could see him pull back defensively. She picked up an apple from the bowl in the center of the table, as though that were what she'd been after all the time, and stared at it, rolling it around in her hand.

"So tell me about this guy you're trying to 'find yourself' for," he said quickly.

She recognized his statement for what it was—a distancing technique. But that was all right, because she wanted to keep space between them, too.

"What's his name?"

Taking a deep breath, she smiled as she looked up again. "His name is Mark." No last names here. He might have heard of Mark Cameron. You never know. And she would just as soon keep that connection quiet.

If Mark found out she was here and came looking for her, he would ruin everything. She needed to be alone, away from him, to be able to think this whole thing through.

Joe took a last bite of egg before he asked, "What is he, some lawyer or doctor or something?"

"No, not exactly." This wasn't going to work. She had to tell him something. "He, uh, he works in government."

Joe raised an eyebrow. "And you... ?"

"I... more or less work for him."

"Ah. The old boss-falling-for-the-secretary routine." He threw down his napkin. "Is he married?"

She set her jaw and stared right back at him. "No. He is not married. And I'm not a secretary."

"Then what exactly do you do?"

She started to answer, then thought better of it. "No references, remember?"

"Ah," he said softly, still watching her. "A mystery woman."

There it was again, something in his eyes. She felt a flush beginning to rise in her cheeks and she looked away, saying quickly, "So Jeremy is going to be okay? I'm so glad."

"He's fine. He can even go to school tomorrow if he feels like it."

"That's a relief." She hesitated, then charged on. "You know, Beth was really worried. She felt just awful that she couldn't call 911 for him. You're—you're not angry with her, are you?"

His eyes widened. "Why on earth would I be angry with her?"

"I don't know. You just were a little short with her and I think she—"

He rose abruptly, taking his own plate to the sink. "I'm not angry with Beth," he said evenly as he turned back. "Don't go putting ideas like that into her head."

Carly rose to face him. "Oh, but I didn't—"

That was as far as she got. From outside, somewhere in the fields, there came a long, high, hideous sound that brought to mind every horror movie she'd ever seen and chilled her to the bone. She spun, eyes wide, and grabbed Joe's arm. "What—what is that noise?"

He looked down at her quizzically. "Just some old coyote out there baying at the moon."

He very carefully pried her fingers off and pulled away from her touch, but she hardly noticed. The sound came again, and her heart thumped madly, even though she knew now what it was.

"But...what's he doing here?" she demanded.

Joe looked down at her blankly. "What do you mean?"

She shook her head, feeling indignant. "This isn't the Wild West."

If she had looked up she would have seen that the smile was back in his eyes.

"No. It's the tame West. But no one's told the coyotes about that yet."

She shuddered, seeing all her dreams about solitary wanderings through the orange groves falling to ashes about her. In the city you had to watch out for muggers and crazy people, but if you were careful and knew what you were doing you were pretty confident of being all right. This was different, somehow, a primeval call to a wildness she didn't think she understood at all.

"Do you carry a…a rifle or something when you go out there?" she wanted to know.

Joe looked at her as though she'd suddenly revealed a streak of insanity. "Coyotes do not attack fully grown people," he told her patiently. "Dogs, cats, even small children you have to be careful with. But I think you'll be safe." His grin was back, but this time there was a definite touch of condescension evident as he looked down at her, still hovering close to him. "And don't worry tonight. Tasty as you may be, no coyote could get into this house and climb up to the second floor to find you."

"I know that." But she still shuddered.

He shook his head and turned, starting for the hall-way, turning off lights as he went, and she followed right behind him, then went on ahead, starting up the stairs.

"Thank you for the omelet," he said. "It was very good."

She had begun to go up the stairs and she turned, surprised, to look down at him. "You liked it?"

He smiled and nodded, amused by her obvious pleasure in his comment. "I liked it."

It was silly to feel so proud of such a small thing, but Carly had never been praised for her cooking before, and this was a sort of milestone for her. "I'll make you another one tomorrow," she said gaily, not noticing that his smile faded quickly at her words.

She turned to go up, but misjudged, and her foot slipped on the threadbare carpeting. The next thing she knew she was airborne, falling, her heart in her throat.

And then she landed against Joe's wide chest with a thump that knocked some of the air out of her lungs.

"Oh!"

He steadied her and she clung to him, fighting to get her breath back. His large hands spread across her back and she leaned close against him, her face pressed to his chest.

Her breathing was back quickly, but she couldn't move away. She stayed very still, very much aware of how large and masculine he was. She felt his heart beating against her cheek, and suddenly she was breathless in a different way. She looked up at him, confused, her eyes clouded, her mind in a fog, filled with a strange longing she didn't understand.

He stared down into her eyes and she felt him stiffen, then heard him swear under his breath.

"Oh no, you don't," he said aloud, quite deliberately, shaking his head and putting her firmly but gently away from him. His eyes were dark and hard and there was no smile at all. "You're going to have to get a handle on your emotions on your own, lady. I'm not going to help you there."

Turning, he went on ahead, taking the stairs two at a time, leaving Carly behind to blink after him in a bewilderment that quickly developed into outrage.

He thought she . . . he was under the impression . . . he had mistaken . . . Why how dare he! Rage filled her and she ran up the stairs behind him, tempted to pound on the door he had already closed. Luckily, she stopped herself in time, contenting herself with making a face at his bedroom as she passed on to her own.

Of all the insensitive, arrogant, self-absorbed, conceited... She swallowed her anger and tried to think of cutting comments to make to him in the morning. There had to be some way to prove to him how wrong he was about her—prove it to him and make him eat crow.

Opening the door to her own bedroom, she went in and looked at herself in the mirror. Bright spots of anger highlighted her cheeks. She looked like a clown.

She turned, and suddenly it hit her. There was something wrong. Her bags were there, but just looking at them she could sense they had been tampered with.

She pulled one up and opened it. Someone had been going through her things. Nothing was folded the way she had done it. Her sweaters had been put back in an order she would never have used. Someone had searched her bags. Who in the world would do a thing like that? And why?

CHAPTER FOUR

"WAFFLES. That's what I want. Waffles."

Carly turned from Jeremy's earnest little face and looked longingly at the carton of eggs and the frying pan. This was an ungodly hour to be learning new skills.

She'd shot up in her bed when the alarm had gone off like the whistle of an oncoming freight train at six in the morning. For just a moment, she'd been completely lost. Then it had all come back to her. She was in a stranger's house, and responsible for the health and happiness of a stranger's children. The thought set butterflies fluttering through her innards.

She'd slipped out of bed and gone to the window to look out over the lovely orchards, and had been just in time to see Joe drive off in the truck. Already up and at 'em at six—it made her want to go back to bed. The truck circled the yard before heading out onto the ranch road, and for just a moment, it seemed to hesitate beneath her window. Was he looking up? She couldn't quite tell, but her nerves got jittery anyway. She had a few things to settle with that man.

Meanwhile, there was breakfast to prepare.

"How about some nice scrambled eggs?" she asked hopefully.

"Uh-uh." Jeremy shook his head, completely decided, his hands forming small fists in front of him on the kitchen table. "I want waffles."

"Not me." Beth flounced into the room and plunked her books down. Her golden hair flowed about her shoulders and her eyes were bright. "I want pancakes. Can we have pancakes? We haven't had pancakes for so long."

"No, waffles!"

"I want pancakes."

"Waffles!"

"Pancakes!"

Carly licked her lips as she contemplated informing them that she had no idea how to make either item. Something told her this was no time to go rummaging through cookbooks. Their choices seemed so passionate. Did they turn on the cook when she refused to obey?

"I don't know about waffles or pancakes, guys," she said. "I can't find any mixes. How about some nice cereal in these pretty bowls...?"

"I hate cereal."

"It rots your teeth."

"I want waffles."

Beth gazed at her brother with scorn. "Pancakes are easier. I bet I could make them. I think you just need milk and flour."

"Uh...I have a feeling there's more to it than that." Carly looked around the kitchen, getting nervous. There must be something easy for these kids. Why on earth were there no bagels in this place?

"'Morning, kids."

Joe was at the door of the kitchen, a smile for his children, a patronizing nod for Carly. He'd come back from his morning patrol and gone upstairs, and now he looked fresh and clean, straight out of the shower. Carly regarded him with a measure of resentment, but there was no denying the man had a strong, steady sense of presence that sent a quiver through the room.

"What's the problem?" he asked.

"No problem," Carly said hastily, a quick smile on her lips. She practically chirped. "We've got everything under control."

His eyebrow quirked. "Oh, really?"

Sarcasm so early in the morning? She lifted her chin. "Yes. I can handle it." My, what lovely confidence her voice exuded. She only wished a little of that self-assurance was real.

"I want waffles, Daddy!"

Jeremy put his hand to his bandaged head, unconsciously going for the sympathy vote, but Beth had her own ace up her sleeve.

"And I want pancakes," Beth insisted, turning to smile winningly at her father. "Daddy likes pancakes best. He told me so."

Joe's dark glance swept the kitchen and saw through every mask. "You'll have eggs and toast," he said shortly. "Pancakes and waffles are for weekends. Carly's got no time for that sort of thing today."

"Oh."

They heaved a collective sigh, but it was evident the master had spoken and there was going to be no whining. Impressed in spite of herself, Carly bit her tongue to keep from thanking him.

"Okay. I'll have scrambled eggs," Beth offered grudgingly. "But please don't leave any little wiggly things in it. Okay?"

Joe's gaze was mocking but Carly couldn't look away. She had to pretend, at least, that she wasn't rattled. Especially after last night.

"Scrambled eggs, stiff and dry, coming right up," she said cheerfully.

Skepticism laced Joe's grin, but he shrugged. "Since you've got it all under control," he drawled, "I'll go on out and get that tractor out of the ditch." He looked back just before he went out the kitchen door. "Call me if you need anything," he told her.

I wouldn't call you if green Martians landed and began scrubbing down in the sink, she thought to herself, but aloud she said, "Sure" as he turned and left the house, and then she went to work on breakfast. "Let's see—warm the pan, get out some butter..."

"Can you help me braid my hair?" Beth was asking, jumping down from her seat.

"I didn't do my homework," Jeremy was muttering. "But it wasn't my fault. You have to write a note to my teacher."

She glanced at the two of them distractedly. "Uh...okay, just let me get this toaster..."

"Good grief!" Beth suddenly looked stricken. "I forgot my library book! Where's my library book?" She ran from the room, calling back, "Carly, can you come help me find it?"

"No," Carly mouthed, but she didn't say it out loud. Instead, she put the toaster on the counter and began peeling slices of bread off the loaf.

"I didn't find my Pirates cap," Jeremy told her solemnly, still sitting very still with two fists in front of him. "I can't go to school if I don't find it."

Carly blinked rapidly. She'd never had a lot of trouble working on two things at a time at her job, but this was different. This was unfamiliar territory, and she was beginning to feel harried.

"Okay," she said quickly. "Just wait while I get this going..." She began mixing eggs like crazy. The toast popped, but the pieces were untouched by heat. She jiggled the handle, pushed in the plug again, and the filaments began to turn red.

"Carly!" Beth shrieked from the den. "Jeremy took my library book! I can't find it!"

Carly turned and looked at the boy. "Did you take her library book?" she asked, beyond frazzled, approaching meltdown.

Jeremy shook his head slowly. "Did not."

"Well...go find your cap."

"I don't know where it is."

"That's why you're going to have to look for it."

"How can I look when I don't know where it is?"

That sounded logical. At the moment, she had no answer for him.

Meanwhile, Beth's voice, coming from the den, was beginning to develop a note of hysteria. "I can't go to school if I can't find my library book! Write a note to my teacher!"

The eggs were browning too fast. Carly worked feverishly with a spatula before she remembered to turn down the heat. The toast was burning. She lunged for the toaster and popped them up, still smoking. Should she scrape them or start over again? Jeremy was playing with the silverware, banging a spoon against the table.

"Carly, come quick, help me look for my library book!" Beth called, tears in her voice. "I can't find it! What am I going to do?"

"Breakfast is burned," Jeremy informed Carly calmly. "I can't eat burned."

Carly's breath was coming faster and faster and her memory buffer was about to hit overload when the kitchen door opened and Joe looked in. "Everything okay?" he asked.

Carly whirled, shielding breakfast with her body, and forced a smile. "Everything's just fine," she said in a voice that sounded much too high to be hers. "Don't worry about a thing."

He sniffed the air but this time he didn't grin. "You don't need any help?" he asked, searching her face.

"Oh no!" She managed a quick, strained laugh. "We're fine."

He shrugged, the corners of his wide mouth twitching. "If you say so," he said, and went out again.

She took a deep breath and turned. Jeremy was staring at her with wide eyes, but he didn't say a thing. She turned, put two fresh slices of bread into the toaster and began dishing up the eggs. Beth flew back into the room like a miniature hurricane.

"My hair! It still needs to be braided."

"The bus leaves in ten minutes," Jeremy intoned from his seat, looking up at the big rooster-shaped clock on the wall.

"Ten minutes!" Beth shrieked.

Carly steadied herself against the edge of the kitchen counter. "Sit down and eat," she said, hoping she sounded as firm as Joe had when he had proclaimed the morning menu. "One thing at a time."

Beth gaped at her, her pretty face anguished. "But there are too many things to go one at a time," she cried.

She was right. Panic was bobbing around in Carly's chest like a seal in a sea tank. There was just too much to do and too little time.

"Here, eat," she said desperately, propelling the girl to her chair. "I'll work on your hair while you get that food down."

"No hairbrush at the table," Jeremy chanted.

Carly faltered. Those words must have come straight from the mouth of his mother. But there was no time to be squeamish now. She grabbed a hunk of Beth's hair and went to work.

"About the library book," she began.

"Oh. I found it," Beth said casually. "It's in my backpack."

Carly nodded and tried to center herself. There was no reason to get angry at the child. Was there? So why was she gritting her teeth? "Okay. Okay. Now just Jeremy needs a note for his teacher, right?"

Jeremy was shaking his head. "I'm not going to school," he told her flatly. "I can't find my cap, so I'm going to stay home."

Any moment now, she was going to start screaming, and once she started, there was no telling how long the screaming might go on. But Beth's hair was braided. And it was time to go.

"It's almost time for the school bus. Let's go."

They were going to make the bus. Carly felt a vast sense of relief welling up. She'd made it through one hectic morning. It really hadn't been so bad. In fact, she'd done pretty well, if she did say so herself.

"Goodbye, kids," she said cheerfully. "I'll see you this afternoon."

Beth slid off her seat and looked at the kitchen counter. "Where's our lunches?" she asked.

"Lunches?" Reality swam in and out and for a moment, she thought there was a black hole at her feet. One more step and she was a goner. She drew in a shuddering breath. "Ohmigod. Okay, okay." The black hole receded as she made her way to the counter and began pulling slices of bread out again. Peanut butter and jelly. That would have to do. Where were the lunch boxes? The plastic wrap for the sandwiches—apples from the bowl on the table—the milk for the little thermoses—and then, at last, she was done. She slammed the boxes shut with a feeling of triumph. She'd made two lunches in less than three minutes. It was a miracle.

Joe entered the back door just in time to witness her handing out the boxes to the children. "The bus already came and went," he said calmly. "I'll have to get out the car and take you myself."

She wilted inside. All this effort, and she hadn't really managed to get it together. But before she even had time to feel disappointment, he dropped another bombshell.

"Oh, by the way. I want to keep Jeremy home today. I think it would be a good idea if we kept an eye on him and that cut on his forehead."

Jeremy solemnly handed back the lunch box and skipped out of the room. Carly wanted to throw the thing at Joe's head.

"Anything else?" she asked evenly.

Joe shook his head, but Beth suddenly gasped and put a hand over her open mouth. "Oh no."

Fear gripped Carly's heart. "What is it?" she asked with icy apprehension.

Beth's eyes were huge, staring at Carly, and she still didn't speak.

"What, Beth?" Joe asked, removing her hand from her face. "What is it?"

"I forgot," the little girl whispered, eyes full of agony. "Today is Teacher Appreciation Day. I'm supposed...I'm supposed..."

"What?" they both asked.

"I'm supposed to bring thirty-six cookies," she whispered. "I forgot."

Carly slumped against the counter, all fight seeping away. Thirty-six cookies. There was no way...no way....

They were both looking at her expectantly. What did they think? Was she supposed to wiggle her nose and make three dozen cookies appear out of nowhere? She couldn't say a word. Hope dimmed in their eyes.

Joe coughed, then laughed shortly. "No problem. We'll stop at Millie's. She always has cookies in the cookie jar."

Beth's eyes brightened. "Millie always has cookies," she agreed. "Oh, I just love Millie!"

Carly watched, still in shock, as they piled into the truck and started down the drive. Beth turned to wave goodbye through the back window, but Carly could barely manage a limp-wristed salute in return.

What had just happened here? She'd tried hard, but she hadn't quite made the grade, had she? And she'd been one-upped by some marvelous creature named Millie who hadn't even had to lift a finger to get in on the action.

She looked around the messy kitchen and groaned. Maybe it was time to admit that she wasn't cut out for this sort of life. Things weren't working out at all. She'd come here for some peace and quiet in order to think over her priorities. But quiet was impossible with children this age. They were too intense. They needed too much attention and supervision. And what kind of peace was achievable with Joe around?

She paused for a minute, thinking about him, letting the reactions that she had been repressing all morning surface. If he'd been a different sort of man...but he was disturbingly masculine, impossible to ignore. And that constant sense of mocking laughter playing hide-and-seek in the shadows of his eyes—laughter directed at her. She shuddered. No. She couldn't stay. This wasn't the place for her.

Marching into the den, she dialed Doris's number. When her cousin's voice answered, she started to speak, but quickly realized she'd reached the answering machine, so waited for the beep to give her message. "Hi, Doris. It's Carly. I'm afraid this isn't working at all. There's got to be somewhere else I can stay. A park bench, maybe. The café after-hours. Anyplace. Preferably without men or children. Let me know when you can come and get me. Thanks."

There. It was done. She was going to get out of here. She turned slowly, almost apprehensively, and wondered why she didn't feel more elated. But never mind. She would look in on Jeremy, who was watching cartoons in the family room, then clean up the kitchen and go upstairs and repack her clothes. She had plenty to do to keep her busy until Doris called.

IT WAS ABOUT AN HOUR later when the stranger skulking through the house nearly scared her out of her wits. Carly had been backing out of the den, looking back with a small sense of pleasure at how neat she'd made it, when the woman had materialized just behind her.

"Hello," the cheery voice rang out, and Carly jumped a foot into the air, letting out a little shriek as she did so. "Oops, steady there." The middle-aged woman in a white uniform reached out and gave her support for a moment. "Sorry if I startled you. It's just me, Nurse Hannah. I come in every morning to check on Mrs. Matthews and bring her supplies." She jiggled the brown paper bag she carried and smiled as Carly drew back and tried to look pleasant. "Joe told me about you. Nice to have you aboard." And she was off, heading for the mysterious green door and the strange mother at the top of the stairs before Carly had time to form any one of the many questions she wanted to ask.

Perhaps that was just as well. After all, she'd be leaving by the end of the day. There was no point delving into all the secrets of the Matthews home if she had no intention of staying.

And that reminded her—it was about time to confront Joe. She'd heard the truck drive up the driveway half an hour before, but he hadn't come into the house again. Looking out the kitchen window, she could see him working on the tractor just outside the entrance to the barn. It seemed as good a time as any.

Tucking the tails of her crimson silk camp shirt into the waistband of her beige twill pants, she unconsciously smoothed her hair before stepping out onto the porch and starting for where Joe was working. One speech, short and to the point—that was all it would take. She would precisely and succinctly explain why she couldn't stay, and then she would laugh out loud at his idea that she had been coming on to him the night before. That taken care of, she would turn grandly and walk back with all the dignity at her command. He would be...oh, probably chagrined, chastened, not to mention sorry, to see her go.

The chastening would take time, of course. It couldn't start until she'd said her piece. And that was probably why he looked so completely unchagrined as he stood back and watched her approach. He wasn't going to make this any easier than it had to be.

She stopped a few feet away and looked at him. The ancient jeans hugging his legs had been rubbed to a fine, silvery patina from years of work. The fresh shirt he'd been wearing earlier was hanging on a nail. He'd changed into an old stained jersey shirt which had the sleeves torn off and a jagged rip across the chest. And that revealed something startling. The man had more muscles than she'd realized—hard, rounded muscles that glistened in the morning sunlight.

Carly felt her diaphragm contract, pulling a short, sharp gust of air into her lungs, and she tried to cover it with a hacking cough that let her cover her face with her hands. Quickly she told herself her reaction was because she had been hit with the unfamiliar. After all, she was accustomed to men who wore more clothing when they went to work. Her system wasn't used to confronting sex appeal this early in the morning.

"You okay?"

He was coming toward her with a determined look on his face. It was obvious he was perfectly capable of giving her a good hard whack on the back if he thought she needed it. She stepped back, stifling her cough, and forced a smile.

"I'm fine, really."

He stopped and she could have sworn his eyes held regret at his lost opportunity.

"You sure?"

She cleared her throat. "Perfectly."

He waited. Her mind was blank. She'd come here to tell him something. What on earth . . . ? She had to say something.

"I . . . I'm sorry about this morning," she said, trying to clear her mind. "I guess things got away from me a little."

He made a dismissive gesture. "Don't worry about it. It's like that every morning."

"Every morning?" How appalling. Who could live that way?

"Sure. That's the way it is when you have kids."

Carly bit her lip. Surely not. There must be some way to organize things better. If she were staying one more day, she would . . . .

Hey…she wasn't staying. And that was the point of her being here, talking to Joe. Right. It all came back to her.

But her speech had somehow lost its zing. She had to think of a new way to present her viewpoint. In the meantime, to cover her uncertainty, she babbled on.

"I guess it was mostly that it was just so different from what I'm used to. I mean, a quiet cup of coffee, half an hour with the newspaper, and then I leave for work..."

His teeth flashed white against his tanned skin. "I knew you wouldn't be able to hack it, city girl," he said, his sweeping glance up and down the length of her as scornful as it was amused. "I'll take you back into town as soon as I'm finished working on this tractor."

Maybe it was the tone of his voice, or maybe it was just that she hated to see this as a failure. But she couldn't let his statement pass. "No. Oh no." Her pride rose and she couldn't restrain it. "No, not at all. I...I was just trying to explain why things didn't go as well as they might have. Next time..."

What was she saying? Next time? Was she crazy? A part of her was yelling "Stop!" but she didn't seem to be able to.

"Tomorrow I'll get things under control," she heard herself saying. "You'll see."

He studied her face for a moment, then shrugged. "Whatever," he said carelessly, and pulled himself up, turning to grab a toolbox and carry it into the barn. She watched him go, her shoulders sagging. What had she done? Here she'd been primed for escape, the reasons for leaving all set out logically, and then she'd locked herself in again. What was the matter with her?

Maybe she could salvage something out of this if she followed him into the barn and just kept talking. She went inside, peering into the gloomy space. There were old piles of hay here and there, but mostly it seemed to be used to store ranch equipment.

"No horses?" she asked as she wandered toward where he was going through tool bins.

He looked up as though surprised to see her there. "No, I don't keep horses anymore. It's too much bother. When the kids want to ride, they go over to Millie's. She still has three or four of them."

Millie again. She turned and looked at him, back to rummaging among his tools. There was something about his voice when he said her name. "Is Millie your girlfriend?" she asked.

He looked up and his eyes changed. "I don't have a girlfriend," he said shortly. His tone brooked no nonsense. He had no girlfriend. He wanted none. That was final.

"Okay, okay." She raised her hands in a mock surrender, backed away, and stepped off a four-inch ledge she hadn't noticed.

The sensation of falling was getting to be a familiar one. This time she didn't even call out. She landed with a thump on her bottom and bounced backward, flailing idiotically in a pile of hay.

"Are you hurt?" he demanded, standing over her.

She shook her head, hoping her cheeks weren't as bright red as they felt. "It's nothing," she muttered, ignoring his outstretched hand as she raised herself into a sitting position. "I can get up by myself."

His grin was creeping back. Pulling back his hand, he stood back and watched her, eyes hooded. "You are clumsy, aren't you? First last night on the stairs, and now this."

She looked up and sighed. "I wanted to talk to you about last night on the stairs," she began earnestly. "It wasn't what you thought it was."

He was still grinning with that particular male arrogance that made any sane woman want to begin screaming in frustrated rage. "Okay, if you say so. But it looks kind of like you want a replay of last night on the stairs, to me."

This was exactly the kind of thinking she had to stop in its tracks. Attempting to retain at least a shred of dignity, she scrambled to her feet on her own and faced him. "That is absolutely untrue," she stated heatedly. "Listen. I came here to decide whether or not to marry one man. Why would I want to get involved with another?"

He shrugged. "You got me. I don't claim to understand it. I'm just observing." Without another glance her way he picked up a large wrench and started back out toward the tractor.

She brushed herself off and hurried after him. Was she staying for another day? Maybe. But if she was, she wanted to make sure he understood the terms she had to work under. He had climbed up and was bent over the engine of the tractor, so she stood at the nose of the machine, hands on her hips.

"You might as well get one thing straight, Joe. I'm not attracted to you," she said stoutly.

He turned and gazed directly down into her lying eyes. For once she couldn't tell if he were laughing or not. "I'm not attracted to you either," he claimed. "So I guess we have no problem."

They stared at each other, both fully aware of the blatant untruth they had staked out between them, both determined to make it true if they possibly could.

"This is purely a working relationship," she went on when she had found her voice again. "No entanglements."

He nodded slowly, still captured by her gaze. "No entanglements," he echoed. "It's a deal."

She nodded too. There didn't seem to be anything left to say. Still, she couldn't turn from him. And then he had dropped back down to the ground and was moving closer, reaching out toward her, and she frowned, starting to twist away.

"You have straw in your hair," he said, his voice huskier than usual. "I'll get it."

She stood very still while he pulled out the hay, piece by piece, forcing herself to watch each straw as it fluttered to the ground, forcing herself to pay no attention to the wall of male skin and sinew presented so close to her face. But her heart was beating very quickly.

Oh, hurry, she urged silently. *Hurry up and go away.*

Perversely, he took his time. When he finally drew back, he lingered, looking at her for a long, tense moment. She could hardly breathe. There had to be something she could say to break the electricity and send the sparks flying off into the air, but she couldn't for the life of her think of a thing.

A humorless smile twisted his lips and he finally turned away. "Don't worry," he said softly, not looking at her. "I'll keep my part of the bargain. You can trust me."

She never doubted for a moment that she could trust him to do the right thing in any given situation, but that wasn't the point. The way her heart was beating, she had to wonder if she could really trust herself.

She'd thought he was going back to work on the tractor again, but instead he pulled a sack from the seat and turned back toward her. Reaching inside, he pulled something out and held it out for her to see.

"Look at this." In his palm he held a bright green avocado. "I picked it this morning. Isn't it a beauty?"

She blinked, staring at it. "I guess so. I don't know much about avocados."

"This," he told her confidently, "is a beauty."

He handed it to her. She rolled its firmness and admired its bright green skin. Glancing up, she caught the look on his face, like a parent showing off his first-born child. She almost smiled, but she held it back, unwilling to let him know how endearing his pride was.

"Why are you branching out?" she asked. "Aren't the oranges enough?"

"You've got to diversify. You never know when a freeze or a drought or Medflies or some disease will wipe out your main crop in any given year. I want something to fall back on. I love citrus, but avocados..." He took it back from her and held it up to the light, gazing at it with shining eyes. "This year's crop alone will let me do things I haven't taken time to do for too long. Things like fix up the house for the kids. It's been going downhill ever since..." His voice faded and he glanced at her, then looked away again without finishing. His eyes were haunted by something shadowed in the angles of his face.

Carly's heart went out to him. Ever since his wife had died. That was surely what he'd been about to say. She wanted to reach out and touch his shoulder with her hand, just a quick, comforting gesture. But she knew he wouldn't want her to do that. So she resisted, looking away toward the horizon instead, pretending not to notice his pain.

A plume of dust was rising from the road.

"I think you've got company," she noted, and Joe turned to look at the blue sedan roaring toward where they were standing.

"It's Millie," he said, and Carly could have sworn a sense of quiet satisfaction warmed his tone. He started out to meet her. Carly followed, curious to see what this paragon of virtue looked like.

CHAPTER FIVE

THE WOMAN WHO STEPPED OUT of the car appeared to be in her mid-thirties, about Joe's age. She wore a crisp plaid shirt and cotton slacks and had her dark hair pulled back from her pretty face in a youthful-looking ponytail. Her smile for Joe was warm and full of affection, but her attention was really on the woman coming behind him. It was obvious she was even more curious about Carly than Carly was about her.

They shook hands as Joe introduced them. "Joe tells me you grew up here in the valley," Millie said. "Do you remember it much?"

Something stirred in Carly's memory. Had she seen this woman before? "Not really," she said slowly, trying to fit the face with a specific incident, and failing. "I was only ten when my mother and I left." She searched the woman's wide, dark eyes. "Did I know you?"

Millie looked startled. "No. No, I don't think so." Her smile flashed toward Joe and then back to Carly. "But I do remember a...a Howard Stevens who sometimes preached at the little church in town. Were you related to him?"

"Oh. He was my father." Carly was unprepared for the sudden surge of delight she felt. After all these years of completely ignoring her father, never giving him a thought, meeting people who knew him was opening doors she had closed ages ago. "Did you know him very well? Can you tell me anything about him?"

Millie looked as though she were sorry she'd brought the subject up. "Not really. I was sixteen. I sang in the choir at the church. That's all."

"Oh." Carly was disappointed. "There must be people in town who remember him," she murmured, frowning. "Maybe I'll have to ask around..."

"You...you haven't seen him since you left?"

"No, not at all. I have no idea whatever happened to him. Do you?"

"Me?" Millie's face paled. "No, why would I know?"

Carly shrugged, gazing at her. Millie seemed strangely interested in this line of thought. But even as she was thinking that, Millie's attention focused on something else. She was looking at Carly, and her eyes changed.

"What's this?" Reaching out, she took another piece of hay from Carly's hair. "Your hair is full of straw." Millie looked at Joe questioningly, the array of exotic possibilities that flowed through her mind showing clearly in her bright eyes.

"I fell in the barn," Carly said quickly, feeling foolish. She certainly didn't want to get in the way of whatever budding romance was being nurtured here. She fluffed her hair, trying to get rid of the rest of the evidence, but she felt uncomfortable and decided it was time to leave these two alone. "I've got things to do at the house. I guess I'll go on back. It was nice to meet you, Millie."

The woman stuck out a hand again. "I'm sure we'll be seeing more of each other," Millie said quietly. "Goodbye."

She and Joe stood and watched as Carly headed back toward the house.

"She's very pretty," Millie said softly.

Joe shrugged. "She can't cook much and doesn't know a thing about kids," he said gruffly. "But she's trying hard."

Millie nodded.

Joe looked at her more sharply. "What's all this interest in her father?" he asked.

Millie looked up at him. "You don't remember Howard Stevens?" she countered.

He shook his head. "No, I don't think so."

Millie smiled, reaching out to touch his arm with quick affection. "Good," she said. "The man is long-gone. If his daughter hadn't shown up like this, I doubt if anyone would have thought about him again."

But something in her eyes told Joe that wasn't true. He frowned, watching her. They'd been friends since childhood, closer now than ever. But he never had understood her.

But then, who understood women? It was best to keep relations cordial and give them a wide berth. At least, that was what had always worked with him. The one time he had tried to get close, tried to develop something more committed, he'd had it thrown right back in his face. He was never going to get caught in that trap again.

CARLY CLEANED and straightened and tried to get Jeremy to open up a little, sitting beside him as he worked on puzzles on the play table. No luck there. Jeremy answered politely most of the time, but his answers consisted of nods and uh-huhs more often than not.

"Want a snack?" she asked at last.

He looked up at her with a cool and cynical gaze for one so young. "No thanks. I'm going to take a nap."

She looked at him with concern. "Oh, is your head bothering you?"

"No." He got up and walked toward the door of the room. "Goodbye."

She watched as he headed for the stairs and his room, then retreated to the kitchen, a less frustrating place where there was always something to clean.

She'd been emptying out the vegetable bin in the refrigerator when Millie came in for a drink of water.

"Oh, hi." She was a little startled, wondering why the woman was still here.

"I'm putting in some flowers," Millie explained, pointing with laughter to the dirty knees of her slacks. "I've been promising Joe I was going to give him petunias for a long time, and I thought today would be a good day to get them started."

Carly nodded. They both knew why she'd chosen today. There was no need to pretend otherwise.

"Joe says you're fitting in fine," she said, sipping slowly at her water and watching Carly over the rim of the glass. "I'm glad. Those children need someone."

It was a friendly comment, a concerned comment, from a close friend of the family, and yet something about it still put Carly's back up a little. "Do you have children of your own?" she asked quickly, to mask her reaction.

"Yes. Trevor is my son."

"Trevor." The teenage boy they'd seen in town the day before. "You seem so young. . . ." She stopped, wondering if she'd been tactless.

But Millie was smiling. "So young to have such a big boy? I am." She laughed. "I had him when I was much too young." The laughter faded and her eyes became serious. "But I'll never regret it," she said softly. "He's the best thing in my life."

Without being told, Carly could imagine what Millie Gordon had gone through, becoming a mother when she was still almost a child herself, losing out on school, missing proms and graduations, forgoing college, growing up too fast. Even if she married the boy's father, all those things would probably have happened. And if she didn't marry him—there was the shame, the need to provide for two young lives, the constant responsibility, the exhaustion. And yet she loved her son, treasured him. Carly's heart went out to her.

"He . . . he looks like a very nice boy."

Millie smiled. "He is." Her face changed. "But so are Joe's two. Beth is a dear. How are you getting along with Jeremy?"

"All right. He's not a very outgoing child."

"No. He takes a lot of work to get to know. But it's worth the effort." She hesitated, and when she asked the next question, Carly had the feeling they had finally arrived at the reason she'd come into the house after all.

"Have you met Phyllis?"

"Phyllis?"

"Joe's mother."

"Oh. No, I haven't. But I have met Nurse Hannah."

Millie laughed. "She's a pale imitation, believe me! Once you've met Phyllis, you'll see what I mean."

Carly smiled. "Is she very ill?" she asked.

"Who? Phyllis?" Millie paused, considering. "That's probably the mystery of the ages around here. Nobody knows for sure what is wrong with Phyllis, and Nurse Hannah isn't saying."

"Joe must know."

Millie shrugged. "Maybe." Her grin was quick and friendly. "But if so, he's not saying either."

"Oh. I see." Actually, she didn't see at all, but she wasn't sure how far she should go with this private family matter. Millie was very nice, but Carly had a feeling she was confiding a little more than was natural for her. Why was that? She seemed to want very badly to be friends, and Carly was too experienced to think it was just because of her own pleasant face. Millie wanted something. But what?

Millie's dark eyes became serious. "When you do meet Phyllis, you'll find . . . well, she's not an easy woman. And she's liable to say things that might surprise you. Don't pay any attention to the things she says. And if you have any questions, feel free to ask me anything." She smiled and put down her glass. "I'd better get back to the petunias before the roots dry out. Thanks." And she was gone.

Carly stared after her, wondering what on earth that little outburst had been all about. Millie was obviously worried that Phyllis would say something to Carly that she didn't want Carly to hear—and didn't want her to believe, if she did hear it. But Carly was just a stranger here, just passing through. What did Millie care about what she was told by Joe's mother? It was very odd.

Carly turned toward the stairway that led to the green door. She was tempted to pay a visit to the mysterious Phyllis. But she wouldn't do so without talking with Joe first.

In the meantime, she had to make a decision. Should she stay or should she go? Looking out the window, she could see Millie taking flats of petunias out of the trunk of her car. And out toward the barn, there was Joe, riding off on the tractor he was testing out. She could walk away from this scene and never look back. But something told her that if she did so there would be things she would leave behind that she wouldn't be able to get out of her mind for a long, long time. Good grief—another set of things to think about—as if she hadn't set herself up with a whole agenda of problems to begin with. Half laughing, she pulled off her apron and threw it on the counter. She was going to go out into the orchards and have that long, lonely communion with Mother Nature that she'd been looking forward to since she'd arrived yesterday. She was going to think about Mark—remember Mark? she reminded herself mockingly. He was the reason she was here. And if she'd come to think through her relationship with the man, she could at least give him a moment or two of her time.

She checked on Jeremy. He was sound asleep on his bed, his face angelic. Then she went down the stairs and out the side door from the family room, so that she wouldn't have to explain herself to the others, and headed for the trees. The scent of the orange blossoms buoyed her spirits. Yes, she would be able to think out here.

JOE RESISTED the impulse to kick the tractor. Instead, he slid down from the seat and began to trudge back toward the house. The damned thing was damaged worse than he'd thought. He was going to have to tow it in to his mechanic.

The flash of something bright caught his eye and he turned in time to see her coming around the stand of cottonwoods, heading for the orchards.

For one soul-searing second he thought it was Ellen.

It wasn't Ellen. Carly looked nothing like Ellen. Thank God.

"Hey!" he called to her. "Where are you going?"

She spun, startled, and spotted him. "Oh! It's you." She glanced into the rich green rows of trees. "I'm going out to do some thinking."

"Ah. You want to be alone." But he kept walking toward her. "Scheduling a little time to search for your true identity?"

She watched him coming closer, one hand on her hip and a wary look on her face. "I know who I am. I just don't know where I'm going."

He stopped a few feet away, thumbs hooked into the pockets of his ancient jeans, head to the side as he gazed at her. "I can tell," he said softly. "Otherwise you wouldn't have ended up here with me." He'd meant to say "us"; he could swear he had. But it came out "me" and he wished he could recall the word. Her being here was nothing personal and he knew it. There was no need to let it turn into something it was never meant to be.

But it was too late. The word had been spoken, and her eyes were filled with surprise and apprehension. "I...uh...I have to go."

He swore softly, kicking at the dirt with his boot and laughing at himself, the situation, life in general. "Hey, don't worry. I didn't mean that like it sounded. We've got our deal. I mean to stick by it."

"Good." She relaxed a little. "Are there any workmen in the groves?" she asked. "I was hoping to find someplace very private."

"Trevor has a day off of school today and he's out along the access road, digging some channel out for new irrigation pipes. Other than that, you should have the place to yourself."

"Great." She favored him with the ghost of a smile. "I guess I'll get going then."

She turned toward the trees, looking young and fresh with the sunshine in her hair. He couldn't help but smile. "Not scared of those coyotes anymore?" he asked, as much to make her turn back and look at him one more time as anything else.

"Not in the daylight." She waved and he watched as she disappeared among the greenery.

He swore again, softly, obscenely, but it didn't make him feel any better. This had to stop. Sure, she was pretty and attractive and even interesting—and he was a normal, healthy male with natural urges. But that didn't mean he had to walk off a cliff into disaster. He'd done that before and found himself drowning in heartbreak. He wasn't going to let himself in for that sort of misery again.

"Go find yourself, Carly Stevens," he said aloud to the empty air. "And leave me alone."

Turning on his heel, he began striding quickly back toward the house.

CHAPTER SIX

IF THIS WAS GOING TO WORK, the man was going to have to stop being so darn provocative. Taking a deep breath, Carly tried to cleanse her mind of Joe and his dark eyes, but it was a struggle. She was here to think about Mark. Mark!

Walking faster and faster, she lost herself among the trees, reaching out to catch hold of a crisp leaf as she passed, crushing it in her hand and inhaling the fragrance.

It wasn't fair, of course. Joe was here in the flesh, as it were, someone she had to deal with in the here and now, and Mark was in danger of becoming a memory from the past. That was the only reason Joe seemed to blot Mark out the way he did. If they were both here with her, it would be a completely different story. Mark. What was he doing now? Had he read her note over a hundred times, trying to figure out why she'd run? He'd never be able to dig up the reasons because, to tell the truth, she was pretty fuzzy on them herself.

Why had she come all this way? And why here, to Amberville again? The reasons were more emotional impulse than any thought-out strategy. She'd had a feeling growing in her for weeks, months, and finally, when Mark had asked her to think about planning a future for the two of them, she'd realized she would have to confront her inner needs and get straight just exactly what she did want to do with her life.

She knew she'd been gliding for years, sailing along as though there were a purpose to her days, some goal she was after, when actually there was nothing but the constant need to have a place to go in the morning. It had been a nice ride. She'd learned a lot. The world at large saw her as an ambitious woman who worked hard, did well, moved up quickly. What they didn't know was that her work ethic had as much to do with her reluctance to go home to an empty apartment as it did with anything else.

Did Mark see the truth? She doubted it. They had been going together for almost a year, and they did well together. They liked the same things, enjoyed the same jokes, looked good in public. She might even be in love with him—at least as close to it as she'd ever been with any man. But what did he really know about her? What did she really know about him?

When he'd popped the big question, she'd felt as though someone had suddenly dashed cold water on her face and told her it was time to grow up. Suddenly she was being asked to consider a real if long-overdue step into honest-to-God commitment. She had to affirm an actual goal, announce where her life was headed. She had worked for Mark for quite some time, respected him and had a lot of affection for him. But was it love? Instead of jumping at his offer, she'd been torn, confused, not sure where to turn for advice. Her instincts had told her to go home. And since her mother's death had taken away that refuge, the only home she could think of was Amberville, the country town that existed like a haven in her memories.

This was where her childhood lay, where she had lived happily before her mother had snatched her up and taken her off, away from her father. And so she had left a letter for Mark, begging for his patience, closed up her apartment, and come "home" to think, to get her feet firmly on the ground and decide what she wanted to do with the rest of her life.

She hadn't counted on Doris, the only relative she'd kept any kind of contact with, being unable to put her up. She also hadn't counted on being thrust into the middle of a family going through its own sort of turmoil.

But that wasn't really accurate. The turmoil had a lot more to do with how she reacted to Joe than anything going on within the family structure itself. At least, she thought it did.

But to get back to Mark. He was a good man, a good politician, which was a trick not easy to pull off. If she married him, she would be caught up in the exciting center-stage of world events for a long, long time. She'd lived on the fringes of that world. She knew what it was like. Was it really what she wanted?

Coming to Amberville was supposed to bring all this into perspective for her, but it would probably take a little time. She took another deep breath, breathing in the ambience along with the citrus scent, and then she saw Trevor through the trees, a spade in his hand, working on a trench in the red earth.

The feeling of relief that swept over her when she realized she would have an excuse to stop thinking about her problems almost made her feel guilty. She didn't waste time mulling that over. Instead, she stepped forward and called out a greeting to the boy.

He swung around and stared at her as she came charging out of the undergrowth.

"Hi," she said brightly. "You're Trevor, aren't you?"

He nodded, leaning against the handle of his shovel, his dark eyes keen with interest.

"I'm Carly Stevens."

"I know."

He was a good-looking boy, tall, with wide shoulders and blond hair neatly cut. She liked him, liked the look in his face, liked the way a shy smile was beginning to curl the edges of his mouth.

"You look like your mother," she said.

His face changed and the smile disappeared. "No, my mom has blue eyes. I think I take after..." His voice trailed off and he looked worried.

She waited a moment, but he didn't go on. Surely he'd been about to say he took after his father. What had stopped him? She came closer and tried to read his mind from the expression on his face.

"Does your father have dark eyes?" she prompted.

He turned away and thrust the shovel into the dirt, hard, stared at it for a moment, then looked back at her. "My mother never told me who my father is," he said at last, his voice even, his gaze steady.

"Oh." Whoops. What could she say now? She should have realized that this might be the case. After all, Millie had been so young when she'd had Trevor. Obviously, the father of the baby hadn't stuck around to see things through. When would she learn to curb her tongue? Groping through her creative resources, she tried to think of a way to change the subject, fast, but her next comment didn't quite fill the bill.

"It's hard growing up without your father." She winced, but since she'd started on this road, she had to go on. "I know a little bit about that. I lived in town when I was young, but when I was ten, my mother took me away. I never saw my father again."

Trevor nodded solemnly. "So you came back to find him?"

"No, I..." She stopped, thinking. Everyone seemed to assume she was looking for her father. What if she did find him? She wasn't even sure she would want to do that if she could. "I came back to find my past, but I don't know if I need to find my father," she told him honestly.

He frowned. "But don't you think you would know yourself better if you found him?" he said tentatively. This was obviously something he had thought about a lot. "I mean, you could see where you got things, like the way you look, the way you act..."

She nodded slowly. "You're right. That could be helpful. But I'm not sure it's necessary. I've gotten along fine without knowing my father all these years. I'm sure you'll do okay, too."

She smiled at him, but he wasn't really listening. He studied her for a moment, then took a step toward her, his eyes alight with some impulse toward revelation. "I—you know, I never told anyone this, but I think I know who my father is."

Just a bit startled, she said, "Oh?"

He nodded. "Yeah. I figured it out. But I think I've always known, you know? I could just tell. And...it's kind of neat because I think I'm getting more like him every day."

"Oh." Surely she could dredge up some other word from the depths of her vocabulary. But for the moment, it seemed to be impossible. She stared at him, wondering why he gave every indication of being infected with the same need his mother had exhibited to open up to her in ways she was pretty sure he didn't ordinarily do. Was it because she was a stranger in town? Did they pour out their souls to every passing tourist? It seemed very odd, but somehow endearing at the same time.

"So he's someone you see all the time?" she asked weakly, though she really didn't want to know any more. It was none of her business, after all.

Trevor stared at her, not answering. His eyes darkened. "I don't know why they don't come right out and tell me it's him," he murmured, almost to himself.

Neither did she. Still, she was an outsider and it really had nothing to do with her. There had to be reasons. There were always reasons. "Have you tried talking to your mother about it?"

He laughed shortly. "No. We never talk about that stuff. I couldn't ask her. She'd just get that hurt look..." His voice faded away and he merely shook his head. "But one of these days," he went on softly, his eyes focusing into the distance, "I'm going to get up the nerve to ask him."

He didn't continue, and she was just as glad. What he was telling her was much too personal. She felt very uncomfortable hearing it.

It was funny, though. She wanted to reach out to this boy she hardly knew, to comfort him, to make all this old pain well again. There was something about him that drew her closer, made her care.

And that made her angry at his mother, his father. Could he be right about the identity of the man? If so, why hadn't the man acknowledged the tie between them? But on the other hand, what if he were wrong? Her heart ached for the boy. What if he laid his soul bare for this person, and the man rejected him?

"You know what, Trevor?" she said earnestly, touching his arm with her hand to get his attention back from his dreams of reconciliation. "Before you confront this man, you ought to do some digging."

He gazed at her blankly. "Digging? What do you mean?"

"Looking for clues, something concrete to base your hunch on. Old newspaper files. Old letters. Old pictures. I don't know. Maybe get a look at your birth certificate. You want to be absolutely sure before you... before you ask someone if he is your father."

"Is that what you're doing to find your father?"

She sighed. "Well, now that you mention it..." She stopped. What was she denying here? What was she resisting? She kept insisting to anyone who would listen that she had no interest in finding her father. But why not? She could at least ask around and find someone who knew him. What would it hurt to find out a few things? "Actually," she said slowly, "I just might."

A new feeling of excitement filled her. Why hadn't she allowed herself to consider the possibility before? She wasn't sure. But all at once it had become something she was looking forward to. And what if she actually found him?

Suddenly everything looked different. Why shouldn't she look for him? Knowing him might be exactly what she needed to give herself a new perspective on things, help her attain that peace of mind she'd been searching for.

"I tell you what," she said impulsively to Trevor. "I'll help you, if you help me. What do you say?"

Trevor's grin was impossibly lovable. "Deal," he said, sticking out a muddy hand.

She took it warmly and smiled back at him. He was such a nice kid. She felt as though she'd known him all her life.

JOE PAUSED just outside the green door to his mother's room. He always had to steel himself to face her lately. Taking a deep breath, he rapped sharply and let himself in, even though she hadn't invited him.

She was propped up against a dozen fluffy white pillows, her silver hair flawlessly combed and styled. The television was tuned to a game show. A plate of cookies sat on a tray to her right. The telephone and remote for the TV sat on the bedside table.

"Hello, Mother," he said, standing in the doorway.

"Darling." She smiled and patted a place on the bed. "Come here and see me. You've been away so much lately."

His steps were slow and reluctant, but he sat where she'd indicated and leaned close to kiss her cheek. The scent of lilac filled his head, making him want to sneeze.

"I've just been talking to Gloria Engles on the phone," his mother told him with a sense of quiet satisfaction. "Do you know that her son Sam is remarrying? He's been so lonely since Grace died, and now he'll have someone to take care of that dear little baby...."

"Mother," Joe broke in, stemming the flow of words he knew were meant to make him feel guilty, to manipulate him into doing what his mother had been trying to get him to do almost all his life. "That's great about Sam, but I don't want to talk about that right now. I have to tell you something. Jeremy had an accident yesterday."

Her expression didn't change from the relentless cheerfulness she always exhibited. "Oh, yes, dear, I know." She gave him a sunny smile. "Tanya at the emergency room called me last night and told me all about it. How is he today? I noticed he didn't go to school with Beth."

"He's fine." Joe turned and looked at her, trying hard not to be annoyed. She was his mother. He loved her. He owed her... well, respect at least. "You didn't notice when it happened? You didn't hear Beth banging on the door?"

She shook her head with exaggerated regret. "I must have had the television on too loud. I'm so sorry I didn't hear them. Of course, I couldn't have done anything much but called 911 for him."

Joe didn't respond. A part of him wanted to let go the anger he felt for her inattention to his children, and at the same time he had to remember her disability. It must be horrible for her to be cooped up this way all the time. He had to be careful not to let resentment blot out that fact. So he didn't say anything, but stared out the window, waiting for the emotion to fade.

"Has Millie been by this morning?" Phyllis was asking brightly.

He nodded slowly, clenching and unclenching his hands. "She put in some petunias for us."

Phyllis laughed softly. "That darling. But why didn't she come on up and see me? We haven't had a visit for days."

"She had to get back home." He looked out the window again, noting the panoramic view she had of most of the yard. The ditch where the tractor had gone over was too far to the right to be visible. He calmed down a little. Of course, she hadn't seen a thing. How could she have had any idea Jeremy was in trouble and not have done anything? She was annoying at times, but not completely heartless.

"Millie is such a dear," Phyllis was going on. "If only you had married her back then all those years ago when she needed you so badly."

Joe turned and glared at her. It had been a while since she'd played this old tune. What had brought it up again? "Mother, she was sixteen and I was eighteen. If I'd married her then, I wouldn't have Beth and Jeremy today."

Phyllis laughed softly, as if to say it was all just a whim, nothing to get excited about. "Well, of course, there are advantages and disadvantages to everything, aren't there? Think what a difference it would have made in your life, in Millie's life, and of course, in Trevor's life." She sighed and her gaze sharpened as she looked at him before continuing very carefully. "And now we have this new person in the house."

Joe almost grinned. He'd wondered how long it would take her to get around to this. "How did you know about Carly?"

"I take phone calls, darling. I talk to people. And I see what goes on out my window. Now, tell me all about her."

He shrugged, willing to do that at least. "Her name's Carly Stevens. She won't be here for long. She's just in town for a sort of vacation, and she needed a place to stay. She heard that I needed help with the kids, so...Doris at the coffee shop put us together."

Phyllis's dark eyes gleamed. "Doris. Ah...of course."

Joe moved restlessly. "So...that's about it."

Phyllis gave him a look that told him she wasn't about to be satisfied with such meager information. "Has she told you anything about her background?" she asked him.

"You mean, did I ask for references?"

Phyllis pursed her lips. "No. I mean, did she tell you about her father and how she used to live here when she was small?"

Joe blinked, surprised. "A little. How did you know all this? What did you do, recognize her from the window?"

Phyllis ignored his questions. "What did she say exactly?"

"She just said she'd grown up here, that her parents split up when she was ten and she hasn't seen or heard from her father since. Why?"

She was gazing at him sharply. "She said that? She has no idea where he is?"

He nodded. "That's what she said."

Phyllis frowned, thinking. "Then she came to look for him, didn't she?"

"She says not. She came to revisit the old home-stead, so to speak. And to think over where her life is going. And that's about it."

Phyllis let out a rather unladylike snort. "So she says."

Joe shook his head, puzzled. "What makes you doubt it? What do you know about this?"

Instead of answering his questions, Phyllis posed one of her own. "Do you remember him?"

"Howard Stevens? No. Everyone else seems to, though."

"Everyone?" Phyllis clutched the hem of her bed-jacket in her pale hand. "You mean ... have you told Millie?"

This whole topic was getting muddled and more and more mysterious. Joe was beginning to lose patience with it. "No," he said evenly. "Millie is the one who told me."

Phyllis gasped and threw herself back against the pillows. "Why don't you turn off the television?" she suggested, her voice strained. "I think I'd better fill you in on things you seem to have forgotten."

Joe stared at her for a moment before he rose to comply. He had a very bad feeling about this. He was pretty sure he was about to hear something that would change everything. And at this moment, he wasn't sure he was ready for changes.

JOE WAS IN THE DEN with Jeremy when Carly came back from her sojourn in the orchards. He stood at the window and watched her walk toward the house. Her step was light and she had a spray of orange blossoms in her hair. She looked like a woman without a care in the world.

His shoulders tightened. He should get rid of her, get her out of here, and he knew it. How was he going to tell her?

"Jeremy?" he said, still watching Carly.

The only response he heard was another page being turned in the coloring book Jeremy was working diligently at finishing before Beth got home.

"Jeremy?" He turned and looked at his son, and the little face rose slowly, reluctantly, to acknowledge his attention, crayon poised. "Do you like Carly?" Joe asked him.

He gazed back into his father's eyes and shrugged. "She's all right, I guess," he said noncommittally. "She can't make waffles."

Well, Joe thought, *there you have it. The kids aren't all that attached to her yet. Why let things go on until they are? It would be best if she left quickly, quietly, with a minimum of hassle.* And he would have to be the one to tell her so.

He heard her come in the back door and he went out into the hall, walking slowly, trying to find the words he would use. He could hear her doing something in the kitchen, humming as she worked. He hesitated for a moment, listening to her. She sounded happy. There was all too little happiness in this house these days. It was too bad....

Swearing softly, he shook his head and made the move into the doorway, and there he stopped, leaning against the jamb, watching her.

She turned and gave him a smile that reminded him of sunshine coming from behind a cloud on a gloomy day.

"Hi," she said gaily. "It's way past time for lunch. Will sandwiches be okay?"

He hesitated. He should go ahead and tell her now. The longer he waited, the harder it was going to be. "Sure," he heard himself saying. "Sandwiches would be great. Thanks a lot."

She smiled again. "No problem." Spinning, she pulled open the refrigerator and began rummaging through the shelves.

He went on out through the kitchen door and into the yard, his hands thrust deep into his pockets. This was going to be harder than he'd thought. He'd been standing right there and yet he hadn't been able to get the words out. But he would. Just give him some time. He would.

CHAPTER SEVEN

"HOW DOES THAT HEAD FEEL, Mr. Jeremy?" Carly asked as she plunked a peanut-butter-and-jelly sandwich in front of where the boy was sitting at the kitchen table. "Have you had any problems with it today?"

She stopped and waited for a reply, watching his face. He looked at her quickly in a searching, questioning way that surprised her. For a moment, she wondered if he were trying to figure out what she'd said, but then his face relaxed and he answered.

"I'm okay."

He turned his attention to his food, but she stayed where she was, interested and a little concerned. There was a haunted look to the boy's eyes, as though he knew something he wished he didn't know, or had seen something best left unnoticed. Impulsively, she reached out and caressed his shoulder with her fingertips, searching for some way to make a connection with this child who seemed so lonely.

"Jeremy, I'm very glad you're okay. But you let me know if anything bothers you, all right? It's part of my job to help you when you need help. Okay?"

He stared up at her for a long moment without speaking, and she wondered what he was thinking. She couldn't read him at all. And then she realized he was looking behind her. Startled, she turned to find Joe standing in the kitchen doorway, watching them.

How long had he been there? It didn't really matter, but she colored slightly anyway. There was nothing to be embarrassed about. Was there? So what the heck was wrong with her?

This wouldn't do, this jumping out of her skin whenever she saw him. She was going to fight it. Withdrawing her hand from the boy's shoulder, she smiled a welcome to his father and tried to pretend there was nothing unusual going on inside her.

"I hope you like ham and Swiss," she said, going to the counter and picking up two plates, one for him and one for her. She carried them back to the table and sat across from him, with Jeremy between them.

"It's my favorite," Joe told her, but there was something in his eyes that made her look away quickly again, and kept the redness in her cheeks.

They ate in silence. She considered telling him about Trevor and the things they'd talked about in the orchard, but on second thought she decided not to. So she picked at her food and Joe ate heartily and Jeremy ate little tiny bites and stared at his plate. The ticking of the clock on the wall was as loud as cannon fire, and the sound of milk splashing into Jeremy's glass as Joe refilled it reminded her of the surf at the beach. Even louder was the echoing silence of the tension at the table. Carly wasn't sure why, but she knew they all felt it. And she couldn't think of a thing to say to break it.

Joe was the one who finally spoke, and the sudden sound of his voice made her jump again. She closed her eyes for a second, giving herself a good talking to. This had to stop.

"I'm going to have to take the tractor in to town to the mechanic," Joe was saying, glancing down at his son. "It's got more wrong with it than I can fix."

Jeremy's face crumpled with guilt. "I'm sorry, Daddy," he mumbled. "I'm sorry I wrecked it."

Joe's stern look didn't soften. "I hope this will teach you not to fool around with machinery you're not old enough to handle," he said evenly.

Jeremy nodded, looking miserably down at his plate, a shining suggestion of tears pooling on his lower lids.

Carly itched to reach for him. She looked at Joe. He was in that damned male mode that brooked no softening. There was a lesson to be taught here. He wasn't about to unbend and comfort the child.

Well, as far as she was concerned the lesson was learned and over with. It was time to lighten the mood. There had to be something she could say... something she could do.... An idea came and she smiled to herself, looking quickly at Joe who was finishing up his sandwich. Good. His mouth was full. She'd have time to get started before he could say anything to stop her.

Leaning down near his son's ear, she said softly, "Hey, Jeremy. Do you know how you can tell an elephant from a banana?"

The boy was looking at her, blinking away the tears and hanging on her words, but clearly puzzled. Quickly, he flashed a glance at his father, who looked just as startled as he was, then shook his head.

She smiled at Jeremy, encouraging him. "Bananas are yellow," she said matter-of-factly, and then, not giving that time to completely sink in, she went on. "Do you know what the banana said to the monkey?"

His eyes shifted again, but this time there was definite interest in them. "No."

"Nothing." She shrugged as though it were self-
evident. "Bananas can't talk. Do you know why the
elephants quit their jobs at the ballpark?"

Laughter was beginning to bubble just below the
surface. Little-kid laughter that went with silly jokes.
She could see it in his eyes. He was sitting up straighter,
looking at her, his misery starting to fade. "Why?"

"They were tired of working for peanuts."

There was a real, honest giggle this time. Pleased, she
grinned at him and ventured just one more.

"Do you know how to tell when a rhinoceros is getting ready to charge?"

He giggled at the very concept. "No. How?"

"He takes out his credit card."

They all laughed that time. Carly met Joe's gaze and
he was laughing too. The ice was broken. The rest of
the lunch hour passed quickly, and the longer they sat
together, the more they laughed. Carly felt a sense of
peace and happiness she hadn't felt in a long time.
She'd done something good here. She could feel it.

Joe watched her, glad despite everything that he
hadn't sent her away just yet. She was good for Jeremy. She was good for the mood in this house. It was
too bad she couldn't stay.

She threw out a mock insult, making him laugh
again. He teased her and reached across the table to
dab at her milk mustache with his napkin and saw how
his son looked at her with laughing eyes. Damn it all,
it was really too bad.

JOE LEFT to load the tractor onto the trailer he was attaching to the back of the truck. Jeremy went to his bedroom to play video games. Carly straightened the kitchen, then went to the den to peruse the older books, looking for anything that might shed some light on the history of Amberville and the valley. She wanted to lay a firm foundation for her search for her father.

She found plenty of material covering the old Spanish land grants of the early nineteenth century, about the pioneers who came across the mountains to settle the valley after gold was discovered in the 1840s, how the Californios lost most of their land to taxes and greedy speculators by the turn of the century, the coming of the Okies from the Dust Bowl during the Great Depression, the post-war building boom. It was all very interesting, but not specifically related to her problems, and therefore not very helpful. But the afternoon slipped away quickly and suddenly she realized it was almost time for Beth to come home from school.

That meant one thing. Dinner loomed. Tonight she was determined to make something herself and not rely on frozen dinners.

A quick perusal of the kitchen brought good news. All the makings of a quick spaghetti sauce were present and accounted for, as well as a nice big package of very long noodles, bread perfect for smothering in garlic butter and lettuce and tomatoes for a crisp salad. This she could do, and she set about doing it, humming all the while.

The phone rang. It was Doris.

"Carly? Are you all right?"

No. Actually, she was in a tailspin of sorts. But she wasn't so sure any longer that she wanted rescuing from it. So she lied.

"I'm fine, Doris. It's hectic around here, but . . ."

"You sound like a drowning woman on my answering machine, honey. I can be out there in half an hour."

"No. Actually, Doris, it's okay. I was just a little panicked this morning. I'm sorry. I think I'll stay."

"You're sure?"

She wasn't sure of anything any longer. She'd come out here to get her head together, and instead of clearing her mind she was cluttering it up with all sorts of new puzzles that were meant to drive her crazy.

But she couldn't tell Doris that.

"I'm sure," she said wistfully. "I really appreciate your concern. But I think I'll stick it out."

She hung up the telephone and looked around her a bit nervously. She'd made a big decision here. She had a feeling there would be times when she would regret it. But she'd taken a step and she wouldn't look back. She would take care of these kids as long as she stayed.

Suddenly she realized she hadn't seen Jeremy for a long, long time. Memories of what had happened to him the day before surfaced, shaking her. She ran up to his room, but it was empty.

"Jeremy?" she called, walking quickly through the upper floor, then through the lower rooms. There was no answer, no sign of him. Her heart began to beat a little more quickly.

She ran outside, shading her eyes against the afternoon sun, calling again and again. But nothing moved except the wind in the trees. Silence lay over the land in a sleepy hush.

Now she was really beginning to get worried. There was something vulnerable about the boy that made this disappearance seem more ominous than it might have otherwise. And just yesterday he had proved how easily he could bumble his way into danger....

"Jeremy?"

There was no answer, no sign of life in any direction. Pictures of the boy lying in a ditch spun into her mind—Jeremy being hit by a truck on the highway, Jeremy being picked up by a shifty-eyed stranger and carried off, Jeremy being shot by a hunter who mistook him for a coyote... The grisly possibilities were endless and they panicked her.

She turned back to look at the house and suddenly had a thought. That mysterious green door—it was time to find out what was behind it.

She ran into the house and up the stairs, not pausing to think for a moment before rapping sharply on the door. There was no answer, but she thought she could hear the sounds of a television on the other side. She rapped again more firmly, calling out, "Hello in there. I hope you don't mind but I'm coming in."

Taking the knob in her hand, she turned it and stepped into the room.

The room contrasted dramatically with the rest of the house. Drapes and couches in designer colors, thick, plush carpeting, raised wallpaper, filtered light. A small, tidy kitchen was set up in one corner. An elaborately carved wardrobe stood in another. The older woman who inhabited the room leaned back against pillows so white that they almost blinded the eye. A thick down comforter was casually draped across the bed, its pattern bold and expensive-looking.

And there, in front of a big-screen television, sat Jeremy, eating chocolates out of a five-pound, foil-covered box.

"Jeremy!" she cried with relief. "I've been looking all over for you. I was so worried."

"Why, he was right here, visiting his grandmother," the woman said brightly, her black eyes sparkling. "What's so surprising about that?"

Carly looked at the woman and knew instinctively that she had set this up. But why?

"I'm Carly Stevens," she said, putting her hand out. "You must be Joe's mother."

Phyllis Matthews took it with her pale fingertips and released it almost immediately. "Nice to meet you, dear. I hear you've been taking splendid care of the children."

"Well, I don't know much about child care, but I've been doing my best."

"Of course you have."

Carly moved uncomfortably. She couldn't put her finger on why, but she felt a lot of animosity from the woman. What could she possibly have against her? They'd barely met. She couldn't see the expression in her shoe-button black eyes. They glittered and shone and reflected light, but they didn't allow any sort of penetration.

Her impulse was to get out of there, but she couldn't do that. Phyllis Matthews, regardless of how she felt about her, was a resource she couldn't afford to ignore. Now that she had definitely decided to try to track her father down, she was going to have to do some serious digging.

"I don't know how much Joe has told you about me," she said, standing near the bed. "I lived here when I was a child, and I'm looking for information about my father. I haven't heard from him since I was ten years old. Howard Stevens was his name. Do you remember him?"

Phyllis sank back into her pillows with a look of resentment on her face that seemed to say she thought Carly was rushing things here. "Howard Stevens?" She pursed her lips and spoke reluctantly. "Now let me think. I do seem to remember that name. There was a man who ran a little grocery store—"

"That was him!" In spite of herself, Carly got excited. "What do you remember about him?"

"It seems to me he preached in that little white church on the corner of Sierra and Placer on Sundays...."

"Yes." Carly forgot her wariness and sank onto the bed, smiling eagerly, moving the ivory-handled cane that lay in her way. "What else?"

Phyllis stiffened, as though annoyed somewhat by her familiarity. But she answered readily enough. "He was a tall, good-looking man. Though I wouldn't say he looked a bit like you."

"No. I take after my mother."

"Well, all I remember is that he was there for a while, and then all of a sudden, he wasn't there any longer. I don't think I ever gave it a second thought."

Carly felt a bit deflated. "You have no idea where he might have gone?"

Phyllis waved a negligent hand. "No. Not a clue."

Carly blinked, looking at her with a slight frown. Somehow she had a feeling the woman was lying to her.

But maybe that was just because she wanted so badly to get further than this, and it seemed that it just wasn't going to happen.

"Do you have any idea of anywhere I could go, anyone I could talk to about him?" she persisted.

Phyllis's mouth tightened. "No, as I told you, I hardly knew the man."

Carly drew back, looking toward the window. "That's what Millie said...." she murmured.

Phyllis sat up straighter. "You've talked to Millie about this?" she demanded.

Carly looked at her, surprised by her vehemence. "Yes."

The woman made a visible effort to calm herself. "You—you shouldn't bother Millie with such things."

"Bother her?" Carly was puzzled. "I just asked—"

"Millie has had a hard life. It does no good to remind her of things...like this...." Phyllis seemed agitated, her hands fluttering uselessly.

Carly's inclination was to leave her alone to her delusions. But she couldn't give up now. After all, she might find out something useful if she pressed a bit further, and so she stood over the bed, using body language along with everything else. She was glad that Jeremy was absorbed in his television show, leaving her free to talk. "Remind her of what things?" she prodded. "What do you mean? Why should this upset Millie?"

Phyllis shook her head wordlessly, and Carly leaned a bit closer. "What is there in Millie's past that you don't want her reminded of?"

The woman's eyes showed fear. Carly almost gasped aloud, it was so obvious. She held her breath, waiting for what Phyllis might say, knowing it was going to be something spectacular, something that would set her back on her heels.

But the moment of possibilities faded as quickly as it had come, and the eyes looked hard and shiny as pebbles once again. "Oh, you just don't understand anything," the woman fretted. "It's not Millie's past I'm worried about. It's her future." She gave Carly a triumphant look. "Joe and Millie will be getting married, you know," she said smugly. "It's just a matter of time."

Carly drew back. This wasn't what she'd wanted to hear at all. "Oh?" she said.

Phyllis was smiling now, confident once again. "Yes, of course. They've been sweethearts since they were children. Through one thing and another—the crazy twists of fate—they haven't been able to get together to fulfill their destiny. But finally the way is clear for them. They'll be announcing their engagement any day now."

Carly felt cold. It wasn't that she believed what the woman was saying. But she could see that it was very much what Phyllis wanted for her son. "I see."

"It's fate, you know. They belong together. They always have." Phyllis sighed happily. "I really think you should leave. Just pack up your cute little silk city clothes and get out. Joe doesn't need you here. He can count on me to take a bigger part in caring for the children until Millie moves in. I'm feeling much stronger now. I can handle it. And, to tell you the truth, you're just in the way."

Carly stared at her, suddenly sure she knew who it was who had gone through her suitcases the night before. She was supposed to be almost bedridden, but she had been up and about not long ago. It gave her an odd little shiver down her back to think of this woman sitting up here like a giant black widow spider, spinning her web and watching everyone else from her perch. She turned and took in the view Phyllis had of the yard and the barn. She lay here all day keeping tabs on what was going on, didn't she? She'd seen her talking to Joe this morning. She'd seen him taking hay from her hair.

Whirling, she looked into the woman's eyes. Yes, she'd seen it all and she was determined to get Carly out of here before she did anything to ruin her plans for Millie.

"Thank you for your own personal insights into the situation," she said carefully. "I'll keep your opinion in mind."

Throwing back what she hoped looked like a carefree smile, she went to the door.

"Let me know if you need anything," she added, just before she went through the doorway and closed the green door behind her.

What a controlling woman. To think that Joe could have been raised by a woman like that. Carly shook her head and turned back toward the kitchen. Funny, but that place was beginning to be her refuge.

BETH WAS ALREADY HOME, eating a snack over the sink, and Joe came home not long after. An hour of chatting with Beth and thinking over what she'd been through all day was just about enough to give her a perspective on what was going on around here and she was ready for him when he came back into the house.

Beth was off doing her homework. Jeremy had come down from his grandmother's room, but he hadn't said a word and Carly assumed he had gone to play in the den. So she was alone when Joe drove up and came in through the kitchen door.

She turned to face him. Her eyes met his. He hesitated, looking at her questioningly, and she felt her pulse quicken. Relentlessly, she forced back the reaction that seemed to come naturally when he was near. It was an automatic response, nothing more. She was going to have to train herself not to do it.

"Joe?" she said. "I—I need to talk to you."

He half turned back toward the doorway and she reached out, afraid he was going to try to escape, and curled her hand around part of his forearm, holding him there.

"Joe, I have to know. Am I in the way here? Do you want me to leave? Because if you do..."

She didn't get any further. Suddenly she realized someone had come in behind Joe. She didn't have to look at her fully to know it was Millie, with Trevor bringing up the rear.

"Hi, Carly," Millie said cheerfully. "I hope you don't mind. Joe invited us to dinner." Her gaze darted from Joe's face to Carly's hand on his arm, and then fixed itself on Carly's eyes. "I thought you might need a little help on your first night cooking for the family."

Carly had a perverse impulse to leave her hand right where it was, but she fought it. "Of course we're happy to have you for dinner," she said brightly, pulling away from Joe. "And I appreciate your offer to help." She managed a fairly sunny smile at the woman. "But I've already taken care of that. Dinner is ready anytime the rest of you are.''

Millie and Joe both looked surprised, and Carly felt vindicated. She knew it was childish, but she made a vow right then and there to study the cookbook in the morning and never, ever, let this woman know just how inexperienced she was in the culinary arts.

Millie helped set the table in the dining room and then helped serve, and Carly relaxed, letting their natural liking for each other grow and make things easy between them. Dinner was pleasant enough. All the others at the table had known each other forever and were comfortable together, the children as well as the adults. Carly found herself getting quieter and quieter as the others talked about the history they shared. She wasn't interested in the incidents so much as she was in watching Joe and Millie, trying to analyze their relationship.

Were they in love?

Joe had said he had no girlfriend, but that didn't necessarily mean anything. His mother certainly thought he and Millie were an item. And Millie was hanging around like someone who wanted to keep an oar in the water. Mutual affection—yes, they had that in spades. You could see it in their shared laughs, their nods and recognitions, the way they talked with each other. But love—she wasn't so sure. Shouldn't there be a sense of excitement when their eyes met? Shouldn't there be a feeling that they longed to touch each other? Wouldn't they be grabbing odd moments alone?

But maybe this wasn't that sort of love. Maybe they had known each other so long, and so well....

"You see what I mean?" Trevor was leaning close to her and whispering in her ear as Joe and Millie teased each other about some picnic where Millie had dropped a cake on the grass.

Carly turned and smiled at him. "What?"

The boy's face was endearingly earnest. "You see how much I'm starting to look like him? In the eyes, I mean. And my shoulders..."

Carly went numb. It came to her in a flash who he thought his father was. It was Joe, of course. Why hadn't she realized it before?

Reaching for a glass of water, she drank it dry. She had to fight to keep her breath from coming in short gasps. Joe... Trevor's father? Oh my God, no!

He was still whispering near her ear, comparing himself to Joe, but she couldn't take in his words any longer. The idea filled her mind, filled her senses, and she couldn't do anything but think quickly, trying to find reasons why it couldn't be true.

Yet the facts kept coming back to haunt her. They'd always been friends. They'd known each other back then. Phyllis seemed to think they'd been close. And she should know. She'd said they were destined to be together. Was this what she'd meant, that it was only right, that Joe would be coming full circle when he married Millie?

Something nagged at her, something wouldn't let her decide it had to be true. Maybe it was only her strong desire to deny it. Maybe it was something else. But whatever it was, she welcomed it. She didn't want Joe to be Trevor's father. She didn't want that at all.

They all helped with clearing the table and doing the dishes, and finally the kids were in bed and Millie and

Trevor were leaving through the kitchen door. Carly stood beside Joe as they called out their last good-nights. He closed the door and turned off the lights, and they started back through the darkened kitchen toward the lighted hall, but before they got there, Joe reached out and stopped her with a touch to her shoulder.

She swung around to face him, her silvery hair flying out and settling about her shoulders.

"You were saying?" he said, head cocked to the side as he looked at her. Even in the dim light he could see that her cheeks were flushed. She'd been looking that way all evening. Why did she have to be so damned pretty anyway?

She was staring at him blankly. "What?"

"Before we were interrupted. About whether or not you were in the way."

"Oh."

She didn't seem to have anything to add and he shifted his weight restlessly from one foot to the other. This was it, his opening. He should tell her now—tell her she had to go, tell her things weren't working out and she should look for another place to stay.

But he wasn't going to tell her that at all. He didn't want her to leave. He didn't know what he was going to do with her if she stayed, but he was sure he didn't want her gone.

"Why don't you stay," he said simply, blocking out all the rest.

She stared at him without saying anything for a long moment, then frowned. "I need to know the truth, Joe," she said, moving closer as though she wanted to see his reactions better, see beyond the shadows. "Are you and Millie . . . are you getting married soon?"

He frowned, searching her face. "Why do you keep asking me about Millie?" he countered.

"Because—" she took a deep breath "—I met your mother today. She told me . . ."

He laughed shortly, turning away. "Don't listen to my mother. She's been trying to get me to marry Millie since the day they brought her home from the hospital as a baby. My mother has some crazy idea that we've been betrothed since childhood."

He looked back at Carly. Her hair looked like spun gold in the hazy light. He knew in one stabbing moment that he was going to regret not sending her away—and yet he also knew he couldn't do what ought to be done.

"Don't pay any attention to that talk. Millie and I are not getting married."

Carly wet her lips with her tongue. She believed him. Maybe she was a crazy fool, but she believed him. Still, there was more to it than that. She had to try and find out the truth. She couldn't come right out and ask him if he were Trevor's father. Subtle questions would have to do.

She took another deep breath and dived in. "Did you and Millie ever date much—say, in high school?" Subtle as a blowtorch. But she saw no other way to do the digging she had to do.

He didn't seem to mind. He shrugged. "Sure. Now and then. But that was a long time ago."

"About seventeen years ago?" She held her breath and braced for the explosion.

But there was none. Joe nodded, his eyes clear, not surprised or insulted by the question. "Yeah, about that. Why?"

Carly blinked and went back to breathing. This was not the reaction of a man tortured by guilt over having left a pregnant lover to fend for herself in the world. Either he wasn't Trevor's father—or he had no conscience whatsoever.

"I just want to get it straight. I don't want to... to get between the two of you..." Oh Lord, there was no delicate way to say this, was there?

"Between me and Millie?" That got a reaction. First he looked incredulous, then wary. He'd moved closer, so close she knew that if she let herself, she would be able to feel the heat of his body. When he finally went on, his voice was low, husky, mocking.

"What are you talking about, Carly? How could you get between Millie and me? Just exactly what are you planning?"

She looked up at him and all she could see was his mouth, his full, smooth lips, the way his teeth flashed in the dark. Her heartbeat skipped and she felt her cheeks heating up again. What would it be like to kiss him? Excitement shivered through her and she was breathless as she forced her gaze away.

"I—I'm planning to take care of your children," she said huskily, looking everywhere but at him, trying to pretend she hadn't just been staring at his mouth. "That's all."

His grin twisted knowingly. "Meaning you have no plans to take care of me?" he asked softly.

He was teasing. She knew he was teasing. Still, his words, the sense of his body so close, the soothing sound of his voice, all made her terrifyingly light-headed. She had to get out of here, quickly, before something happened.

She couldn't answer him. Wordlessly, she backed away and turned, heading for her room. When she reached the stairs, she glanced back, sure that he'd be laughing at her. His eyes were following her progress, but there wasn't a hint of humor in their cloudy depths. And that shook her even more.

She hurried to her room, not allowing herself to think until she'd stepped inside and closed the door behind her. Then she leaned back, eyes closed, and tried to put things into perspective.

Why did the man keep doing this to her? She'd never been like this with Mark. They'd dated and laughed and worked together and there had always been a warm sense of sharing between them—never this wild, tingling excitement she felt just looking into Joe's eyes. What was the matter with her?

Physical attraction. That was it. He was certainly attractive and she was just responding in a natural way to what her hormones were telling her when he was near. She took a deep breath and threw herself on her bed. That was it. Pure chemical reaction. Had nothing to do with anything real or lasting. She would get over it soon, as she got more used to him.

But in the meantime, it was playing havoc with her ability to think about Mark and her future with the man who had asked her to marry him. She had only been here for a little over twenty-four hours. What was her state of mind going to be like after another few days?

CHAPTER EIGHT

"'AND THE GROUCHY OLD BEAR sent Billy home with hugs and kisses for his entire family.'" Carly closed the book and smiled at Beth, snuggled down into her snowy covers.

"And they all lived happily ever after," Beth chanted.

Carly laughed. "Of course they did." She leaned over and gave Jeremy a quick hug. "And so did the grouchy old bear," she teased him.

She almost got a smile. His little shoulders stayed stiff with her hug, but at least he didn't pull away as he had the first day or so she'd been here.

It had been seven days since she'd arrived—seven days full of hard work and learning something new about kids—and herself—every moment. In a funny way she was beginning to feel at home.

"Off to bed with you," she told Jeremy, giving him a nudge to get him started toward his own room. "Tomorrow we're going to make the bus without having to run for it."

"For the first time," murmured Beth, already half asleep.

"For the first time," Carly agreed, smiling down at her precious face. "Good night, sweetheart."

She bent down to kiss Beth's cheek, and as she rose and turned she realized Joe was in the doorway, watching. She started, as though she'd been doing something wrong. But she hadn't been, dammit. She was getting darned sick of the way he kept her off balance all the time.

She straightened, making herself as tall as possible, forcing a calm and cool facade she had to manufacture out of thin air. "Oh look, Beth. Your daddy is here to kiss you good-night."

She stood back as Joe went to his daughter and gathered her up into his arms, murmuring endearments, cherishing her. Carly watched for a moment, surprising herself when she realized a lump was threatening in her throat. She wasn't sure if she were yearning for the father's love she had been without for so many years or touched by the affection Joe didn't try to hide. Either way, she felt like an interloper, and she left the room quickly, stopping by Jeremy's room to tuck him in.

"Good night, tiger," she said. She didn't dare try to kiss him, but she ruffled the hair on top of his head and smiled down at him.

He looked up but didn't smile. "Good night," he said.

She hesitated, watching as he closed his eyes and pulled his teddy bear closer. He was such a beautiful child, but he worked so hard at keeping the world at arm's length. She'd talked with the others about him. Phyllis said he was just going through a stage. Millie said he had been traumatized when he lost his mother. Therapy, she suggested. She'd been trying to get Joe to take him to a therapist for months. "Therapy?" Joe

had snorted when she'd raised the idea with him.
"Jeremy doesn't need therapy. He's no nut case. He's
doing fine."

That was where Joe was wrong. The boy was not
doing fine. Carly wished with all her heart she knew
what she could do to change things around for him.
Her instincts told her that love would do the trick. But
how could it help if he wouldn't let her close enough to
love him?

Joe was coming down the hall toward his son's
room. She turned, blew Jeremy a kiss, and went the
other way so as not to have to face Joe again.

Avoiding Joe—that was one of the main things she
did all day. And yet, at the same time, she always
seemed to be finding excuses to be near him. It was
crazy. Insane. She didn't understand it. She didn't understand herself. Funny, before she'd run from Mark
and come back to California, life had really seemed so
simple. She'd come here to give herself time to clear up
just a few things, and instead a thousand new dilem-
mas had developed. Wouldn't it be great just to go
back to simple?

But even more than that, what she wished more than
anything else in the world was that she could read the
emotions behind those dark eyes of Joe's. What was he
thinking? She had no idea.

She went downstairs to the kitchen and spent some
time straightening things, wiping down the counter,
and setting out the toaster and frying pan for breakfast. She was getting used to the routine. To her surprise, work like this, and planting flowers in the garden
and interacting with the kids, was taking up her days
and leaving her hardly any time at all for thinking

things through. After seven days, she was already settling in. Who would have believed this city girl would
feel so comfortable here?

She heard Joe coming down the stairs but didn't
think twice about it. He usually went into the den and
watched the news or read for awhile before going to
bed. So she was surprised when he came into the
kitchen and sat down at the table. Turning, she gave
him an uncertain smile.

"Can I have another piece of that cherry pie?" he
asked.

All wariness fell away. "You like the pie?" she asked
with ill-concealed delight. It was her first pie-making
attempt and she was proud of it. She'd only had to call
Millie once for advice on how thin to roll the dough for
the crust.

"It's pretty good," he allowed, his dark eyes soft
and accessible.

This time her smile was genuine. "Okay. For that,
you can have all the pie you want."

She cut him a thick slice and sat down across from
him to watch him eat, chattering with more exhilara-
tion than nervousness. He responded in kind. They
were feeling free and easy together for a change. She
liked that.

He ate a few bites and she watched, content in his
pleasure. When he looked up and met her eyes, he
smiled.

"You've been working real hard, Carly," he commented. "I've been meaning to tell you how much I
appreciate it."

"I've been enjoying it," she told him.

"Really?" He searched her face as though he couldn't quite see how that could be true.

"Really," she assured him. "It's so different from what I'm used to. It's kind of like a businessman taking a vacation on a dude ranch, don't you think? Total immersion in a foreign culture."

He laughed. "Kind of, I guess. So that makes you the greenhorn dude..."

"And you the crusty old cowboy."

They grinned at one another, and just when Carly was congratulating herself on how nice and friendly they were keeping it, making sure not to let that electric charge develop between them, it happened again, just zinged out of nowhere, and she was shivering inside once more, just as always.

She looked away quickly, so he wouldn't see. She didn't think he noticed. He was saying, "Still, don't work yourself too hard. You ought to take some time off now and then."

She nodded, tracing her thumbnail along the pattern in the tablecloth. She could keep her equilibrium if she tried hard enough. Just block it out, she told herself. Ignore it, and it will surely go away. She took a deep breath and looked up at him, steeling herself. "I am, actually. In fact, I'm going to need to take some time off tomorrow," she told him, hoping he didn't notice that she was looking at his left ear instead of into his eyes.

But he wasn't noticing things like that. Her words had caught his attention. "Tomorrow?" His fork poised in the air.

"Yes. I want to go into town and talk to some people who might know something about my father."

He took another bite in silence. She could tell it troubled him. "Why do you want to do that?" he asked at last. "I thought that wasn't really in your plans." He frowned, putting down the fork. "I thought you said you'd come here to get your head together so you could go back and marry that guy who loves you."

She stared at him, surprised by his reaction. Why did he care? After all, she was just going into town to talk to a few people. It was true that when she'd first arrived she'd claimed to have no interest in finding her father. At that time, she'd actually believed it herself. But things had changed. She had changed. She was busy changing every minute. Wasn't that what life was all about?

"That's true," she answered him slowly. "But the more I've been thinking about it the more I've come to realize that finding out about my father, who he was, why my mother left him, where he's gone, is all part of what I need to do to put myself together."

Joe shook his head, avoiding her eyes. She couldn't see his face fully, but she had the feeling that he was upset.

"That's hogwash," he said shortly, wiping his mouth with the napkin. "It's all old news. Old history has nothing to do with you anymore. Live for today." He turned and stared at her. "You should go on from here and forget the past. Don't wallow in that sort of thing. It won't do you any good."

Now he was really beginning to annoy her. This was hardly any of his business in the first place, and she didn't like being second-guessed this way about her own feelings and her needs. She leaned forward and said her piece with conviction.

"How can I forget the past? How can anyone? The past is part of what you are today. The past is part of what makes your present."

He leaned closer, too, facing her across the table. "Not if you don't want it to," he said, his eyes hard as glass, his voice almost fierce. "It's up to you."

She shook her head slowly, staring at him, wondering what he was really talking about, her search for her father or his loss of his wife. Still, she couldn't back down just because he might be trying to rationalize his own pain into oblivion. She wasn't him. He might be trying to hide from his past. She knew she'd been hiding much too long. It was time to open the vaults and see what she could find there.

"You can't wish the past away," she told him evenly.

His head came up at that, his gaze challenging. "*I* can."

Well, maybe he could. But she didn't think so. Did he really think he was fooling anyone with those smoky dark eyes? Her heart went out to him, but she couldn't back down. She couldn't pretend to agree with something so patently incorrect. Still, he wasn't going to agree with her either. Changing the subject would be better than going on with this. Looking away, she let her gaze travel around the kitchen, trying to think of something that would put them back on that friendly footing they'd started out on.

"You know what I would like to do?" she said as casually as she was able. "Put new wallpaper up in this room."

"Wallpaper?" He looked startled. He probably thought she was a little loony. But at least he had his mind on something new. "Why?" he asked.

She hesitated. It was all very well to change subjects, but if she really wanted to win on this issue she knew she should have waited for a better time to bring it up. She should have waited until he was in a better mood. But what the heck. She couldn't walk on eggshells with him all the time. He certainly wasn't walking on eggshells with her.

"Because the room needs it," she said firmly. "This old flowered pattern was great about ten years ago, but you need something fresh and a little more colorful to liven up this room."

He looked from the cupboards to the wall with its copper forms and flowers, looking at a loss about how to understand how she could possibly say such silly things. "No, absolutely not." He frowned. "This is supposed to be a country kitchen, and that's what it looks like. Leave the wallpaper alone."

His wife again? Was this her favorite room, her choice of print? Somehow she didn't really think that was it. But maybe she was wrong. His face looked hard. She felt suddenly cold. She shouldn't have said those things. She shouldn't mess with his past. What did she know about it, after all? What right did she have to bring up things that might hurt him? She really ought to learn to keep her silence.

But what he had just said about the wallpaper sank in. She looked at him from beneath her lashes and shook her head slowly. She knew she ought to keep quiet, but she just couldn't let him get away with it.

"So you won't let me change this old wallpaper?" she asked.

He didn't say anything, but he shook his head.

"What's the matter?" she said quietly, looking him straight in the eye. "Can't let go of this old remnant of your past?"

He blinked, then glared at her, but the effect was ruined by the flash of amusement that edged the expression in his eyes. That was one good thing about him. He had a sense of humor. And he knew right away when she had him cornered. Coughing to save a little time, he put on a look of innocence that couldn't have fooled a kitten. "That's not it at all."

"Oh no?" She smiled, feeling smug. "Why else would you be so set in your ways?"

His shoulders went back in astonishment. "Set in my ways? You don't know me at all. I'm a freethinker. I'm open to change." He hid an imminent grin in a twist of his wide mouth. "I hired you on, didn't I?"

She laughed. Their eyes met. She felt something lurch in her chest and the laughter died. It was definitely time for her to go to her room. Rising, she put his half-eaten piece of pie in the fridge and turned toward the door.

"I think I'll go and—"

Before she had a chance to make a clean getaway, he reached out and caught her, his fingers circling her wrist. "Sit down and talk to me," he said, his dark eyes unreadable.

She stared down at him. "You still want me to talk to you?"

That was unusual. They had already talked longer than they had any other time for at least three days. She pulled away from his grasp, then sat down rather nervously on the edge of her chair. "What do you want to talk about?"

He leaned forward and his eyes seemed to bore into her. "We have lots of things to talk about. Like for instance . . . why is it that you jump like a cat every time I come into the room?"

That almost made her jump again. She could feel herself coloring. He knew what was going on. He felt it, too. Why was he trying to get her to verbalize it? "I—I'm just trying to keep out of your way."

An expression almost of pain flashed across his face. "Why do you want to stay out of my way? Have I done something mean to you?"

She looked at him hard, trying to ascertain if he were joking or just trying to torture her. Could it be that he really didn't understand the sexual attraction that flashed between them all the time? Or maybe he knew that but thought she was dealing with it like a wimp.

"No. No, of course not. You haven't been mean. It isn't that." And he knew it.

But his eyes were dark again, unreadable. "Then what?" he asked.

How could he pretend not to know? How could he ignore the spark of electricity that snapped between them every time their eyes met? A nightmare possibility presented itself. Suppose it were all one-sided. Suppose he didn't feel a thing. She looked at him furtively, searching for an answer.

"And one other thing," he went on before she could find one. "Why is Trevor calling you all the time?"

She sat up, startled. How did he know that? There had only been two phone calls from Trevor, both times asking for advice on where he could go and what he could do to look for information about his father. But that was his secret to tell, not hers. And if Joe were so opposed to her looking into her own past, instinct told her he would be even more so about Trevor.

And why was that? Because he was the boy's father? She shied away from thinking that. She didn't really believe it, despite all Trevor's hopes and dreams. She averted her eyes. "Trevor and I just really hit it off," she said evasively. "He's a friend."

He didn't come right out and say he didn't believe her, but his eyes told her as much.

"Trevor is all Millie's got," he told her softly. "Just don't take him away from her."

She stared at him, completely confused. "How could I possibly do a thing like that?" she asked.

He shrugged. "I don't know. Things happen. Millie might think you're turning Trevor against her somehow."

"But...why would I do that?" Worse yet, why would Millie suspect such a thing? She liked Millie. She certainly didn't want to hurt her. "Do you really think she might feel that way? I'd better talk to her."

"Maybe you'd better." He studied her for a moment. "But my question still stands. What do you and Trevor have between you?"

"Friendship," she said shortly. And it was true, as far as it went, so she didn't even have the need to avoid his eyes. "Haven't you ever had friends?"

"Yes, I've had friends," he said slowly, and just a trace of the humor he had been hiding for the last few moments was glinting in his eyes. "It's a lover I'm doing without."

Her cheeks were reddening again and there was nothing she could do about it. She wanted to yell at him, but she bit her lip and held it back. He felt the electricity all right. So much for his act of innocence. Doing without a lover, indeed.

"Well, you know what they say," she answered more flippantly than she felt. "Abstinence is good for the soul."

Now his eyes were sparkling. "Yeah, but it doesn't do much for the nervous system," he drawled, causing her to blink rapidly several times.

What was he implying here—that they could get rid of this mutual attraction if they just went to bed together? She looked at him sharply, ready to take umbrage. But he wasn't leering. He was teasing. Just kidding around. She hoped.

"Of course, it might be abstinence that makes the heart grow fonder," she improvised as she rose and started for the hall again, carefully skirting the area around his chair. "I get those old sayings mixed up sometimes."

She glanced back and caught his exaggeratedly pained look.

"No, that can't be it," he said. "Isn't it abstinence that's the root of all evil?"

"Nope." She grinned at him from the doorway just before disappearing around it. "Abstinence makes the world go 'round. And that's the truth."

He listened to her go up the stairs, swearing at himself softly and laughing at the same time. What the hell had he said those things to her for? Those thoughts hadn't even been in his mind when he'd first come into the kitchen. There was something about her that made him say the most absurd things—things he didn't really think, things he didn't really mean. Or did he?

"FLOWERS AREN'T REALLY all that different from houseplants," Carly mused to Millie the next morning as they worked on planting an edge row of some purple pansies Millie had brought over. Millie had been teaching her about gardening all week, taking her to the nursery to pick out flowers, showing her tools and soil amendments. Together they were transforming Joe's front yard. "And I've always had a way with those."

"They're the same little green carbon-dioxide users," Millie agreed with a laugh as she handed Carly a pony pack of colorful blossoms.

Carly nodded, digging her hand tool deep into the worked soil. "Weeding and digging and playing around in the dirt must be therapeutic," she said, placing first one plant, then the next, in its small hole and then patting soil around the roots. "I've done some of the best thinking I've ever done while gardening this week."

Sitting back, she put her head to the side and considered the aesthetics of her work. "Why have all you home gardeners kept this a secret for so long?" she teased Millie. "I'm going to have to tell my friends when I get home. Think of the money they'll save in tranquilizers and sessions with their shrinks."

Millie laughed again, fidgeting with the gloves in her hands. "Do you miss it?" she asked as Carly began to clean herself up as well.

"Miss what?"

"City life."

Carly looked up quickly. Why was it that everyone knew without being told that she came from the city?

"I miss some things," she said slowly. "I miss the busy streets and the restaurants."

Did she miss Mark? There was no time to miss him. There was too much to do and learn. She had given him a call when she knew he would be out and left a message on his answering machine, thereby avoiding his inevitable questions about where she was and when she was planning to come back. "I just wanted you to know that I'm okay," she'd said. "The question you asked is a serious one and I want to give it serious consideration. Thanks for giving me this time to really get in touch with my own feelings. I miss you, but I'll be back soon."

She felt like a hypocrite saying those things, because the truth was, she wasn't sure if she really meant them. Did she miss him? Being honest, she had to admit that she didn't. But in some ways, she didn't feel as if she ought to miss him. Carolyn Stevens, young political worker on the fast track, spending her days with people who ran things, made the big decisions, spending her evenings at fancy parties or four-star restaurants—that was the woman he loved. Not Carly. Not the woman who was content to spend an evening helping Beth with homework or helping Joe fix a piece of farm equipment on the kitchen table. This was not the person Mark knew. So how could she miss him?

But she didn't like to think that way, because all it did was confuse her. So she shoved Mark back into the shadows again, and lived for the moment. For now.

"I guess some people are just meant to live in the city," Millie was going on. "Joe's wife Ellen, she never did get used to living out here in the country. She was always missing things, yearning for things. I guess that's why..."

Her voice faded and she looked away. Carly waited for more information about Ellen. This was the first time anyone had actually brought up that name in her presence. But Millie didn't seem to want to talk about her any more than anyone else did.

"Better get some water on those new plants," she said instead of finishing her thought. "If you want, I can bring by that rosebush this afternoon."

Carly shook her head as she got to her feet and went for the hose. "Thanks, but I can't do it today. I'm going into town."

"Oh?" Millie seemed to freeze. "What are you planning to do there?"

"Ask around about my father."

The silence from Millie seemed to last too long. Carly turned and found her friend staring off toward the highway, her face ashen, her fingers playing nervously with her hair. Glancing back at Carly, she gave her a tremulous smile that flickered and died.

"I...do you think that's such a good idea? I mean, if you go digging around in the past, you might find out things you wish you didn't know."

"Wish I didn't know?" Carly took a step closer to where Millie was standing, frowning. "What are you talking about, Millie? What is there about my father that I'm going to be that upset about?"

She shook her head quickly. "Oh no, I didn't mean...I don't know anything. It's just that..." She gave a gesture of exasperation as tears began to fill her eyes. "Oh damn, now I'm crying. I'm sorry. I...it's just...Trevor..."

She began to fight off the clumsy gloves and Carly stepped forward quickly with a handkerchief. She was pretty sure she knew what was wrong now. Millie was afraid her looking for her father would make Trevor start thinking too much about his own. Or maybe she was aware that it already had.

"I'm sorry, Millie," she said quietly, offering comfort but no surrender. "I didn't mean to upset you. But I have to do this."

Millie nodded, wiping her eyes and calming herself. "Of course you do." She managed a smile of sorts. "Listen, I'll drive you into town. I'll help you."

That was certainly a turnaround. Carly hesitated, not sure she wanted Millie along. But when she came right down to it, she didn't have much choice, unless she wanted to call a cab to come way out here in the country. Joe had never answered when she'd asked about borrowing his car. He'd left it when he'd taken off in the truck to visit a neighboring ranch, but the keys were nowhere to be found. So in the end, she took the ride Millie offered with gratitude, and they had a good talk going into town.

Her heart started to beat faster as they approached the area that had a few familiar landmarks. She was going to find something out today. She was sure of it.

The corner grocery store was indeed long gone, just as she'd thought, but Millie helped her find the little white church.

"It looks just like I remember it," Carly breathed as they leaned against the parked car and stared at it. Paint peeled from its clapboard exterior. Someone had painted graffiti on the side. The rude markings had been whitewashed, but the dark paint underneath showed through like a blemish that wouldn't be hidden by makeup. "Only it's so much smaller."

It was locked up tight. They peered in through the dusty windows but there wasn't much to see.

"I guess no one uses it anymore," Millie said, looking up and down the street rather furtively. "We might as well go home."

Carly shook her head slowly, turning to look at the neighborhood as well, taking it all in like a drink of sweet water. It was hard to bring back the particulars of houses or trees, as they had all changed so much during the years. But the feeling—there was something in the air she recognized.

"Let's take a walk," she said impulsively. "Some of the old houses are still standing on the south side of the street. Maybe I'll see someone I remember."

She started walking briskly up the sidewalk, hardly noticing that Millie was coming along only reluctantly. Her mind was filled with a recollection that had come on her suddenly from out of the blue.

She'd been young, maybe five or six. She'd been out on the street with coins held tightly in her sweaty little hand, waiting for the ice-cream man. She didn't often get to buy from the ice-cream man. Her mother said it was a waste of money when there were so many children starving in Africa. Besides, she could get ice cream for free from her father's store.

But buying from the ice-cream man, with his jangly music and his crazy colors, was something special. And today she was going to get to do it.

She was so wrapped up in happy anticipation that she didn't notice the clump of prepubescent boys coming toward her until it was too late to run.

"Hey, she's got money in her hand," the one in the Black Death T-shirt said to the others. "Hey kid, give us that money," the fat one in the jeans jacket demanded. "We need it more than you."

They crowded around her. She went cold with fear. They seemed to tower over her. But her fingers tightened on the coins.

"No," she whispered. "It's mine."

"Come on, kid." Dirty hands began grabbing at her, trying to force her fingers open. "Give it up."

She began to thrash out blindly, whimpering, but locked into a stubborn defense she maintained by instinct rather than design. "It's mine, it's mine!" Something, probably a hand, came in contact with her mouth, and she bit down, hard. A cry of pain, and she was off and running, running harder than she had ever run before, running with tears flowing from her eyes, running up and down streets she'd never seen before. She tripped and scuffed her knee, but she was up again and running before the pain could register. She could hear them running behind her and she dodged between two houses, ran through a backyard, into an alleyway, out into a vacant lot. They were gaining on her. In a minute they would catch her and she knew they would hurt her. But she wouldn't let go. Never! She sobbed as she ran. There was no way to avoid what was sure to happen next.

And then it was over. Hands grabbed her, arms took her up into the air, and she cried out, "It's mine!" before she realized the arms were protecting, not threatening.

"Carly, baby, what is it?"

She blinked past her tears and saw her father's face just inches from hers. A sob of relief shook her and she buried her face in his shoulder and cried and cried. She was with her daddy. She was safe.

Safe. She shuddered a little now, thinking of that little girl. Had she ever felt that safe again?

She and Millie walked for blocks, and here and there she thought she recognized houses she might have visited in her childhood. But there wasn't a familiar face, nor a familiar name on a mailbox. As they came back down the opposite side half an hour later, she was feeling discouraged. Was it really possible that there was no one left who had lived here all those years ago?

"Got any ideas for my next move?" she asked Millie. "I've already searched the telephone directory for his name and called the city office of records to see if he had taken out a license or bought any property lately."

"They lost all the old records in a fire at city hall ten years ago," Millie said quickly. "You won't find anything there."

"So they told me." Carly sighed. They were almost back in front of the church. She hated to see hope die this way. She glanced at the little white structure, and suddenly realized something. The double front doors were standing open.

"Look!" she cried. "Someone is here." She almost ran to the doorway and looked inside. An old, bent woman was polishing the burnished brown wood of the altar. Rows of well-worn pews lined the room. A huge cross hung from the wall. It was obvious, now that she was inside, that the church was still very much in use.

"Excuse me," she called to the woman as she approached. "Hello. My name is Carly Stevens."

The woman stopped her polishing and turned to watch Carly, but she didn't smile. Carly came to a stop a few feet away and did enough smiling for two. "My father was the preacher here about seventeen years ago," she said. "Did you work here then?"

The woman didn't speak for a long moment. Her watery blue eyes took in Carly and then went to where Millie was hovering in the background.

"I've only worked here for the last ten years," she said in a whispery voice.

"Oh." Carly was deflated again. "Well, maybe you know something about him. Howard Stevens? Have you ever heard of him?"

The watery eyes looked puzzled, confused, and kept wavering away to glance at Millie. "I've heard of him," she said reluctantly.

"Really?" Carly's hope rose again. "What do you know about him? Do you have any idea where he is now?"

She shook her head. "He left town. That's all I know. He left town."

Hope left Carly like air from a spent balloon. "Oh. Well, is there someone else I could talk to?"

The woman went back to polishing. "Nope. There been six different preachers in the last few years. Ain't no one left who was around in those days."

Carly turned and looked at Millie, who shrugged and turned to go back outside. This couldn't be it. This couldn't be the end of the line, could it? "Uh... thanks," she said to the woman. "Sorry we bothered you."

But now that Millie had left the church, the woman was coming toward her quickly. Carly stood where she was as the woman approached, watching the doorway as though to guard against Millie's return. The woman's bony hand clutched at her arm. "Ask Phyllis Matthews," she whispered hoarsely. "She knows a thing or two, that's for sure." She started to retreat once again.

Carly reached out to stop her. "What? Phyllis Matthews? What does she have to do with this?"

The woman shook her gray head and backed away. "Ask her," was all she said before she ducked back down the aisle.

Carly stared after her. Phyllis. Of course. She'd sensed from the beginning that Joe's mother knew more than she was letting on. She turned back toward the car with determination.

"Let's go home, Millie," she said as she slid into the seat. Some instinct held her back from telling her friend what the woman had just advised her. "I don't think we're going to get anything else here."

Millie's smile looked relieved. Or was that just her imagination? Lord, she was getting paranoid. Still, the woman in the church had definitely wanted to tell her about asking Phyllis out of Millie's earshot. Carly sat back in the seat and watched the town flash by as Millie drove them back out into the country. She was beginning to realize she was doing more here than merely conducting an innocent search for information about her father. Looking into her own past was opening up things in the pasts of others, things they didn't want brought out into the light of day. She was going to have to be a little craftier from now on if she was going to get anywhere.

She thought of Joe. How much did he know that he wasn't telling her? That thought tore at her in a painful way, and she wasn't sure why.

CHAPTER NINE

SHE KNOCKED on the green door with a sharp, forceful rap.

"Phyllis?" she called out. "May I come in?"

There was a sort of scuttling sound and then the plaintive voice called out. "All right, Carly. Come on in."

Carly pushed open the door and entered. Phyllis lay back on her pillows, a handkerchief to her face, but Carly had no doubt she had just been up and about.

"How are you, Phyllis?" she asked, standing beside the bed.

The woman's eyes were clear, but her voice was faint. "Not very well, I'm afraid. I think I'm coming down with something."

Like a bad case of falsehood perhaps? Carly took a deep breath and tried to smile.

"I'm sorry to hear that. I won't take up much of your time. But I do need to talk to you."

"Well..." She sniffed into her handkerchief. "What is it, dear?"

"I've just come back from town. I've been talking to people about my father. And I've learned some interesting things."

Phyllis went very still, her dark eyes wide and apprehensive. "You know, Carly, I'm really not very well—"

Carly didn't let her finish. "You knew my father, didn't you?"

"What?"

"You knew him." She had to force herself to remain calm. "Why didn't you tell me from the first?"

Phyllis shook her head. "I don't know what you're talking about. I told you I knew of Howard Stevens. I never knew the man, not as one would *know* someone..."

She wasn't going to let her get away with this. "Then how did you know him?" she insisted.

Phyllis blinked and avoided her eyes. "Well, we went to his church occasionally. We shopped at his little store now and then. That was all. I'd hardly call that close knowledge, would you?"

Carly had a sinking feeling. Phyllis was determined not to tell her anything. Controlling herself with effort, she kept her voice soft. "Please, Phyllis. Tell me anything you know."

The woman shrugged, and before she could make another disclaimer Carly added quickly, "Do you have any idea where he's gone? Do you have any idea why my mother left him? Can't you see how important it is to me to find out what happened?"

Their eyes met and the small space between them seemed about to burst with possibility. Carly held her breath, willing the woman to talk. Phyllis stared into her eyes for a long time. *Oh please,* Carly begged silently. *Please, please...*

And then Phyllis was coughing, avoiding her eyes again. "Could you please get me a drink of water?" she asked hoarsely. "My throat is so dry."

Carly hesitated, then went to the sink and poured a glass of water, coming to the other side of the bed to give it to the woman. Phyllis sipped slowly, staring down at the pattern in her sheet. Carly stood where she was and waited for her to speak.

"About my father," she said at last when it looked as though Phyllis might have forgotten she was there.

Phyllis looked up quickly and shook her head pathetically. "I'm feeling so weak, my dear," she whispered. "I'm afraid we're going to have to call the doctor. I can't really talk any more."

Carly went cold with disappointed anger. She wanted to yell at her, wanted to force her to speak. But what could she do? Turning without saying another word, she left. Phyllis knew something all right. Carly was just going to have to find another way of getting to the information.

THERE WAS SOMETHING about giving a car a good wax job that was soothing to the male soul, Joe decided. Maybe it was the sight of the shine coming through the layers of filmy paste, or the fine detail work, or the mindlessness of rubbing for hours. Or maybe it was all of those things combined. Whatever. He liked it.

He tipped the can and put another blob of thick blue liquid on his cloth and began to wipe it onto the silver-blue surface of the hood of his year-old Camaro. Yeah, this was good. This was making him feel better. Given a little time, this might even blot out the puzzle that was making him crazy—the puzzle of why he had let himself get roped into keeping Carly Stevens at his place.

No, that wasn't really it. He sat back and reached for the can of wax again. Why didn't he just admit it to himself? He knew why he'd let her stay. He even knew why he wanted her with a deep, throbbing ache of need that was keeping him awake at night. What he didn't get was why he didn't just go ahead and let nature take its course. Get it over with. Do what came naturally.

There was no guarantee that she wanted what he wanted, of course. She felt the pull between them. That much was obvious. But she was supposedly in love with the schmuck back home. So she could be receptive or not. That was her right. But at least he would have put it to her and got it out in the open. Yes or no, he would be able to sleep at night, because he would know where they stood.

Oh hell, he was still fooling himself. He threw down the cloth in disgust and reached for the buffing pad. She felt the attraction, sure. But she didn't want to do anything about it. Why couldn't he be honest with himself and admit that that was what was bugging him the most? He wanted her, and she didn't want him.

He heard the back door slam and he recognized her footsteps on the porch but he didn't turn around. He was going to turn over a new leaf and he was going to do it right now. She was going to mean nothing to him. She was hired help and that was all. When he looked at her he was going to think of Greta, the large Nordic female breathing fire and brimstone who had been the kids' last caretaker. Conditioning—that was all it took. They did it for smokers. They did it for drinkers. He would do it for himself. Think Greta, he reminded

himself as he heard her approach. Just think Greta and
stay calm.

"Joe?"

She'd stopped just behind him. He kept right on
rubbing.

"Yes?" he answered, thinking of the heavy blond
mustache Greta had sported with pride.

"Beth brought a little friend home from school.
Sunny Bayles. Is it all right if she stays overnight?"

"Uh ... sure. Why not?"

"Okay. I'll tell her."

He waited, but she didn't leave. Unshaven legs, he
told himself grimly. A large mole with two long, black
hairs right in the center of her chin.

"The car is going to look great," she said.

"Uh-huh."

He could smell her scent. Even above the waxy
aroma of the polish he was using, her fragrance seemed
to slip in and blot everything else out. Or maybe it was
all in his mind.

Mind. That's right. Mind control. He was conducting an experiment here. He was going to think of
Greta, not Carly. Greta.

Good old Greta smelled like sweat and laundry soap.
And her voice—it snarled and bellowed like a fog-
horn. She used to call to him across the yard. "Hey,
you, mister! I gotta problem here. You gonna come
help me or am I gonna walk?"

The kids hid bugs in her bed. One time, Jeremy
found a garter snake and put it in her bathtub. She'd
screamed for Joe, and he'd come to the rescue. The
sight of that semi-naked body had lived on in his

nightmares for months. He shuddered now, thinking of it. Yeah, that was the spirit. Keep thinking of it....

"Joe?"

He closed his eyes for a fraction of a second. There was something about the way she said his name....

"I went into town today to look for someone who knew my father."

The experiment went up in smoke. So much for Greta. She was fading fast. There were deeper emotional issues here than smooth skin and a pretty face. He was a goner, and he knew it.

He put down the buffing pad and turned to look at Carly. "Did you find anyone?" he asked, watching her face for the information as much as anything else.

She hesitated. "Not exactly. But I did find someone who said your mother could help me."

Bad news. He'd hoped she wouldn't get that far. So now what? How long could she keep looking at him with those bright, honest eyes before she realized the truth?

"I went to your mother," she continued.

Damn. That must have been some confrontation. He shook his head slowly. He could see in her face how it had gone.

"She refused to tell me anything. And now she's playing possum, pretending to be too sick to talk."

And she can pretend with the best of them. He sighed, feeling guilty at how relieved he was that his mother hadn't told her anything.

"Joe, will you say something? I need your help. I want you to get your mother to tell me what she knows about my father."

It made his heart skip to see her like this. She wanted
to know the truth so badly.

But so what? Everyone wanted something they
couldn't have. He'd wanted Ellen. He would have given
anything to keep her here with him, with the kids. But
he hadn't been granted his heart's desire either. And
they'd survived, him and the kids. They were doing
okay. Carly would survive not knowing.

He hesitated, taking a long, deep look into her crystal blue eyes. She was going to hate him if she found
everything out and found how he'd kept it from her.
But there was no alternative.

"Let it lie, Carly. You're only asking for trouble."
He turned back to the car and began polishing with
long, controlled strokes.

"How can finding out the truth make trouble? I'm
not planning to do anything. I just want to know the
truth."

Her voice had a small break in it that tore at his
heart. He couldn't look her in the eye anymore. There
ought to be some way he could tell her. But how could
he? It wasn't really any of his business. He hadn't even
known much of it himself until she'd come on the
scene. And if she did find out, what would she do?
There was no telling how many people would end up
getting hurt—including Carly herself. It would probably be better if she stayed in the dark and just went on
back to wherever it was that she came from. And married the wonderful and extremely patient guy who was
waiting in the wings. He glanced sideways at her, noting the silver glint the sunlight made on her hair. Geez,
if it were him, he'd be ripping the countryside apart
looking for this woman by now. Either the man had the

patience of Job, or he was a complete idiot. He leaned harder into the work and kept on rubbing. "Sorry, darlin', but the truth doesn't always set you free."

He didn't turn to look at her, but he did strain for signs that she was leaving. Unfortunately, she showed no evidence of being bowled over by his witty repartee. Neither did she head for the house. Instead, she came up close beside where he was working and asked a question he would just as soon have avoided.

"Joe. What exactly is wrong with your mother anyway?"

He gritted his teeth and answered truthfully. "I don't know."

"You don't know?" Her face mirrored her disbelief.

"That's right." He went on working, not wanting to get caught up in the meeting of eyes again. "She's in control of her own illness, whatever it is. She's got the best medical care I can get her. She's got anything she wants anytime she wants it. She's living the way she wants to live right now." His cloth stopped for a moment and he finally looked at her. "She's my mother, Carly. I take care of her, and I will as long as she wants me to. I'm not going to contest her life-style."

"But she sits up there for days...it's—it's not right."

Her face was so open, so uncomprehending. She thought she was experienced and sophisticated with all her city background, but she really didn't know much about people and what made them tick, did she? He sighed and looked into her eyes again, braving the reaction he knew would follow.

"Listen, Carly. My mother's had plenty of disappointment in her life. If this makes her happy right now, that's okay with me. As long as she doesn't do anything to hurt my kids, she can do what she wants.''

Carly shook her head, ready to protest, but he went on, cutting her off.

"She's been hurt, she's been disappointed, she's worked for years for others. And now she should have some time to do what she wants to do.''

Carly still shook her head, unconvinced. "But she's wasting her life away up there,'' she said. "You should be encouraging her to live her life more fully, to come down and—''

"Carly.'' He resisted the urge to touch her, to convince her with his hands. Steeling himself, he turned back to the polished car, rubbing for a higher shine in places where he'd already just about rubbed the finish right off.

"Let me tell you about my mother, Carly,'' he said softly, determined not to look at her again. "When she was young she had a beautiful voice. When she was just sixteen she used to hire a hall in town and people would come from miles around to hear her sing show-tunes and light-opera stuff. She was so good, she got a scholarship to a big music college in the East.''

He hesitated, then went on, supplying the details. "Her father was against her going. He was a farmer and he didn't see what good all this singing did. Who would want to listen to her singing songs nobody could understand the words to, anyway? He wanted her to marry my father and settle down. So she made a pact with him. If Geoffrey Matthews still wanted her in four years when she was through with her training, she would come back and marry him and be a country wife.'' His buffing cloth paused as he remembered things. "You see, Geoffrey was older than she was, about twenty years' worth. He was the last man on earth she wanted to marry. But she figured he was so old, he didn't have much time left, and he would surely find another girl in those four years. So she went east and studied opera. That was what she loved. And she did real well. So well that a European opera company offered her a job. It was a dream come true."

He paused and stared out at the mountains. It had been years since he'd thought about his mother in these terms. His life had been so caught up in his own problems lately that he'd forgotten other people had their dreams smashed, too.

"Well," Carly asked impatiently. "Did she go? How did she do abroad? Did she get to sing in Vienna?"

He looked at her. She was really interested. Despite everything, he had to smile.

"No. She never sang in Vienna. She called home to tell her parents the exciting news and her father reminded her of her bargain. There was to be no tour of Europe. She was to come home and take care of her responsibilities."

"She came home and married that older man?"

He nodded, amused at her horror. "I told you he was my father, didn't I?"

"Yes, but..." She made a face.

"She came home. She hated every minute of it, hated the man she married, hated life on the farm. But she came home and did what she was supposed to do. And the only time she ever sang again was in a church choir."

"That's crazy!"

He shrugged. "Times were different then. She was raised to do what was expected of her."

"Did she . . . did she ever love your father?"

"I don't think she ever loved him in any sort of wildly romantic way. But she eventually came to have a great affection for him. And they did okay toward the end."

Carly shook her head, marveling at another age, another way of doing things.

"Why doesn't she go on with her singing now? She probably couldn't do full opera, but surely she could sing in shows, maybe in dinner theater . . ."

"I guess the way she looks at it is—too little, too late. She missed her only chance."

A look of quick anger passed over Carly's face. It was all very well to understand backgrounds and feel sorry for this woman, but when you came right down to it Phyllis wasn't your completely sympathetic character.

"So instead of being happy herself she's going to make the rest of the world miserable?" she asked evenly.

Joe looked at her. "She doesn't make me miserable."

"Doesn't she?"

"No."

Carly was sorry, but she couldn't be quite that generous to the woman. She looked up at the window of Phyllis's room and knew Phyllis was watching them every minute. Watching them and wondering what Joe was revealing to her.

Which brought up another subject. How much of anything did Joe know himself? She turned back to look at him. She'd never known a car could need so much polishing. He was avoiding her as much as he could and she knew it. But there were questions he might be able to answer—questions she hadn't had the nerve to put to him as yet. Maybe it was time.

"Tell me this, Joe," she said softly, standing as close to him as she could get and still give him room to do his work. "Do you know who Trevor's father was?"

He didn't turn around, but his hand stopped rubbing. "That is none of your business, Carly," he answered as softly as she'd spoken.

"Then you do know."

He turned to stare at her with his dark, deep eyes. "Carly, go away."

"What about my father? What do you know that you haven't told me?"

He dropped the pad and turned to grab her by the shoulders, holding her fiercely where she would have to meet his dark gaze.

"Carly," he said earnestly, "there are a lot of things going on here that you don't understand. You've got to stop digging into the past. It's only going to hurt people. It's only going to hurt you."

She stared up at him, her blue eyes beseeching him to understand. She wanted him in her corner. But maybe that was impossible. "Don't you see, can't you understand, that I can't stop? It's too late."

He shook his head. "You were happy, weren't you? You told me yourself that you never cared that much about finding your father before. It wasn't until you got here that things changed."

His dark eyes looked tortured. "I don't know, maybe if you just would go back where you came from..."

She shook her head. "You know it's too late for that. Now that I've begun, I have to know the truth. I'll never have another chance to do this. I've got to find out, and I've got to find out now."

"What about this guy who's waiting for you? How long do you think he's going to wait?"

"Mark?"

He nodded.

Avoiding his eyes, she looked away distractedly. "I don't know. I can't think about Mark right now. That almost seems like another life. A life I'm going to get back to one of these days. But right now, I have to find out about my father."

"Carly." He touched her hair, her cheek. His eyes were clouded, so troubled she could hardly stand to look into them. "Carly, don't do it. It's only going to hurt you."

"I can be hurt, Joe. I'm strong. I can take it."

He let her go, stepping back. She stood where she was for a long moment, looking at him. And then she turned slowly and started walking back toward the house.

Joe felt tired as he watched her go. They were in for some rough times. And she was going to be hurt. Only time would tell if she were as strong as she thought she was.

CHAPTER TEN

IT ALL STARTED innocently enough, later that afternoon. Beth and her friend Sunny wanted to make cookies. Carly stuck around to supervise, though she was actually trying to pick up a few pointers on the fine art of cookie baking herself.

Chocolate-chip cookies. Was there anything that smelled better in the oven? Was there anything that tasted better freshly baked?

They put in the first batch, set the timer and retired to the den where Beth wanted to show Sunny pictures of the horse she kept at Millie's. When the buzzer went off, they trooped back into the kitchen, pulled the delicious cookies from the oven, and turned to the bowl to prepare the second batch.

"Wait a minute!" Beth cried.

"Uh-oh," agreed Sunny.

"Wasn't there more batter left?" Carly chimed in.

They all stared at the bowl. There seemed to be about half as much batter left as there had been when they'd left the room.

"Who could possibly be eating the batter?" Carly asked slowly. She and Beth looked at each other and Carly gave the little girl a big wink. Beth grinned.

"Let's put in the second batch," Carly said. "Then we'll see what we can do about this mystery."

They dropped the teaspoons of lumpy batter onto the cookie sheet and put it into the oven and went to the den, but this time they didn't stay there. Instead, they hid behind the hallway door and listened intently, trying hard not to giggle. When they heard the soft pad of footsteps going into the kitchen, they came out from behind the door and began to sneak toward the kitchen as quietly as they could manage. When they reached the kitchen door, they sprang out and surprised Jeremy with a fingerful of batter halfway to his mouth.

"Aha!" cried Beth and Sunny and Carly, all at the same time.

A look of pure demonic delight spread across his naughty face. He dashed for the door, breaking through the line they made and heading down the hall with an evil cackle.

"He got away!" the girls both yelled in chagrin, and off they went after him. Carly laughed and watched from the doorway, enjoying Jeremy's grin as he ran from one room to another, just ahead of the girls. This was a side of the boy she hadn't seen enough of.

When the pillows started flying, her first impulse was to stop things. But they were having so much fun, and Jeremy needed this kind of release so badly. And what harm could a pillow do?

The crash of something solid hitting the floor answered that question soon enough, but when she reached the living room she found it was only a tray that wasn't damaged at all. She closed the door to the dining room with its china cabinet and glassware.

By now there were pillows littering the floor from every room in the house. To make matters worse, the fight was looking one-sided, with Jeremy trying to fend off the two of them. Carly bit her lip, then made up her mind. She had to throw her lot in with the underdog.

"Hold on, Jeremy! I'm coming to the rescue!" she cried, picking up an armful of pillows as she ran toward where he was cornered by the girls in the den.

The girls squealed with indignation at her betrayal, but they all laughed and threw more pillows—pillows from the couch in the den, pillows from the chairs in the living room, pillows from the seats in the kitchen, pillows from the spare bedroom. It was raining pillows and laughter.

Jeremy made a run for the stairs and Carly stopped by the kitchen to take out the batch of cookies that needed attention. Before she could get back into the fray, the outer door opened and Joe came in just in time to see a pillow whiz in through the doorway.

"Hey, what's this?" he asked, staring down at it.

"What do you think it is?" Carly reached down and picked it up, tossing it into his unsuspecting face before he had a chance to react. "Haven't you ever had a pillow fight before?"

She didn't wait around for an answer. She was almost to the stairs before the pillow was returned to her. It bounced off her shoulder and she laughed as she ran toward the second floor. He was right behind her. They dashed in and out of bedrooms along with the girls and Jeremy, shrieking and tossing pillows as fast as they could. Then the kids headed back downstairs, but Joe had Carly trapped in his bedroom.

"I've got you now," he told her, eyes shining and pillow in hand. "Say 'uncle' and I win."

"Never." She feinted left, she feinted right and then she made a dash for it, trying to emulate Jeremy's

tricky escape in the kitchen, but he dropped the pillow
and tackled her, and the next thing she knew she was
falling onto the bed with Joe coming down on top of
her.

His body was hard and heavy, but it pinned her with
such delicious strength, the gasp she heard come from
her lips was more of wonder than of lack of breath. He
made no move to roll off. His face was very close to
hers. When she tried to look into his eyes, all she could
make out was a dark, penetrating blur and lashes that
cast a shadow.

Her hands curled around his shoulders. "Uncle,"
she whispered.

"The feeling is mutual," he whispered back, his
breath hot on her forehead.

Her fingertips pressed into his shoulders and she
arched slightly toward him, face upturned, lips parted
just enough.

He had to kiss her. He had no choice. If he had
drawn back at that point, she was afraid she might have
cried out in anguish. His mouth was even hotter than
his body, smooth and slick and sultry as the sun. She
closed her eyes and let his heat wash over her. Her body
felt alive, every inch of her experiencing him with a
sensual awakening she'd never known before. He
didn't feel heavy any longer. He felt like heaven.

His lips released hers lingeringly, his head slowly
rising until his eyes met hers again.

"Sorry," he said softly.

She wanted to whisper back, "Don't be," but she
didn't dare. She couldn't let him know how good his
kiss had been. She couldn't admit to him that she'd

wanted it to go on and on—that she wanted to feel his body even heavier, that she wanted...

There was no use going on with that train of thought. As he bounced up away from her and off the bed, she followed quickly, avoiding his eyes. The screams of laughter from downstairs turned both their heads in that direction.

"I guess it's about time to settle them down," she said, starting for the door on legs that didn't seem to have any knees. "I'll go."

"Carly." He stopped her with a hand on her arm. She turned and looked back at him questioningly, waiting, almost holding her breath, for what he might have to say. He hesitated, staring into her misty eyes.

"Listen, why don't we gather the kids and go into town for pizza?" he said at last. "Does that sound good?"

She smiled, almost with relief. "Yes," she said simply. "Yes, that does."

She went on downstairs and started calling to the children to calm down, but her mind was still back in Joe's room, wondering why kissing Joe was so much better than kissing had ever been before.

PIZZA—the staff of life. How did the pioneers live without it?

Joe took the last large piece of mushroom and sausage and bit down with relish. There was nothing like it. He could just about eat it every day—as long as he had a steak-and-potato meal thrown in every so often.

The table was full. They'd stopped by Millie's so Sunny could see the horses, and they had ended up inviting Millie and Trevor to join them for dinner. Trevor had begged off.

"I can't believe he'd rather go see his girlfriend than spend an evening with us, can you?" Millie had teased.

Trevor had turned red, but he hadn't given an inch. He'd made Carly laugh. There was something about that boy she really liked.

Carly was sitting with a little girl on either side of her, and Jeremy was between him and Millie. The smiles and laughter were making Joe feel very good. It had been a long time since he'd seen his kids this happy.

"The pitcher's empty."

He looked down the table as Beth's woeful face and smiled. He'd do almost anything for that little girl. That was a condition he would have to watch carefully. No matter how you sliced it, doing too much for your kids was as bad as doing too little. Ellen used to tell him that all the time and he knew she'd been right. Whenever they'd taken the kids out, there had been no extras, no seconds. She had been very strict.

But Ellen wasn't around anymore. His smile widened to a grin. "You want more soda?" he asked his daughter.

She nodded hopefully, her blond curls bouncing, and he put down his pizza and reached for the empty pitcher.

"You got it, kid," he said and started off toward the beverage counter.

"Hey, Joe." A large, rawboned man in a plaid shirt and a cowboy hat stopped him for a hearty handshake. "How you been?"

"Just fine, Andy. And you?"

"Gettin' 'bout ready to harvest my avocados. Got some beauties."

Joe grinned at him. "Hey, you haven't seen anything until you've seen my Fuertes. You ought to come on over some day soon and I'll show you around."

Andy nodded. "I'd like that." He glanced back at the table Joe had come from. "So who's the pretty lady?" he asked out of the corner of his mouth.

Joe turned to look back at the table, too. Carly was bending close to rub something off Jeremy's cheek with a napkin, her silky hair falling down over the side of her face in a shiny curtain of silver. She was wearing a soft, loose dress that kept sliding off her shoulders and sometimes seemed to barely catch at her breasts. As she sat back, she put her arms around the two girls sitting on either side of her, laughing as Beth told her something comical. She was free and easy with the kids in a way Ellen had never been. He stared for a moment or two longer than was called for, because he couldn't pull his gaze away.

"So?" Andy prodded. "Is she just the current nanny, or are you claiming territorial rights? Because if you're not interested, buddy..."

"She...uh...she's more or less engaged," Joe said quickly, then felt like an idiot. "I mean, she's considering a proposal right now. So..."

Andy's grin was pirate-wide. "So she's still fair game, is she?"

"No." Joe felt something knotting up inside his stomach. He glared at the big man with his wide shoulders and piercing blue eyes. "No, Andy, she's not. She wants peace and quiet. So leave her alone."

"Hey." Andy shrugged, palms out. "I get the picture, buddy. I get the picture." He backed away from Joe's scowl. "Say, I'll be over one of these days to check out your crop. Nice seein' ya."

"Yeah." Joe watched him disappear, then turned and filled the pitcher, content in the knowledge that he'd just made a class-A fool of himself.

He studied her again as he walked back to the table. She was certainly pretty, but there was more to her than that. He'd never known a woman with such a light shining inside her. Whatever man ended up with her might even have himself a happy marriage. God knows, he thought bitterly, there seemed to be few enough of those around.

There was music wafting in from the adjoining room. An old jukebox was playing slow dance tunes from the fifties and sixties. Joe looked at Carly and suddenly a wave of longing came over him. He wanted to do man-woman things with her. For maybe the first time in his life, he wanted to dance.

He asked her. She was surprised, but Millie said she would stay with the kids, and the two of them made their way through the crowd into the next room. When she turned and raised her arms to him, he felt the bottom drop out of his stomach.

The song was a doo-wop tune about moonlight and kisses and she melted in his arms as though she belonged there. He felt himself redden, like a teenager, like a kid at his first high school dance. He held her closely, feeling her breasts against his chest, her warm breath on his shoulder. Things were stirring inside him, things that had been anesthetized for too long. He thought of the kiss, of how her body had felt held

down by his, and for a moment he thought he was going to have to pull away from her in order to control
himself.

She felt good, much too good. *Oh Greta, Greta,* he
thought with a sigh, *where are you when I need you?*

She heard the sigh and lifted her head to look into his
face. "What are you thinking about?" she asked curiously.

He smiled at her. Those blue eyes looked as clear and
clean as high Sierra lakes. He was feeling much too hot
right now. It was tempting to think of a leap into the
cool water she represented. A long, luxurious leap...

Suddenly he realized she was beginning to frown,
wondering what his problem was, no doubt. That he
wasn't about to explain to her. But he could answer her
question. What was he thinking about?

"A previous caretaker the kids had." He grinned.
"I've been thinking about her a lot today."

Carly felt a pang. Jealousy? Couldn't be. But she
definitely felt something, and it wasn't good.

"Was she very beautiful?" she asked carefully.

"Well..." He pretended to consider. "She was tall
and blond."

"Oh." Amazing how jealousy could spring out of
nowhere. There was no reason for it. She would have
to work on keeping this silly emotion under control.
"And I suppose she was Swedish."

"Yes. She was Swedish, all right. In fact, I think she
claimed to have been a lady wrestler in Sweden."

Carly blinked. "Mud wrestler?" she asked, confused.

Joe's grin spread. "No, just a regular wrestler. My guess, she was probably at the top of the heavyweight class."

"Oh." Carly gave him a look, did a double take and then they both laughed. "You did that on purpose, didn't you?" she accused him.

He was all innocence. "Did what?"

But the music was over and she was slipping out of his arms.

"We should go back," she said, looking around. This had been lovely, but she knew she shouldn't be getting this close to intimacy with this man. The storm warnings were out all over the place and it was time she stopped ignoring them and ran for cover.

He let her go reluctantly. Her body felt like silk and fire all wrapped into one. She was beginning to get under his skin. Something was going to have to give, somewhere.

He didn't try to put an arm around her shoulders as they walked back toward the table where the children were still having a wonderful time. He could feel her trying to hold him at arm's length, and he knew she was doing the right thing. But a part of him didn't care about the right thing. A very big part of him wanted her. Wanted her very badly.

LATER THAT EVENING, Carly was cleaning up the last remnants of the cookie-baking project in the kitchen when she heard a soft rapping on the door. Turning on the porch light, she peered out.

"Trevor?" She let him in quickly. "What's wrong? Is something the matter with Millie?"

He shook his head, ducking into the room and looking around. "She's fine." He looked toward the hallway. "Where's Joe?" he asked conspiratorially.

"Out checking on the new guard dogs he hired for the avocado lot. Why? What is it?"

Trevor pulled a package from under his jacket and showed it to her. "I found some stuff," he told her, eyes sparkling. "My birth certificate, for one."

"Oh, Trevor!" Her heart leapt for him and she reached out to touch his arm. "Let's see. Put it out here on the table."

He spread out his treasures one by one. His birth certificate was still white and crisp. Millie was listed as the mother, and the father was written in as "unknown." Carly stared at the word, thinking what it must have cost a woman like Millie to have them write that there. She shook her head slowly, wondering if she could have been that brave.

"My shot record," Trevor noted proudly, showing off the yellow cardboard form. "And these newspaper clippings were stuck in a box with these things."

Carly hardly dared to touch the brown and brittle clippings. She picked up the first one and unfolded it, hoping it wouldn't crumble in her hands. There was a picture of a bright-faced girl who must have been Millie at about eighteen. The short attached article very circumspectly complimented her on being chosen valedictorian of her graduating class when she had a one-year-old child to care for along with her studies. The town was very proud of her for continuing her education under these circumstances. Carly smiled. Millie really was a brick.

The second article was an obituary written when Millie's parents were killed in a car accident twelve years before. Then there was a picture of Joe ready to leave for college. Carly gasped and looked at it closely. He looked so young. The fresh hope in his face made her want to hold the clipping to her heart. How quickly that optimism faded as one grew older. How tragic that it had to be.

The last yellowed piece of newsprint was very carefully folded in fourths. Carly looked at it for a long moment before opening it. She had a strange feeling....

"Go on, open it," Trevor urged. "I think it's you and your family."

Carly's fingers began to shake. Her breath came faster as she pried the ancient piece of paper open. And there it was—her mother's smiling face, her father's more serious expression and a little nine-year-old Carly held up in her father's arms. What article it came from she had no idea.

She stared at the picture, stunned. Why? And why hadn't Millie mentioned it?

"Neat, huh?" Trevor saw nothing extraordinary about Millie having kept a picture of Carly and her parents all these years. "But look at this one of Joe. Don't you think that proves he's my father? I mean, why would my mom have kept this picture if not for that? Joe was about seventeen when I was born. I checked. So it wasn't long before this picture was taken." His face looked so earnest that she wanted to cry. "I figure he couldn't marry my mom because he had to go away to college. Don't you think? And then he met Ellen, and maybe he and my mom had a fight right around then or something, and so he married Ellen and brought her back here where he could keep an eye on me. Does that make sense?''

"Oh Trevor." She touched his cheek, but it hurt too much to look into his eyes, so she busied herself folding the newspaper clippings into their previous shapes. ''Tell me, Trevor,'' she said as she worked. ''Look deep in your heart and tell me what really makes you think that Joe might be your father.'' She handed the package back to him and he held it in his lap.

He thought for a moment, then shrugged and smiled. ''I guess it's because he's always been there for me, ever since I was little. Even when Ellen was still here. He acted like my father. I mean, he did all the things that a father would do.'' His eyes were clear as crystal in sunlight. ''And he loves me. I know he does.''

"I know he does too," she whispered, holding back tears. This was hard, but she felt it was something she had to say. ''I'm sure of it. Joe and your mother are really good friends and I'm sure they always have been. But... oh, Trevor, I would hate to have you read too much into that...''

The kitchen door swung open and Joe stepped in. ''What the hell are you two up to?'' he demanded, his question mixed with anger, turning his face dark in the shadows of the kitchen light.

Trevor sprang to his feet, stuffing the package inside his jacket. ''I was just going,'' he mumbled, slipping past Joe and out toward his car. '''Bye,'' he called back.

But neither of them returned his greeting. Joe and Carly stared at one another. She knew he was waiting for an explanation. She would tell him the truth. Just maybe not all of it.

"What was he doing here?" he asked again.

"He brought over his birth certificate to show me," she replied.

His frown hardened. "Now why would he go and do a thing like that?"

She licked her lips. "Because I'm looking for my father and he thought maybe I would be able to help him look for his."

He was searching her face, the frown fading. Instead, there was a look of apprehension taking its place. "What did the birth certificate say?" he asked quietly.

She hesitated. "Nothing. Just that Millie was his mother and his father was unknown."

His relief was palpable. "Well, that's not a lot to go on."

"No." She looked at him levelly. "I think he deserves to know the truth, personally."

He glanced at her and then away. "It's none of your business," he said for the second time that day.

She stood up from her chair. "You said that before, and I still don't buy it," she snapped. "There are too many secrets hovering around this place. You know something about my father, and so does your mother. You and Millie and your mother probably all know who Trevor's father is. What makes you think the people most involved—Trevor and I—should be protected from the knowledge? What gives you three the right to keep things from us?"

He touched her, his hand on her shoulder, his finger flexing gently. "Carly," he said softly. "I really don't

know as much as you think I do. And these aren't my
secrets. I . . . I don't have any right . . .''

"Joe." She put her hands to his chest, her fingers
curling around the lapels of his crisp cotton shirt, her
face turned up to his. "Trevor thinks you're his father."

The shock of her words went across his face in
waves. "What?" he said hoarsely, wincing. "Oh my
God. When . . . what did he say . . . ?"

"Joe." Her hand flattened against his chest, right
over his heart. She searched his eyes as though she
could find the truth if she only looked hard enough.
"Are you?"

His eyes closed for a moment, and he slowly shook
his head. "No, Carly," he said softly. "I'm not Trevor's father. I told you. Millie and I have never been
lovers."

She nodded almost groggily, surprised at how relieved she was to finally have it spelled out for her in no
uncertain terms. "Good," she said. Her bones had
turned to liquid. All energy had suddenly drained away.

He heard her reaction and looked down, reaching
out with a finger to tilt her chin up so that he could
look into her eyes. She stared up, fascinated. His eyes
were so dark, and yet she thought she could see clouds
of smoke swirling in them. Something opened, like a
corridor into the clouds, and she watched as it seemed
to deepen and stretch farther and farther into nothing-
ness. She couldn't look away.

"Carly?"

He was going to kiss her again. She felt as though she
were floating, as though her arms and legs had lost all
ability to move. This time his mouth was hard and

hungry, and she gasped at the white-hot desire she felt in the rasping urgency of his tongue against hers, against her lips, against her vulnerability.

He pulled back and swore softly, repeatedly, before he pushed her away and said in a low, harsh voice, "Go to bed, Carly. Go. Go quickly."

She stared up at him, stunned and not sure what to do.

He reached out and took her shoulders in his hands, turning her and steering her toward the doorway. "Go," he said again. "Before it's too late."

She went, though everything in her screamed out to stay. She hurried up the stairs and down the hall to her bedroom and flung herself onto her bed. It took a long time to still the pounding of her heart. Why did Joe have such incredible control over her emotions? She'd never been swept along this way before, like a leaf in a swirling rush of a river. The only thing she knew for certain was this—she didn't hate it.

When her mind finally cleared, she pushed Joe into the background. Thinking about him only made her feel confused and guilty. She needed to put Trevor's visit into perspective. One by one in her mind she went over the things he had shown her. The one thing that stuck was the picture of her family. What on earth was that doing with Millie's private papers?

She didn't even consider confronting her about it. She hadn't had a straight answer from that source yet. She would have to go to the newspaper and look at their old files. That way she could find out what article went with the picture. But would that tell her why Millie had kept it? Maybe not. Still, it was bound to give her something more than she had at this point. She would get to the newspaper office as quickly as possible.

She groaned as she realized she wouldn't be able to do that until Monday, and here it was, only Friday night.

A whole weekend to wait. Carly sighed and looked at the ceiling. A whole weekend with nothing to do but think about Mark and Joe and why she only got more and more baffled by the situation as time went by.

CHAPTER ELEVEN

"DO YOU HAVE TO WAIT a long time before you get married?"

Joe looked up, a little startled, from his newspaper. Beth was playing with her Barbie dolls on the floor at his feet. She had Barbie and Ken in fancy dress, he noted with relief. It must be those two she was planning nuptials for this morning.

"That depends, sugar," he said, smiling down at her. "How long has your Barbie known your Ken?"

Beth's brow furrowed as she thought about it. "I got Ken on my sixth birthday. So she's known him for over a year."

"Great. That's plenty of time. He can go ahead and ask her any time now."

He turned back to his paper, but Beth wasn't satisfied. She reclaimed his attention with a hand on his knee.

"You have to wait a year?" she asked, her face stricken.

He frowned as he looked back at her. "No," he answered a little impatiently. "Not necessarily."

Her face cleared. "If it's true love," she said, completely confident now that she understood, "then you can ask any time. Even after one week. Right?"

She won him over again. He couldn't hold back his smile. He tossed her curls with a quick move of his hand, then touched her cheek. "That's right, sugar. True love makes anything possible."

She nodded, her lower lip caught by her upper teeth as she thought about it. "Is it true love with you and Carly?" she went on as though it were the most natural question in the world. "She's been here for more than one week."

Joe's eyes widened and he stared at her. "What?" he choked out.

"How long do *you* have to wait?" She gazed at him serenely, waiting for his answer.

Joe opened his mouth but not a thing came out. What could he say to her? Where had she picked up this outlandish idea?

"Uh...Beth, honey, Carly and I...we're not..." The words just wouldn't come. He stared at her dumbly, and from the hallway he heard Carly's voice.

"Beth! Garfield's on in the den! Better hurry!"

Beth's mind dropped the wedding issue in anticipation of her favorite Saturday morning cartoon.

"Garfield's on. Gotta go." Leaving Ken and Barbie in a heap on the floor, she jumped to her feet and ran from the room.

Joe sat very still, not sure what had hit him. Beth...did she think he was in love with Carly? Had he done something to give her that idea? Or did she just want Carly to stay so badly that she thought she'd found a way to make it happen?

And then he didn't have any more time to think it over, because Carly was coming in through the doorway.

"Oh, hi, I've been looking for you." She thrust a stack of letters into his lap. "What are these? I just found them stuffed behind the bread box."

He looked at her first, admiring the way her jeans hugged her hips and the nice curve of her breasts where the plaid shirt had been tucked into the belt of her pants. She wasn't as skinny as she had been at first, he realized suddenly. She was softening, rounding out. And his hands itched to explore her new dimensions. But he wasn't going to do that, he reminded himself. He'd been letting control slip a little lately, and that had to stop. She was only here for another few days at the most, he was sure. Surely she had come to some conclusion about this Mark person by now. One way or another, she must be starting plans for heading home.

"Look at them," she was insisting, and he tore his attention away from the way she filled her clothes and took a look at the papers she'd dumped in his lap.

Picking them up in a lump, he looked at them with distaste. He recognized them right away. Maybe he should have aimed them at the trash instead of holding on to them all this time. "They're nothing. Just notes the teachers send home periodically."

Carly frowned, looking from the papers to his eyes and back again. She couldn't believe what he was saying, that he could be so uncaring. "But... there seem to be some real problems here. Have you been in to talk to the teachers at all?"

He shrugged, on the verge of resenting her for bringing it up. "No. I figure they should be able to handle things at school, and I'll handle them at home. Share the burden, so to speak." He folded the letters in two and glanced around the room for a wastebasket.

Carly frowned, clearly upset by what she'd read. "I can't understand how you can be so cavalier about this." Before he had a chance to get rid of them, she'd snatched them back. "No, listen, Beth's teacher seems to be really worried about the extent of her daydreaming. And look at what this teacher says about Jeremy. She says he's sullen and unresponsive and doesn't interact with the other children." She looked up at Joe. "That isn't how he was last night. He was beaming, full of life and laughter."

Joe shrugged as though he were wrestling with an uncomfortable shirt rather than an uncomfortable idea. "Yeah, but he's a quiet, solemn sort of kid. That's just the way he is. So the teachers are always writing about it, as though he could change if he wanted to." He made a gesture of dismissal. "There's nothing wrong with him. He's doing okay."

Carly shook her head slowly. "I don't think so, Joe," she said softly. "I don't think you're right at all."

Now his resentment was bubbling up in his throat and he had to hold back his anger. Who did she think she was? She was only here for a few weeks. Tomorrow she would be gone. What did she want to do, stir up a hornets' nest and then take off to leave him to try to put things back together again? They were getting along fine. They didn't need her to tell them how to live their lives.

"Stay out of it, Carly," he said evenly. "Everything's all right."

She was still shaking her head. Why couldn't he understand how important this was? Children were only young once, and for a very short time. You couldn't just let things slide and hope for the best. If things went bad, there was sometimes no time to make them right again. She didn't know how or why she knew this. But she knew it, just the same, and that fact surprised her, pleased her. Maybe she had some natural mothering instincts after all.

"I think something's wrong," she insisted. She hesitated, then plunged on. "I know Ellen probably used to do these things and you're not used to handling them. But believe me, Joe, you've got to take over." She waved the letters. "Someone has to go in and talk to his teachers."

Anger cut through him like the flash of a blade. This damned woman—she came in here, getting the kids to love her, making them see what they'd been missing, throwing his life into a tailspin—why the hell had he ever let her in? He'd been crazy to do it. If he had any guts at all, he'd kick her out.

"Joe, someone has got to talk to them."

He jerked himself to his feet and glared at her. "Well then, why don't you go on in and do it? I don't have the time."

He was angry. She licked her lips and tried to think what she could do to quell it. She shouldn't have mentioned Ellen. She knew that. He wasn't over her death. That much was obvious. And how could he be? Her influence was everywhere, in everything in the house. He must mourn her every day. She wished she could think of a way to comfort him, to reach out to him.

She had to keep this in mind, especially when he kissed her and made her feel as though she couldn't live without his mouth caressing hers. He was just looking for the closeness he had lost when his wife died. He was hungering for the touch of a woman, and it had a lot more to do with missing Ellen than it did with liking Carly. She would forget things like that at her own peril.

"Well, I could go if you want me to," she offered tentatively.

He muttered something she couldn't understand and swung around. Two long strides brought him to the doorway.

"Where are you going?" she cried.

He turned back and looked her up and down with unfriendly eyes. "I'm going over to see Millie," he said, his anger fraying the edges of his words. "There are more problems around here than scare notes from teachers. And I think she has a right to know about this little conspiracy you and Trevor have cooked up behind her back."

"Joe—"

But she might as well have saved her breath. He was out the door and out of the house in no time.

She stood very still, listening to the screen door slam. She'd thought they were talking about Jeremy and Beth. How did Millie get into the picture all of a sudden?

Breakfast had been surprisingly peaceful, considering what had happened the night before. There was undeniable tension between the two of them whenever their eyes met, but they'd managed to stay calm and to act in front of the children as though nothing had happened. Sunny's mother had come to pick her up after breakfast and she'd stayed for a long time, talking about Sunny and Beth and life out here in the country. It had been fun talking with someone who had no ties to the questions she carried with her all the time now. She'd been able to relax and enjoy a normal conversation. She'd almost been able to forget all the rest.

But now it was back in a rush of confused emotions. What was Joe going to tell Millie? To beware of Carly? To come on over and confront her? To get Trevor out of town and away from her influence? There was no telling. She sighed, shoulders sagging. In the meantime, she was just going to have to go on as though nothing were happening.

There was certainly plenty to do. She spent some time going through the china cabinet, polishing silver and admiring the lovely pieces. At first she'd thought they must be Ellen's, but the few that were inscribed all had the Matthews name or the name Splindette, which she assumed must have been Phyllis's maiden name. Some dated from the nineteenth century. More history to be delved into.

The intercom buzzed three times while she was working. This was something new. Phyllis was beginning to communicate. Suddenly, she needed things from downstairs, like orange juice or the television schedule or someone to come up and catch a spider.

"It's a new campaign," Carly muttered to herself after the spider incident. "She's bound and determined to drive me away, or drive me crazy, whichever comes first."

She fixed lunch for the kids, vaguely wondering what Joe could possibly be talking about so long with Millie, and then she gathered up some clothes that the cleaner had delivered, and took them up to Joe's room. They were shirts and a suit, and she hung them up. Out of the corner of her eye she could see women's clothing still hanging in the back of the closet.

Ellen's. It had to be. She turned and looked, and then curiosity got the best of her, and she reached in and pulled out a handful of crowded hangers.

Ellen certainly had good taste in clothes. Silk pantsuits, a designer-label rayon dress, cashmere sweaters in bags, fine wool slacks—everything she touched looked expensive and well made, but something seemed slightly out of whack. Somehow this gave the appearance of the wardrobe of a big-city professional woman rather than a country mother. What had Ellen been like?

Joe had loved her. And that was just about all she knew. It was strange that no one talked about her. At first she had attributed it to being careful of Joe's feelings, but now she wasn't so sure. You would think Millie would have a thing or two to say about her, at least when Joe was out of earshot. But she really hadn't commented, any more than Phyllis or the children had.

The children. Surely they missed their mother. Losing her had been traumatic. But they never said a word about her. Now that she thought about it, their silence on the subject seemed rather strange.

Maybe looking at the wardrobe of the woman would give her a clue or two. She laid the beautiful clothes out on the bed and went into the closet for more.

And found more of the same—three-piece suits and hostess gowns and cocktail dresses. Where did she find the opportunities to wear these things here in the valley? And what did she wear when she went to the market or took the children out to watch their father work in the orchards?

Carly draped the rest of the collection over the bed and looked at it. What an astonishing assortment of sophisticated clothes. She wished she knew what Ellen had looked like. Joe had to have a picture somewhere.

She looked around the room, tempted to start going through drawers. But that wouldn't be right. Besides, if he walked in, she would look like a thief.

She turned back to the clothes. They were beautiful and expensive and sophisticated. But that didn't really tell her much. Ellen might have been the same—or a complete opposite who just had a thing for lovely clothes that she stuffed into her closet and never wore. She really knew no more about the woman than she had before she'd started this. Sighing, she began to put the clothes back.

She was half finished when she saw her favorite again—the black-silk pantsuit with a huge parrot hand-painted up the left side. Smiling, she slipped it from its hanger and walked over to the full-length mirror, pressing it to her and posing.

"Just my style," she mocked herself archly in the reflection.

"Then why don't you keep it." Joe's voice made her jump and whirl. "It would probably look good on you."

The horror of the situation staggered her. How could she have been so insensitive? She should have known he would show up at exactly the wrong time. And here she was, trying on his dead wife's clothes. She stared at him, stricken.

"Joe, I'm so sorry. I didn't mean to...I shouldn't have..."

He walked toward her and reached out to finger the gauzy silk of the pantsuit. "No problem," he said casually. "It's no big deal." He turned and looked at the clothes still lying on the bed. "Take them all, if you want to. Burn them. It's all the same to me." His laugh was short and humorless. "No big deal," he repeated.

No big deal? Her heart was beating a mile a minute and she could hardly catch her breath. "No, this is terrible," she admitted, backing away from him. "I meant no disrespect though, really, Joe. You probably think I'm some sort of callous monster."

His dark eyes were taking on a puzzled look. "Carly," he said, reaching out and stopping her retreat with a hand on her elbow. "What's the matter? What are you talking about?"

"I..." She felt so miserable she could hardly speak. "I'm so sorry. I know it must be painful for you to see your wife's clothes being pawed over by someone who is almost a stranger. I mean, it hasn't been that long since she...since she died, and you still have her clothes here close to you..."

"Died?" Joe looked astonished. "You thought Ellen was dead?" In a sudden move that shocked her, he threw his head back and gave vent to uproarious laughter, laughter that was harsh with bitter pain. "Ellen's not dead, Carly," he said when he had calmed himself. His dark eyes glittered with something between scorn and humor. "She's in San Francisco with her lover. Though I think I heard she'd married him the other day. So I guess she's an upstanding citizen again and I shouldn't say anything against her."

Carly stood staring at him with her mouth open. The silk pantsuit slipped from her hands and fell into a puddle on the floor, and she didn't notice. Ellen wasn't dead? Joe wasn't a grieving widower? The children weren't really half orphans? The room took a spin around her as she tried to regain her bearings.

"Oh," she said weakly. "I don't know why, but I just assumed..."

"I know." His wide mouth twisted in a crooked grin. "You couldn't imagine how any woman could leave me, right?"

He was kidding, but for her it was true. Ellen—instead of being a tragic figure, in just a few minutes, with just a few words from Joe, was becoming something else, some kind of deviant fiend who wasn't even very bright. It was difficult to rearrange her thinking quite this fast.

"Actually," she said in a quavering voice. "Actually, you're not far from the truth." She sank down onto the bed. "What happened, Joe? I mean, did she really leave you? And her children?" The full horror hit her. "How could she leave her children behind?"

He reached down and scooped up the pantsuit, holding it in his hands and looking down at it as though it had the answers. "I'd like to say I wouldn't let her take the children," he said quietly. "And I think that would have been true, if she had ever even tried." His gaze rose and met Carly's. "But she didn't try. She left us all, and this life, with hardly a backward glance. She won't be coming back."

He lifted the silk cloth to his face for a moment, as though taking in her scent. "We met in college," he said. "She was beautiful. A little strange, but so bright and enthusiastic." He shrugged. "I loved her from the first moment I saw her. Getting to know her came later.

I don't think I really realized what she was like until after we were married. Long after we were married.''

Carly couldn't say a word. The sight of his tortured face silenced her.

"She hated the country. She'd grown up in Boston. She felt like she was dying out here, like she was starving for something I couldn't give her.''

He walked over to the other side of the bed and carefully laid the pantsuit down.

"She used to lie right here in this bed and cry,'' he said, standing back and looking at the piece of silk he'd placed there. "She would cry for hours and she wouldn't tell me why. I'd lie beside her and wrack my brain. What did she want? What wasn't I doing? What wasn't I saying? How was I hurting her?''

He sat down on the bed and stared at the pillow. "I tried so hard to make up for it somehow. I brought her flowers, candy, tried to talk to her more, got tickets for shows. I planned a trip to Hawaii. Paid for the tickets. Handed her the itinerary with her birthday cake. She opened the envelope and looked at the plans...and she started to cry again.'' He shrugged. "I was going crazy trying to figure out what it was, what I could do to help her.''

He hung his head, silent for a moment. Carly ached to go to him, to wrap her arms around him. But she didn't dare. Instinct told her he wasn't ready for that. So she sat frozen, aching with the desire to comfort him and unable to think of a single thing she could do that could possibly ease his pain.

Joe hardly knew she was in the room any longer. He was letting out things he had kept bottled up for much too long, and it almost didn't matter who heard them.

He just had to get them out. Then, maybe, they would quit eating away at his soul.

"Finally she started talking about it," he went on. "She'd tell me she felt trapped. That she couldn't stand it here. She couldn't stand me anymore. She couldn't...she couldn't..." No, he could never say those words. She'd said she couldn't stand the kids, but he never wanted them to hear that. Never. He would rather they blamed him for their mother disappearing from their lives. They'd already paid too high a price. He wouldn't allow them to pay any more.

"I offered to go with her to counseling, but she refused. She didn't really want to make things better. She just wanted to get out. She wanted something new."

He looked up and seemed almost startled to see Carly sitting across the bed.

"So she just left?" Carly asked softly.

He nodded. "She packed up, left me a note, took off for San Francisco. I got divorce papers a few weeks later." He took a deep breath. "I went to see her, to try to talk her into coming back." His eyes met Carly's, wide and candid. "It wasn't that I wanted her back for myself at that point. My love for her had died a long time before. In fact, in some ways I hated her." He stopped and thought about that for a moment. "But the kids needed her. I wanted her back for the kids."

Carly nodded. Of course he did. If there was one thing she was sure of, it was his love for his children.

"She said that part of her life was like a bad dream. She didn't want to be reminded." His mouth twisted. "And then her new boyfriend walked into the room where we were meeting. He's a lawyer with a big corporation." His eyes narrowed and he looked at Carly as though still trying to understand. "They were perfect together. A pair of yuppies. You could see that she was happy. That this was what she wanted." His gaze hardened. "I don't care about that. I'm glad she's happy. But I can never forgive her for what she's done to my kids. Never."

He reached out and slowly gathered the silk pantsuit up into a ball in his hand. He stared at it for a moment, and then threw it back onto the floor where it landed in a pathetic, crumpled pile. After a few moments, he turned to cast Carly a weary smile. "Say, listen. Before you marry this guy, this Mark, make damn sure you know what you're doing. Don't end up like we did." His smile faded. "Don't do to him what Ellen did to us."

Carly shook her head. "I could never, ever do that." She spoke the words with utter conviction.

Cynicism flashed in his eyes. "Yeah, that's what they all say." A bitter smile twisted his mouth.

And in that one phrase, Carly knew why he always seemed to have something guarding his emotions, even as he released hers as they had never been released before. Joe was bound and determined never to love again. It was as clear as the pain on his face.

CARLY WALKED by the telephone three times before she finally made up her mind to go ahead and make the call. Mark deserved to know. She couldn't leave him hanging forever.

It was Saturday afternoon—evening in Washington. He might be home. Well, then she would just have to talk fast and hang up no matter what he said. Taking a deep breath, she picked up the receiver and punched the proper buttons.

The answering machine came on. She slumped with relief, and at the beep she quickly gave her message. "Mark, I just have to tell you this. There are things from my past—things I didn't even realize I needed to know—well, now they make up this puzzle that I have to solve before I can come back. I hope you'll understand. I know you and I know how impatient you must be with this mumbo jumbo I seem to be obsessed with. But I can't help it. It's just the way it is. If you've had it with me, I'll understand, believe me. I have no claim on you at all. Do what you think is best. I'm sorry."

She hung up and sighed. There was more she could have told him. *"Mark,"* she could have said. *"There's a man here with tortured eyes and shoulders so wide they could shelter me in a storm, and I'm getting him all tangled up in my emotions. It may take some time to get him out of my system again. Better not wait, Mark. I have a feeling this is going to take awhile."*

If only there were a way of telling him that without actually telling him that. There should be a way to let someone know hope for renewing a relationship was fading without having to go into the gory details.

She caught her breath and held it. What was she saying here? That things were over for her and Mark? She'd come to find herself so that she could go back to him refreshed and recommitted. Instead, she'd gotten herself hopelessly lost. It was hardly fair to say everything was over. Maybe if she just saw Mark again....

But no, she was afraid not. Could Mark blot out Joe's shadowed eyes? Could she ever forget that kiss that had left her feeling like rubber? She was tangled up all right. And she'd never been all that good at getting rid of snarls.

CARLY WAS OUT WORKING in the garden when Millie arrived. Joe hadn't said anything about his meeting with his old friend, but Carly had been expecting her just the same. She rose as Millie's car came up the drive, pulling off the muddy gloves and going to meet her.

"Get in," Millie suggested. "Let's drive out by the lake. I want to talk to you."

Carly had a sinking sensation in the pit of her stomach, but she did as Millie suggested. Millie backed out of the driveway and headed for the highway, driving slowly, not in any particular hurry. Neither of them spoke more than a few words. Carly sat very still and looked out the window at the changing landscape.

Millie turned her car off onto a dirt road that led them on a bumpy ride up and down a series of hills, threading their way between rows and rows of bright green trees. The air was filled with the scent of crushed lemon leaves and sweet lemon blossoms.

Carly began to relax and enjoy the ride. It was amazing how comfortable she felt in this area now. She'd only been here a little over a week, but she felt at home. Ancestral memory maybe. Or maybe she was just a country girl at heart.

She grinned, thinking that, and Millie said, "What's so funny?"

"Life," she answered promptly, and then wished she hadn't. From all evidence, Millie's life had been anything but a kick.

They had crested the last hill and were looking down at the sparkling blue water of Lake Bonita. Millie pulled into a cutout that gave them a beautiful view and turned off the engine.

"It's a reservoir really," she told Carly. "We get most of our local irrigation from it."

"It's lovely," Carly said.

Millie nodded. "I come up here and just stare at the water when I really need to think," she said. She stared at it now. "Oh Carly, Carly. What are you doing?" she said softly.

Carly suddenly felt very cold. "I'm looking for my father, Millie. That's all."

"No, Carly. That's not all." Her hands gripped the steering wheel. "You're taking each one of us out of our lives and making us into something we weren't before you came here."

Carly blinked. She hardly thought that Millie was being fair. "I don't mean to hurt you, Millie. I don't want to hurt anyone."

"No." Millie's dark eyes turned toward her, huge and sorrowful. "I'm sure you don't mean to hurt anyone. The problem is, you don't understand the harm you're doing."

Carly made a gesture of impatience. "Then explain it to me."

Millie smiled and reached out, her hand gently touching Carly's silver-blond hair with candid affection. "You don't understand anything, Carly," she said, her voice dreamy. "You don't understand how I feel about you. How much I care."

Carly frowned. "I like you too, Millie. I think we could be good friends—"

"Oh Carly." She patted Carly's cheek and turned away with a wistful smile. "We're tied together in ways you don't understand. I care for you almost as though you were a part of my own family."

The woman was acting in a very puzzling way and Carly wasn't sure she liked it. Why couldn't anyone be straight around here? Why couldn't everyone just be open and aboveboard and let the chips fall where they might?

And that was what she wanted to communicate to Millie. Taking a deep breath, she said, "If you care so much about me, why won't you tell me the truth?" She turned so she could keep Millie from avoiding her gaze. "What is it that you know about my father?"

Millie looked pained. "I'm not going to talk to you about your father," she said softly. "I really don't know anything that would do you any good."

Carly sat back and fought hard to hold back the surge of anger that threatened to explode and destroy what little hope she had of making any headway here. "Well, if you won't tell me the truth, at least do it for your son," she said evenly. "You have to tell Trevor who his father is. He needs to know. Do you know that he thinks Joe is his father?"

Millie closed her eyes and nodded. "Joe told me."

"You had no idea?"

She was silent for a long moment. "I think I did have an idea that he might think Joe was his father. I ignored it. I think he's probably thought that for a long time, and I've let him."

Carly wanted to shake her. Did these people think they could go on living in a dreamworld forever? "Why?"

"Because it was easy. Because there was no other man I could lean on, who would be a father image for Trevor, and I knew he needed that. It made him feel loved, it made him feel connected."

"But when he realizes the truth—"

"I know." She sighed. "Life isn't funny, Carly. It's hard. Decisions are hard. Especially when they involve children. That's the hardest . . . to know the right thing to do. You're never sure. You never know until everything is over and it's too late to change whether you've taken the right road."

She was going to resist feeling sorry for the woman. There was too much at stake to give way to sentimentality. Staring straight ahead, Carly said calmly, "Tell me about Trevor's father, Millie."

Millie moved as though trying to ward off her words. "I don't want to," she said, her voice so quiet it could barely be heard.

Carly stood firm. "Tell me anyway," she said. It wasn't what she really wanted to know, but at this point she felt as though the more secrets she could force out into the open, the more likely it was that her own past would come into focus.

To her surprise, Millie didn't need any more coaxing. She started softly, her words stilted, measured. "I was barely sixteen," she said. "He was older, much older, and I was dying for some love in my life."

Carly looked at her in surprise. "But your family . . . ?"

Millie shook her head. "What can I say about my family? My parents came from an old-fashioned tradition. Showing love and affection wasn't in them. They worked hard and expected me to do the same. I'm sure they must have loved me, but they didn't think it was necessary to express that love in any way. I was an only child and it was so silent in my house. So very silent."

Her voice trembled and she waited to calm herself before she went on.

"So I went outside and tried to develop other interests. I tried to find acceptance from others. For some reason that was a lonely year for me. My best friend had just moved away and Joe was a senior and totally involved in senior activities and girlfriends and sports. I felt so alone. And then I met . . . him."

For a moment, Carly thought she wasn't going to be able to go on, her voice was so shaky. But she stiffened her resolve and began again.

"He was so different. He talked about things I'd never thought about before. He opened the world up to me. And when he felt emotion, he let you see it." A teary smile lit her face as she remembered. "He touched. He laughed. He wept. And I was so hungry for everything he was, everything he had."

She sighed and used an embroidered hankie to wipe the tears that were dropping from her eyes.

"It wasn't his fault, you know," she said earnestly, turning toward Carly. "The affair, I mean. I came on pretty strong. I was so dumb. I threw myself at him as only a naive sixteen-year-old girl can. I had no idea what I was getting myself into. To see him respond to me . . . to know someone cared—it was heaven. And so I did everything I could to hold him. And it was so wrong."

She sniffed into the hankie again and Carly felt her heart going out to the woman in spite of all her determination not to be touched by her account. "What happened to him?" she asked. "Where did he go?"

Millie closed her eyes and shook her head. "Here's the part I'm really ashamed of. Carly, he was married." She turned and looked at Carly, her eyes begging for understanding. "At sixteen, you don't even understand what that means. All you care about is your own selfish needs. You can't see ahead, can't see what you're doing to other people." She sighed. "I paid for that. I paid and paid and I'll go on paying. It was a horrible thing that I did."

Well, sure, it wasn't very nice. But she was really taking on too much of the blame for herself. What about this older man who should have known better? A married man, for God's sake! What was he thinking of? Did it ruin his marriage? Was he still around somewhere?

She looked at Millie and tried to edit the flow of questions down to a few pertinent ones. "But what about the man? Did he help you? Did he take some responsibility himself?"

She shook her head. "He didn't know. He left town before the baby... Trevor... was born."

"And you never tried to contact him?"

"No. And I never will."

Carly let out an exasperated breath. "Oh come on, Millie. All this mea culpa stuff is all very well, but there's a limit to how much punishment anyone is obliged to take. You're certainly remorseful. And it's been a lot of years under the bridge. You deserve some happiness."

Millie laughed softly. "You sound like Phyllis. But Trevor is the one who deserves the happiness. Not me."

Carly thought for a moment. "Does Trevor know any of this?"

Millie shook her head. "I can't tell him. How could he understand?"

Carly smiled at her. "He loves you. He would forgive you anything."

Millie stared at her for a moment, a flicker of hope in her eyes. But then her face hardened. "No. I can't risk it."

Carly studied her. "Is that why you won't tell him who his father is, so that he won't go looking for him and find out the whole story?"

"Exactly."

Carly bit her lip. The kid was never supposed to know. That hardly seemed fair. But, she had to admit, letting him think Joe was his father was probably the best solution in Millie's eyes. But it wasn't the truth. And some day he would find that out. And if they weren't careful, he would hate them both.

Millie had dried her eyes and was all business again, sitting up straight and looking downright unburdened to have related the entire tale and made her case so touchingly.

"So, Carly," she said, her voice bright again. "Now that you've heard the whole sordid story, I hope you see why you have to stop encouraging Trevor."

Carly didn't see at all. "You're never going to tell him who his father is?" she asked carefully.

"No. I don't think he needs to know."

That was all very neat and tidy for Millie. But where did it leave the rest of them? "I think you're wrong, Millie. I think you're so wrong. And I think Trevor is going to resent it more and more as he gets older."

Millie drew in a deep breath. "You may be right. But I'll have to take my chances." She glared at Carly, the picture of strength where there had only moments before been a broken woman. "Won't I?"

JOE WAS DRIVING the truck up the drive as Millie was leaving from dropping Carly off. He swung down and caught up with her before she got to the house.

"What did Millie have to talk to you about?" he asked, looking down at her as they walked.

Carly looked up and wished he weren't so darned handsome with the late afternoon sun in his eyes. "She told me all about Trevor's father," she said blithely.

"She what?" Joe stopped where he was, his face registering his shock.

Carly almost laughed aloud. "Not his name, if that's what you're worried about." It was curious how relieved he seemed to be when he heard that. She frowned and searched his eyes. "Why? Who is he?"

Joe took a deep breath and resumed walking. "I've told you before these aren't my secrets to tell."

Carly shrugged. She hadn't really expected to get anywhere. "She doesn't think Trevor needs to know either and I think she's dead wrong."

Joe didn't say anything. When they got to the kitchen door, he held it for her and watched her go in before him.

"Thank you, sir," she said flippantly, turning and looking back at him. "You're such a gentleman."

"I try to be," he muttered, reaching out and touching her lower lip with his finger, running it the width of her mouth before he drew it back again, his eyes smoky with some strange longing that made her breath come faster. "But sometimes it's damn hard," he added.

Turning on his heel, he left her standing there with a hand over her heart. "Don't feel like the Lone Ranger," she whispered to no one in particular.

CHAPTER TWELVE

SUNDAY was a red-letter day. Phyllis suddenly decided she was well enough to join the rest of the family. Everyone stood around, mouths agape, as she descended the stairs from her room, her little legs seemingly as sturdy as trees. She wore a flowing orange caftan and made a lot of dramatic gestures. A real crowd pleaser.

"Hello, all my loved ones. Look! Isn't it wonderful? I'm so much better now. I've decided to come down and make breakfast for my grandchildren."

"Make breakfast?" they echoed as one, still stunned.

Carly glanced at Joe. He was as surprised as she was. But she was pretty sure she knew what was behind this wonderful recovery. The woman wanted to prove that they didn't need Carly.

"Of course I'll make breakfast." Phyllis beamed at them all. "How would you like pancakes?"

"Oh goody!" Beth cried, clapping her hands.

"How about waffles?" Jeremy said grumpily, standing close to Carly, but he never had any hope of penetrating the layer of good cheer Phyllis had wrapped herself in this morning.

"It's a miracle," Joe said, a bit of his sarcasm showing.

"Call it a rebirth," Phyllis corrected sunnily. "I feel as though I've been born again. Like I'm ready for anything."

"You may be ready for anything," Joe said. "But is anything ready for you?"

"Oh, you little devil." She pinched his cheek and laughed, and he grimaced and went outside to see about things that men see about when they want to get away from their mothers.

She shrugged, watching him go, then turned and walked into the kitchen, pulling open cabinets as she went. "Now let's see, where do we keep the mix? Oh, someone's been changing things around, haven't they? Naughty, naughty. It's going to take me some time to get readjusted, I can see that."

"Would you like some help?" Carly offered, coming forward to point out the canister she was looking for. "I'd be glad to help you."

Phyllis turned and gave her a smile that was closer to a sneer. "Thanks, but no thanks. I've heard about your lack of experience in the culinary arts, dear." She laughed as though it were supposed to be a joke, but Carly felt her cheeks redden, and looking down she could see the stricken look on Beth's young face.

"Carly makes good pancakes," Beth said stoutly, joining Jeremy at her side. "Carly makes the greatest. Doesn't she, Jeremy?"

Her brother nodded vigorously and Carly felt something stinging her eyes. She wanted to wrap them both into her arms and squeeze them very tightly, but instead she managed a light laugh and said, "Your grandmother has had lots more experience at pancakes than I have. Years and years of it." Her eyes flashed as they met those of the older woman. It was best that Phyllis know right away that she wasn't going to get away with this stuff without a fight on her hands. "So let's see how she does, okay?"

The children nodded, and Beth turned to frown at the woman who had been mostly invisible and upstairs in bed for most of the two years she had been living with them.

Beth looked at her, head to the side, considering. "Are you going to be our grandmother again?" she asked at last, her little brow furrowed.

Phyllis's laugh was a bit hollow. "Darling, I've always been your grandmother and I'll always be your grandmother. That's one of those things about life—you can't divorce a grandmother."

Carly looked quickly at the children to see how that reference to their mother's absence affected them. Their eyes were bland, emotionless, and she wondered exactly how Joe had explained it to them. On the whole they seemed to have adjusted very well. They had their behavioral problems, but she had seen no evidence that they were in any real trouble. Emotionally they seemed pretty stable.

She asked them to set the table and they went to the flatware drawer, squabbling over who would take what to the table.

Phyllis watched them, shaking her head. "They need a mother, poor dears," she said to Carly in a loud stage whisper. "If only Joe and Millie would hurry up and get married, these kids would have a happy home once again. Don't you think?" She smiled as though to say, "Two can play this game, dear."

She did make great pancakes, Carly had to admit. They all sat around the table, including Joe, and ate until they could eat no more.

"Now, I have big plans for our Sunday," Phyllis announced as they were finishing up, clapping her hands for attention. "We'll play board games and make fudge and—"

"Uh . . . Mother." Joe's voice wasn't quite as diffident as Phyllis surely would have liked. "I'm sorry, but I'm afraid we already have plans."

Everyone turned to stare at him, including Carly.

"Oh?" Phyllis said coolly. "And what are they, dear?"

There was just a moment when it was apparent to anyone watching really closely that he had no idea what he was going to say next. Carly could almost see the wheels turning in his mind as he searched quickly for inspiration. "We're taking Carly fishing," he said at last, his tone triumphant. "She hasn't been since she was a little kid. And Beth and Jeremy want to teach her all about fishing on the Kennison River."

Phyllis frowned, her foot tapping on the floor with frustration. "You know I hate fishing," she snapped.

"Yes, Mother. I do know that." Joe's smile was exceedingly innocent. "But after such a long illness you'll hardly be up to an outdoor trip at this point anyway, will you? So why don't you just stay home and watch a little TV and we'll be back by dinner time. Okay?"

What could she say?

Probably a lot, if Joe had given her the time and space, but he didn't. He hurried them all and had Carly in the kitchen making sandwiches and the kids packing the car, and before she knew what was happening she was on her way to go fishing. In a boat. On a river.

"Do I have to bait the hook?" she asked, wrinkling her nose.

"I'll do it for you," Jeremy assured her, and she smiled her thanks. He was still the quietest little boy she'd ever known, but lately he had taken to sitting beside her at every opportunity, and she was taking it as a compliment, whether it was meant that way or not.

They stopped at a sporting-goods shop to get bait and pick up a license for Carly, and then they were off. The area of the river where they were headed was actually a series of small lakes that emptied into each other. Joe had a boat docked at one of them. The four of them piled aboard and Joe started the motor, taking them out into the center of the lake where the water was like glass and the wild-bird calls echoed from bank to bank.

"It's so beautiful," she breathed, looking from the water to the evergreens that rimmed the lake.

"Yes," he answered softly. "It is." But he was looking at her blue eyes, her silver hair, her full lips.

She turned and met his gaze. He smiled, and so did she, and for just a moment, his fingers locked with hers. And then he drew away.

They fished and laughed and ate sandwiches and got sunburns. Beth caught two small rainbow trout and threw them back to swim again. Jeremy caught a huge golden trout and Joe caught three good-sized rainbows. Carly didn't catch anything.

"And I'm glad," she claimed unconvincingly.

They all laughed at her. It was warm laughter, loving laughter, and it warmed her as nothing else ever had. She and Beth sang silly songs on the ride home and Joe and Jeremy made fun of them. All in all it was one of the most marvelous days Carly could remember ever having had.

They came back tired and happy and found Phyllis had retreated to her room again.

"Gone but not forgotten," Joe murmured, looking about the empty house and the untouched kitchen with dishes from breakfast still in the sink. "Sorry, Carly. About everything."

"Don't be." She smiled at him.

He smiled back, a long, lazy, slow smile that started at his eyes and looked like it might never end. She felt it curl around her and she wanted to touch him. But the kids were nearby and she didn't dare.

"A successful day," he murmured.

She nodded and grinned. "You've certainly done your manly duty and brought home the bacon," she teased.

He pretended to preen. "It's a jungle out there," he told her. "But a man's gotta do—"

"What a man's gotta do," she joined in, laughing. "What a guy."

They smiled into each other's eyes as if it were something they just couldn't stop doing. But they couldn't stand there forever. Joe finally moved, gesturing toward the catch still out in the car.

"If I clean the fish, can you cook them?" Joe asked her at last.

She picked up a spatula and saluted with it. "Clean on, Macduff," she said in her best Scots accent.

"Right." He turned to go out, but hesitated, and then touched her cheek with the flat of his hand. "I'll be back," he promised softly.

She nodded, feeling like a teenager with stars in her eyes, and watched him disappear through the door. Then she made a lunge for the cookbooks and searched madly in the indexes for trout.

Batters and doughs and parchment paper and marinades. Good Lord! Which recipe was the best to use?

"The simpler is always the better," she muttered to herself. " 'Sauté in butter.' Sounds fabulous."

And it was. It actually was. She cooked a delicious dinner, to her own quiet satisfaction. Strange but true—she was getting good at this sort of thing.

The mood of the day carried on through dinner. Even Jeremy told a joke. And when the food was all completely devoured, Carly shooed them all out to the den to watch television.

"You all just stay out here and out of my hair, and I'll be able to get the dishes done much faster," she told them, settling Jeremy with a coloring book. Beth was dancing in the middle of the room, singing a happy song, and Joe had turned on the television. Carly was just turning to go back to the kitchen when she heard a name that chilled her. She whipped her head around to catch the latest item being reeled out on the news.

"Congressman Mark Cameron has announced the disappearance of his fiancée, Carolyn Stevens . . ."

She stared at the screen, panic fluttering in her chest. They were showing a picture of her. Good grief, Mark, not the one from the Capitol ID card! She cringed, and at the same time rejoiced, because there was very little chance that anyone in California would connect the woman on the screen in the horn-rimmed glasses, her hair swept up into a fashionable twist and her face set in professional disdain, with Carly Stevens in her jeans and sneakers, with her silver hair blowing in the wind.

"The Congressman is offering a reward..."

A reward. Oh Mark, Mark, didn't you get the messages on your answering machine? Or did I say something that made you think I was being held by Gypsies? A reward, for heaven's sake.

She looked around the room at the others. Jeremy was lying on the floor with his coloring book and hadn't even looked up. Joe was reading a weekly newsmagazine and had only glanced up a time or two, but his face showed no signs of recognition. Carly breathed a sigh of relief. They didn't have a clue.

She turned to go back to the kitchen, and that was when she noticed Beth. Her eyes were very wide and she was staring up at Carly, her little mouth open in wonder.

Carly's heart fell. She knew. There was no doubt about it. Beth had recognized her behind the glasses, beneath the complex hairdo. Her childish eyes saw right through the superficial to the simple meat of the matter. Carly had just been on TV. Beth was in awe.

Carly was struck dumb. What could she say to the child? Turning, she headed for the kitchen, buying time. But she could hear Beth's footsteps right behind her. What was she going to say?

Before she had a chance to formulate anything at all, Beth's little arms came around her legs, holding tightly. Carly stopped, took a deep breath, and looked down at the upturned face.

Beth's gray eyes were full of questions. She stared up at this woman who had come to live with them and seemed to have another life somewhere else. "Did my mama leave so you could come?" she asked in a quivering voice. "Are you going to stay?"

"Oh Beth." She dropped to her knees and put her arms around the girl. "Beth, Beth, I don't belong here. I'm sorry, darling, but I can't promise you anything like that."

Beth's lower lip began to wobble. "Don't go, Carly," she whispered, tears beginning to roll one right after another down her rounded cheeks. "Please don't go like my mama did. I love you."

Carly closed her eyes and held the little girl to her, held her as she sobbed, and tried to wipe away her own tears without Beth seeing. There was nothing she could say that would take care of this.

Suddenly the interweaving of relationships was clear to her as it had never been before. Every move she made, every decision she took, had a bearing on what happened in other lives. She could never be completely free. Not as long as there was love in her life.

She carried Beth up to bed and tucked her in, telling her loving things and moving carefully to jokes, so that she left her with a tearstained face that was smiling.

On the stairs she hesitated. Her impulse was to go to Joe and talk with him about what had happened. Funny, this new urge to share with him, to see things through his eyes as well as her own. Because, of course, it was impossible. She thrust the impulse back into the dark shadows where it belonged and went on into the kitchen and began to do the dishes, working blindly, thinking about Beth.

"Want some help?"

She whirled to find Joe behind her, his eyes smiling. Help? Was that what he was offering?

She'd been hired to do this work. There was no reason he should help her. But something new was creeping into their relationship, and she had the urge to test it out.

She smiled back. "Sure," she said, throwing him a dishrag. "The more the merrier."

They started out in companionable silence, but by the time they'd finished, their teasing had them both laughing. Jeremy came into the room and sat at the table and watched them, not saying anything, but laughing softly at their silly antics. And when it was time to go to bed, Carly went with a glow that lasted until morning.

CHAPTER THIRTEEN

THE NEWSPAPER OFFICE was open at eight Monday morning, but she couldn't make it before ten o'clock. The paper was a daily and once she got an idea of the mass of microfiche she was going to have to wade through, she nearly gave up.

But where else was she going to go to find the answers she needed? She plunged into the work with a sigh.

The morning had been hectic. Beth had clung to her, wanting to stay home with a stomachache that didn't seem to affect the mountain of French toast she put away. Carly had packed her off anyway, despite the pleading eyes and pouting lower lip.

At the last minute, she'd dropped down to give her a hug. "Beth, darling, I'll be here when you get back. I promise."

Beth had brightened a little and she and Jeremy had gone to the bus stop, and Carly had turned around to deal with Joe.

He was different this morning, brooding, quiet. She had a feeling that he'd had a night to think over their relationship and he regretted the closeness they'd shared the day before. He was drawing back. And that scared her.

He'd left to go out to work with hardly a glance in her direction, though he had agreed to let her take his car into town. She watched him go, then went in to use the telephone once more, dialing Mark's number at a time she was sure of getting the machine.

"I saw the item on the news last night, Mark, and I've got two things to say. Number one, I am not your fiancée. And number two, I'm not missing. I know this has been rotten of me, leaving you in the dark like this. But I think you had better know that I'm getting involved in things here...so involved...I'm not sure when I'll be back. It might be a long time." She closed her eyes as she said the last, not sure herself what it meant. "So consider this a sort of goodbye, Mark," she went on. "I don't think you'd better count on me, personally or professionally."

There. She'd done it. She'd cut the ties, destroyed her career. And she felt lighter than she'd felt in months.

What the heck. She could surely get a job in California doing the sort of work she'd done in Washington. Sacramento was full of politicians. She'd be able to find something there. Once she was finished here.

But what was she saying? Of course she was going back to Washington. That was where her real life was. This was just a...a...an interlude of sorts. Like a vacation. And a person always had to go back when the vacation was over, didn't she?

Besides, there was this issue of her father and what had become of him. She had a full day ahead of her, slogging through tapes of tiny newspaper print that threatened to give her the headache to end all headaches. She spent two hours looking at pages and pages of articles that had nothing to do with anything, before breaking for lunch. An ice-cream cone at the corner soda shop revived her and she was back at work half an hour later.

It was drudgery, looking at the screen until her eyes ached. And then, suddenly, there it was—the picture of her with her family. Excitement shot through her. She'd almost lost faith that it had ever really existed.

The attached article was short. "Howard Stevens is known for running one of the best-stocked corner groceries in town. But starting Sunday, neighbors will know him by a new name: Preacher Stevens. He will be taking over duties at the New Bible Church on Fourth Street where he has filled in on occasion for Reverend Stuart for many years."

There was a paragraph about his education and his experience, then a few lines about Carly and her mother. She skimmed it quickly, disappointment beginning to build. There was nothing here. And certainly no reason why Millie would have kept the picture.

And then her eyes fell on a familiar name in the last paragraph of the article. "Phyllis Matthews has volunteered to organize a choir for the little church. She will serve as choir director and plans a busy choral season."

So she barely knew him, did she? Anger smoldered in Carly's heart. Not that this was a big surprise. Still, she couldn't understand why Phyllis would lie about it.

All in all, the article was a major disappointment. There had to be more somewhere. She was almost blind as it was. She might as well keep looking.

She came upon the article about Joe almost an hour later. And finally the piece on Millie as valedictorian. And that was it. A wasted day.

She got home the same time the children did. Their spontaneous energy brightened her mood. She served them cookies and listened to how their day had gone and packed them off to their rooms to get their homework out of the way. Then she brewed herself a cup of herbal tea and sat down to think over how her own day had gone.

She had to put some order into these jumbled bits and pieces of information she had. There was only one really new thing that she had learned today—and that was that Phyllis had been even more intimately connected with her father than she had admitted. But the original puzzle still remained. Why had Millie kept the picture?

She stared down into her tea leaves, waiting for inspiration. What did Millie know about her father? Why had she been interested in Carly and her family? And why didn't she come right out and say so from the beginning?

But wait. She sat up straight and frowned.

Millie was connected to Phyllis. Phyllis was in her corner all the way. Phyllis wanted her for a daughter-in-law and, from all hints and anecdotes, had always wanted exactly that. So you might say Millie and Phyllis were very close. And she had just learned that Phyllis had organized the choir for her father's church. Millie admitted to having gone to her father's church a time or two. Suppose it were more than that. Suppose Phyllis had brought Millie with her to be a part of the choir... Yes, Millie had said something about singing in a choir.

She went very cold, her breath coming in short gasps. There was something there—a question of timing, a question of opportunity, a question of coincidence—that she didn't want to look at fully. It was horrifying, like a door behind which you knew a monster sat, and yet you had to go through it, and as you reached for the knob your fingers trembled and you couldn't get a grip, couldn't turn the knob.

She was almost grateful when Phyllis walked into the kitchen, her flowered pantsuit bright enough to light a small city.

"Well, there you are," she said cheerfully, giving Carly a look but not really seeing her, or surely she would have noticed how agitated she was. "I was just about to start dinner." She gave her a challenging glance.

Carly was in no mood to start competitive cooking at this point. "Fine," she said, forcing herself to be calm, to push aside the things she had been thinking about. "Let me know if I can do anything to help."

She began gathering her cup and teapot together preparatory to leaving the room, but she paused when Phyllis came near and stood over her.

"I could tell you what you could do to help," she said, her dark eyes flashing. "But I think you know what it is."

Carly looked her straight in the eye. There was no longer any room for polite pretense.

"You want me to leave, don't you?" she said bluntly.

Phyllis was just as honest. "That about sums it up."

Carly sat back and took her mug of tea in two hands. Phyllis was not on her list of well-liked persons at the moment. She saw no reason why she should go out of her way to make life easy for the woman.

"Well, I'll tell you," she said slowly. "I don't think the children want me to leave. And I don't think Joe wants me to leave."

Phyllis sighed, shaking her head. "I'm fully aware of that. And that is exactly the problem, as you very well know."

Carly smiled faintly. She knew that was Phyllis's problem. Maybe it was her own problem too. She wasn't sure.

"Tell you what, Phyllis," she said. "I'll think it over. And I'll do what I think is best for everyone."

"Including me?" Phyllis asked archly, drumming her long, painted nails on the back of the wooden chair.

Carly didn't feel much like grinning, but she managed to do it anyway, just because she didn't want Phyllis to think she was being intimidated.

"Sure. You will be last on my list, but you'll be included." She rose and put her mug and the teapot in the sink. "Give me a call if I can help with dinner in any way," she said brightly, then left the room.

At least the woman wasn't cagey about what she felt. She came right out and let you know what she wanted. She was going to have to confront her about what she knew and get her to be as candid about that—but not right now. She wasn't ready. She was feeling just a little shaky about everything. She wanted to be stronger before she made the final push for the truth. And right now she wanted to go to her room and lie down and stare at the ceiling and pray for inspiration.

Turning a corner, she found Jeremy sitting on the bottom step of the stairs, his back to her. He was leaning against the wall and pulling on a loose piece of the wallpaper.

"Oh Jeremy," she said sighing, letting her arms go limp with weariness. "Don't do that."

He didn't turn or make any other sign that he had heard her. He just kept picking at the piece of wallpaper.

She stopped where she was and frowned. No matter what Beth had said at the beginning about how Jeremy would never mind her, she'd found him to be a very obedient child, helpful and cooperative. He was withdrawn and seemed to live in some private place he kept inside that was just for him, but he was not an unruly or disobedient boy at all. But she'd always had a feeling. . . .

"Jeremy?" she said softly again, not moving a muscle.

He didn't make a move. His little fingers still picked at the paper.

"Jeremy?" she said a little louder. "Can you hear me?"

He kept on peeling the paper off.

He couldn't hear her. She was convinced of it.

"Jeremy?" she said a bit louder.

Still no response.

"Jeremy!" she shouted. This time the vibrations should bounce upon his skin as well as his eardrums.

And they did. He yanked his hand back and turned, wide-eyed, surprised to see her there.

Yes! That was it. He was definitely surprised. He hadn't heard a thing until she'd shouted. He was hard of hearing. What was wrong with everyone for missing it?

She knelt beside him. "Jeremy, darling, do you have problems hearing me?"

He shook his head quickly, his eyes full of fear. "No," he said, his gaze glued to her lips. "I can hear you."

You can lip-read, you mean, she thought to herself. Oh Jeremy. The poor baby. He must have spent most of his life trying to pretend, working so hard at figuring out what people were saying so they wouldn't figure out what was wrong.

Ignoring his stiffening, she threw her arms around him and hugged tightly.

"Jeremy, Jeremy, you dear thing." She drew back and looked at him and smiled, but he didn't smile back.

"It's all right, you know. If you're having trouble hearing, we'll take you to doctors and see if they can—"

He shook his head violently. "No," he said fiercely. "I can hear! I can hear."

Struggling out of her arms, he ran up the stairs and slammed the door to his room, while Carly sat back and stared after him.

INSTEAD OF GOING to her room as she'd planned, she turned and went out the front door. She was pretty sure Joe was working in his office in the barn, going over some figures. She could hardly wait to tell him.

This was more important than the stuff about Phyllis and her father, she told herself, knowing she was rationalizing like crazy. That whole issue was coming to a head, but she found herself avoiding it. It was as though she had the pieces of the puzzle in front of her but she was scared to go ahead and put them together. So she thrust the whole thing into the back of her closet and took up a new toy.

She'd known from the first that there was more to Jeremy than people had told her. They said he didn't listen. Didn't they ever stop to think that that might be because he couldn't hear? Maybe it was just that people who had grown up with him always around just took him for granted. Whatever it was, he'd fooled too many people for too long. Something had to be done.

Jeremy. She had to take care that things changed for him. She had a new burning issue to think about, an issue that shouldered aside the search for her father for now. She ran across the yard and arrived before Joe red-cheeked and breathless.

"Guess what," she announced, eyes shining. "Jeremy is hard of hearing. I proved it."

He looked up with a frown, obviously not amused at being interrupted. His face looked dark and hard in the shadows of his office. His hair was in disarray, as though he'd been running his hands through it, and thick strands fell over his forehead. There was nothing inviting about the look in his eyes. "What are you talking about?"

"Jeremy." His cool response dimmed her enthusiasm only a little. "He can't hear. That's the problem. That's why he's so withdrawn."

He threw down his pencil and grimaced, leaning back in his chair and looking at her from half-closed eyes. "Listen, Carly, you've only been here a week, you hardly know the boy."

"I know this boy," she insisted, refusing to back down. "He's a good boy. He does what I tell him to do. And just now, I came up behind him and spoke to him several times. Joe, he didn't hear me. I'm sure of it."

He sat motionless for a long moment, then shook his head slowly. "He ignored you."

"No. That wasn't it. I was there, Joe, I saw him. And I'm sure of what I saw." His hard face was unbending. She couldn't understand how he could be so inflexible. She put out a hand in supplication. "Joe, please, I want to take him for testing—"

His face became even darker, almost angry. "No. No way. He's been through testing. We took him for all the tests two years ago. They didn't turn up a thing. I won't have him go through that again."

She was bewildered by his adamancy. "But, Joe, I'm so sure—"

He sat up straight and glared at her. "Leave him alone. He's a quiet kid. That's not a crime, you know."

She stopped arguing. There wasn't much use. She should have read the signs from the beginning and saved it for another time. There was something prickly about him today, a new wariness. She wasn't going to get anywhere with him while he was like this.

"Okay," she said, trying to smile. "Listen, we can talk about this later—"

"Later?" He rose from his chair and came out from behind his desk, coming up close to her in a manner that was more aggressive than friendly. "What 'later' is that, Carly? How long are you planning to stay? Another day? Another week?"

There was something in his eyes—was it pain? Was it anger? She couldn't be sure. But as he spoke, he reached out and took her hair in his hand, letting it flow through his open fingers like sand at a golden beach, watching every nuance. Then his hand came in and curled against her neck, moving slowly down, fingers spreading against her skin, and his gaze followed the movement as though he were half hypnotized by it.

She stood very still, afraid to speak, afraid to move, not sure what was going on, not sure if she liked it, but not daring to do anything that might make him stop.

"You're a visitor here, Carly. A transient. Passing through."

His hand cleared her hair away and his face slowly descended to her neck. His lips were warm, but when he opened his mouth and tasted her skin, his touch was hot, searing, and she moaned softly, closing her eyes, letting the delicious warmth pour through her.

"You're only here for a short time, Carly," he went on, rubbing his rough cheek against her silky skin, his voice as rugged as gravel, as soft as night. "What do you want to do, tear my whole life apart and leave it in pieces on the ground when you walk away?"

His eyes were as hard and flat as tinted glass as he lifted his head. His hand slipped down inside her shirt, sliding beneath her bra, cupping her breast, fingers searching for the nipple, setting her pulse on fire. And his gaze still held hers, almost defiantly.

She didn't push him away. She knew she should, but she didn't seem to have the strength. Instead, she moved, gasping as the sensations stirred in her, and then she lifted her face to his, wanting his kiss, hungry for it, needing it with a new, deep, burning ache inside that she had never experienced before. Her lips parted and she sighed, leaning toward him.

But he only stared down at her, offering nothing. His hand moved away from her breast and clenched into a fist, and his eyes grew so dark that they seemed black and limitless.

"Go away, Carly," he said softly, his face twisted in a tortured grimace. "Just go away."

She stared at him, not sure if he meant for now or forever.

"Go." He pointed toward the door, eyes burning.

Numbly, she turned and began to walk back to the house. When she looked back, he was heaving a sharpened ax up over his shoulder. She swung around, hand covering her mouth.

"Joe, what are you doing? Where are you going?" she called back.

His eyes were hooded as he looked at her. "I'm going to the upper orchard to split some wood," he said, his voice as rough as a winter wind. "I feel a sudden need for some vigorous physical activity."

He turned toward the truck. She bit her lip, wanting to insist on going with him, afraid for him. But he wasn't hers. And now he wanted her off his property. Phyllis would have a good laugh over this one. Carly had barely finished telling her that Joe didn't want her to leave. It seemed she'd made a small error in judgment.

CHAPTER FOURTEEN

MILLIE'S CAR WAS PARKED in the driveway. Carly hadn't even heard her drive up, but she could hear the laughter now. While she'd been going through an emotional and physical experience that had shaken her to the roots, Millie and Phyllis were having a jolly talk in the kitchen. It was almost amusing. Almost, but not quite.

Still, facing them would be even less so. She hesitated, wishing there were a way she could gracefully avoid the two of them, but it was too late. They'd seen her. Millie called out a greeting, and she went in, forcing herself to don a friendly smile in return.

"Join us," Millie insisted, offering a plate of brownies she'd brought over. Her voice was welcoming but her eyes were inquisitive, moving quickly over Carly, looking for clues as to what she was up to.

Carly sank into a chair at the table and looked at the two of them. They both loved Joe, each in her own, possessive way. Were they forming an alliance against her? She wasn't feeling very strong at the moment. She wasn't really up to a fight.

"I've just come from the community center," Millie told her chattily. "They're putting on a musical version of *The Turn of the Screw*. I'm trying to talk Phyllis into getting involved."

Carly did a double take. "A musical version of *The Turn of the Screw?* Can they do that?"

Millie looked at her blankly. "Why not?"

Carly blinked. "Have you ever read *The Turn of the Screw?*"

"Oh, it'll be cute—a little girl, a little boy, the governess—sort of a mystery *Mary Poppins.*"

"As written by Stephen King," Carly noted dryly.

Millie's puzzled look showed that she still didn't quite get it. "Anyway, Phyllis would be perfect for the job."

Phyllis looked pleased, but she was shaking her head. "No, no, you're a darling to even think of me, Millie, but you know my singing days are over."

"Phyllis has a wonderful voice," Millie explained to Carly. "And she's done a lot of work with choral groups."

It was amazing how they could sit here calmly talking about this and not see the connection, not remember that choir had been the root of all...what? Something. Something that Carly still needed to find out.

"Yes," Carly said slowly, feeling numb. "I've heard about her choir-directing days."

Both the other women froze and stared at her. So they did get the connection after all.

Carly knew it was time to confront them, time to lay her cards out on the table. But she felt groggy, listless. Her mind wouldn't really focus. She wasn't ready.

"You know what I think she should do," she went on, speaking to Millie rather than Phyllis. "I think she should take Beth in hand and train her to try out for a part. The child seems to have inherited her voice."

Millie blinked rapidly and stumbled over her words, having a hard time readjusting from the shock of Carly's earlier statement. "Uh...yes, you know...I think Carly may have an idea there, Phyllis. I...uh, I mean, I've heard Beth singing. She does have a nice voice. Maybe you ought to—"

"She's too young," Phyllis said, glaring at Carly. "And I doubt I would have the patience for that sort of thing these days. As I said before, my choral days are over."

An uncomfortable silence fell over the table. Carly thought of Joe, of his touch on her breast, and she shivered, but no one mentioned it. She had to get out of here, but for some reason she didn't seem to have the strength to get up and do it. One of them would have to say something sooner or later. Then maybe she would have an opening to leave.

Millie beat her to it. She finally broke the silence when she pushed back her chair and said, "Well, I think I'll go say hello to the children. Are they in the den?"

Carly looked up at her but she didn't smile. "I think they're in their rooms, doing homework."

"Great." That would give her even longer to stay away. "I'll just run up and see them. Be back in a jiffy." She escaped through the doorway.

Phyllis sat holding her teacup and looking at Carly over the rim like a cat who had a mouse between her paws.

"Millie is a wonderful person, isn't she?"

Well, who could argue with that? "She's very nice," Carly allowed, looked at the woman warily.

"She loves the children as though they were her own."

"She's very good with them."

Phyllis smiled as though she thought things were going well. "She's done her best to keep things going here, keep things on an even keel, since Ellen left."

"Yes, she's been very generous."

Phyllis reached out and put her hand over Carly's in a move that made Carly want to yank her hand away. "She's waited so long for Joe, poor dear. She's worked so hard at it. You can see why it disturbs me to see you walking in and destroying everything."

No one could ever accuse Phyllis of skirting an issue. Carly slipped her hand away, resisting the urge to wipe it on her pants. Sitting back, she looked the woman in the face, nodding slowly. "I can see your point, really I can. You want Millie and Joe to marry."

"Of course I do. I always have." She scowled for a moment, remembering. "They were meant for each other from the first. Her mother was my best friend, and we always planned how it would be. Gloria had her dress picked out for the wedding by the time Millie was ten years old. We knew where we would hold the reception. We had the service planned to the minutest detail."

"And then Millie got pregnant?" She watched, knowing Phyllis would nod at that. But it wasn't going to be good enough to silence her this time. "You know, from what I've seen and heard, I don't buy it," she said softly.

Phyllis looked up in surprise. "What are you talking about?"

Carly looked her square in the eye. "I don't think Joe would have married Millie, even if she hadn't gotten pregnant. I don't think Joe loved her that way. Ever."

Phyllis gave her a look of pure, unadulterated scorn. "You know nothing about it," she said. "Past mistakes kept them apart. But, finally, everything was falling into place. Trevor was going to have Joe for a father. Beth and Jeremy were going to have Millie for a mother. And Joe was going to have the wife he's deserved all these years." Her penetrating eyes pinned Carly to the wall. "And then you came along."

Carly nodded slowly. "I haven't done anything, you know."

Phyllis dismissed that as a poor excuse. "You're here, aren't you? Tempting Joe."

Tempting Joe? Somehow she'd thought it was the other way around.

"The best thing you could do, my dear," Phyllis advised, getting up and smoothing her blouse, "is to go on back to Washington and leave the rest of us alone. Think it over, why don't you?"

She gave Carly a brittle smile and left the room, but Carly was still frozen by what she'd said. Washington? Washington? Why did Phyllis always seem to know everything?

Well, that did it. The jig was up. If she knew about Washington, she knew who Carly was, and what she did, and probably all about Mark, too. The next thing she knew, the woman would probably be threatening to go to the tabloids and ruin Mark's career. With what, though? Damn it, she hadn't done anything!

Millie came breezing back into the kitchen and flopped down onto a chair. "Where's Phyllis?" she asked brightly.

"I'd love to say she was in full retreat," Carly said casually. "But I'm afraid this is just a chance for her to regroup and fight another day."

Millie wasn't too sure what Carly was talking about and it was obvious she was pretty sure she didn't want to know. But before she had a chance to think of an inane topic of conversation that would keep them from the meat of any matter at all, Carly leaned forward on the table and spoke bluntly.

"Tell me the truth, Millie," she said wearily, her shoulders slumping, her eyelids drooping with fatigue. "Do you love Joe?"

Millie wasn't shocked by the question. In fact, she seemed almost to welcome it. Her face softened and she smiled. "Of course," she said. "I've loved him all my life."

Carly reared back as though the woman had slapped her in the face. Millie laughed softly.

"Don't worry," she said. "I said I loved him. I didn't say I was in love with him. And you know very well he doesn't love me. At least, not the way his mother wishes he would love me."

Worry? What on earth did she have to worry about? He wasn't hers. Still, it was good to know for sure that he wasn't Millie's, either.

"Would you marry him if he asked you?"

Millie considered for a moment. "No." She flashed Carly a quick smile. "I know it would certainly fulfill Phyllis's dreams. She's been scheming and planning for us to get married since we were kids. When I messed everything up by getting pregnant, she nearly died."

She frowned, remembering. "It was so awful. Sixteen years old and pregnant. They worked hard on me, Phyllis and my mother. They wanted me to have an abortion, not tell anyone. Not even Joe." She smiled gently. "Of course, I went right to Joe and told him, and he helped me fight them. So then Phyllis thought, well, maybe we would end up together after all. But when Joe went away to college, he came back with Ellen on his arm. And that was the end of that."

How awful. If Millie had been harboring dreams all those years, it must have hurt to see Joe with another woman.

"Did you hate her?"

"Who? Ellen?" She smiled. "No, I didn't hate her. She was beautiful, with long, shiny red hair and a face like a model. But she never could adjust to country life. No matter how hard Joe tried, he couldn't make her happy. He changed everything he could to please her, but it was never enough."

That seemed to confirm what Joe had told her. Carly felt a wave of quick sympathy for Joe. And for Millie as well. But this was no time for sympathy. Sympathy didn't get anyone anywhere.

"Well, I suppose he should never have married her in the first place."

Millie didn't comment on that. She thought for a minute, then went on.

"I don't know how much Joe has told you about Ellen, but she had a problem. She had something of a mental breakdown about a year before she left. There was instability in her background, things Joe didn't know about, things he thought they could work through. But things just got worse. It's hard to feel sympathy for a woman who leaves her children behind, but believe me, Ellen went through her own personal hell before deciding to do it. And you know, she could have hurt him so much worse. She could have taken the children with her and left him with nothing."

Carly hadn't thought of Ellen's departure in those terms. "You're right," she said softly. The thought of Joe without the kids was a heart-wrenching one. "But Phyllis must have been happy when Ellen left."

"Oh yes." Millie grinned. "She was ecstatic. She was sure we would get together. She moved back in here to work on it, calling me with bulletins every day. But Joe resisted. He can be so stubborn. And he didn't want any more females steering his life around."

"From what you've told me, I can hardly blame him."

"Isn't that the truth? We haven't done him much good, have we?"

Carly wondered if she were included in the "we," but it hardly mattered. Millie was right. Joe had reason to be wary of women.

They chatted for a few more minutes, and Carly studied Millie. She was really so nice, and she loved the children, loved Joe. Phyllis was probably right. They should get married.

That thought cut through her like a knife, and there was no reason for it. Did she want him for herself? And if she got him, what would she do with him? It was crazy, all of it.

She should leave. But how could she leave Joe and the children? How could she miss the avocado harvest and Jeremy's birthday, which was coming up in a few weeks?

Suddenly she felt claustrophobic. She had to get outside, get into the fresh air.

She rose from her chair. "Millie, I—I think I'll go for a walk. See you later?"

"Sure." Millie looked concerned. "Will you be all right?"

"Oh yes. I'll be fine."

She threw back a wan smile and went for the door. She needed to be alone, and there wasn't much time left.

HE HEARD THE CAR coming up the dirt road and he didn't turn around. He knew who it was. He did look for his shirt, but he'd hung it up a few yards away in the little caretaker's cottage that sat like a reminder of yesterday on the corner of his lot. He certainly wasn't going to go all that way to put it on just for her benefit.

He swung the ax again, savoring the jolt of metal against wood, the hard clang, the shock that went through his body as he hit, the sweat that beaded and dripped from his temples, down his back, across his chest. His old, torn jeans were slung low on his hips and felt tight and threadbare against the swelling muscles of his legs. The late afternoon sun was baking his naked shoulders. As he swung the ax, he could feel every muscle in his body. And that was good. *The more you felt, the less you thought.*

"Joe."

He stood still, not turning, the ax resting against his leg, his head thrown back, his eyes closed. Maybe if he didn't answer her, she would go away.

She should go away. It would be much better if she would go away and never come back. Then maybe he could wipe her out of his mind, out of his soul.

And out of his heart. He swore softly to himself. After Ellen, he'd promised himself there would be no more women in his life. For a long time that promise had seemed easy to keep. Carly was the first real temptation he'd faced. And he'd crumbled with barely a fight. How could he have let her become this important so quickly? Now he had to do something to stop it.

"Joe," she was saying. "I think maybe you're right. It's time for me to go."

Everything in him clenched, but he still didn't turn around and he still didn't say a word to her.

"I've talked to Phyllis and I've talked to Millie, and the more I think about it ... I realize you're right. I'm just in the way here. I'm the foreign element. All I do is throw monkey wrenches into everyone's plans. If I weren't here..." Her voice faded and she shrugged helplessly.

"If you weren't here..." He turned and looked at her at last, and wished he hadn't. She stood tall and beautiful, her silver-blond hair flying out around her shoulders, her lovely face etched in misery. It was all he could do to keep himself from reaching for her, smoothing back her flyaway hair, kissing her forehead, holding her to his chest and soothing her unhappiness.

"What do you think would happen if you weren't here?" he said instead.

She shook her head. "You could marry Millie," she said in a voice barely above a whisper. "The two of you could provide a home for all the children."

Exasperation shot through him and he threw out his arms. "How many times do I have to tell you that I have no intention of marrying Millie?" He took a step closer, face indignant. "Did I marry Millie before you got here? No. So what makes you so sure I'll marry her once you're gone?"

She shrugged. "I don't know. Everybody wants you to."

He shook his head, disgusted with them all. "How about you? Do you want me to?"

Her chin rose. "I think you know the answer to that."

"Maybe I do." He took a step closer, his eyes darkening. "And maybe I don't."

They stared at each other, and then he threw back his head. He was falling again. Goddamn it, he couldn't stick with his convictions for even five minutes.

"Millie has nothing to do with this," he told her shortly. "It's you."

She stared at him, wide-eyed. "Me?" she asked, bewildered.

"You." His eyes narrowed and he turned his gaze toward the trees. "You came here and messed with our lives, Carly. You've got the kids loving you. You've got me..." He shook away that thought in anger. "You've only been here a few days and already we all depend on you. You're not going to stay. You're going to go back to where you came from and make your Mark idiot happy and leave us with nothing.'' His anger was directed at her again, through his dark, scorching gaze. ''No, that's not right. You'll leave us with something. A big empty gap where you used to be.''

She felt as though she'd been hit in the stomach with something hard and heavy. She couldn't quite catch her breath. He was only telling the truth, but . . . but did it have to be the truth? Things could change. She could stay. . . .

She shook her head, trying to clear her mind. What was she thinking? She couldn't stay. She had a life that was waiting for her in Washington, even if Mark wasn't a part of her plans any longer. Besides, Joe didn't really want her to stay at all. He'd made it clear from the first, and things she'd learned about Ellen and his pain over her betrayal only confirmed it. He didn't want to tie himself down to a woman again. Ever.

But right now she couldn't think straight. He was too close, too beautiful, too tantalizing. Her mind would have to go on hold; her body was taking over.

''I'm sorry,'' she murmured, looking at the interplay of muscles across his shoulder, the sinews of his neck, the hollow at the base where his pulse throbbed like the heart of a hawk. ''I didn't mean to. . .''

Her breath was coming in short, shallow gasps. He was so close the heat of his body seemed to shimmer around her. She looked at his chest, at the shiny slick of sweat that covered it, at the dark, curling hairs that matted and glistened, at the brown nipples that were wide and smooth and flat, at the way the dark hair thickened around his navel, and then thickened again going down into his jeans. She could see the hard lines where his hipbones curved, see the angles where muscles were flexed. Her body began to throb and ache with longing. She felt like a dancer in a pagan movie, compelled to act like a wanton, compelled to reach for what she wanted most. And so she reached for him, stretched out a hand until it connected with a charge that snapped through her, and then slid her palm slowly down his chest, catching his heat in her hand.

He stood very still while she touched him, his eyes half closed. Her hand moved up and down, caressing him as though she were in a trance, and his body began to tremble with desire. He caught hold of her hand and held it in his, held it away from his chest.

"You shouldn't have come up here, Carly," he told her, his voice low and hoarse.

"I know." Her eyes were as clear as the sky on a spring day.

He held her hand more tightly, fighting a battle within himself. "Why did you come?"

She looked into his face and she smiled. "Because I couldn't stay away."

His breath was coming faster and faster, but he had to make things clear to her. "You understand that... now that you're here, I can't let you go."

She nodded slowly, still caught in his eyes. "I want you, Joe," she whispered. "Can't you see that?"

There was no hope left after that. He sank toward her like a man leaping into a rushing stream. His hands cupped her face, drew it to him, and his mouth took hers with a hunger that snatched her breath away.

She clung to him, her hands sliding across his wet flesh, her mouth as hungry as his, wanting more of him, deeper, harder. She was frightened, scared to death, but she was exultant, too. Though it had only been a little over a week that she'd known him, she felt as though she'd waited for this all her life.

Joe had waited even longer. At least, that was how it felt. Forever. For eternity. Her body was too soft to believe in, too warm to leave. He slipped his hands up under her sweater and ran them down her back, following her spine and then down under the belt of her slacks, to take hold of her soft, rounded bottom, cupping her with his fingers, pulling her toward him, pressing her to his hips. He wanted her to feel him, to make sure she knew what she was getting into, because he wasn't sure he was going to be able to stop if she changed her mind.

It was crazy. There were so many reasons why they shouldn't be doing this. Not the least of which was Mark, the man she was supposedly going to marry. Mark, for whom he had a deep and abiding hatred.

He had no idea what would happen later, where she would go, what she would do. But for now, there was no Mark. He had killed Mark, and she was his. His, and nobody else's.

He looked around groggily for where they could go. The ground was too rough and rocky here, too open. The caretaker's cottage. It was old and empty and unused, but there was clean straw on the floor. Drawing back, he took her hand and led her quickly to it.

Pulling her inside, he closed the door and looked at her in the gloom. "You're sure you want to do this?" he asked in a husky whisper.

She looked into his burning eyes and reached down to pull off her sweater, bra and all. As her high, pointed breasts swung free, he made a sound deep in his throat, and reached for her with one hand, at the same time he reached for his belt with the other.

They were on the straw, still writhing out of their clothes. Joe buried his face in her, drowning in her softness, tasting one nipple, then the other, then her navel, her long, slim thighs, the moist focus of her need. She cried out, her hips beginning to move, her sanity gone in the spiraling urgency of her longing. She reached for him and stroked, gasping at his beauty, the texture of velvet over steel, taking him, urging him to come where she needed him.

Shudders rippled over him and he murmured her name. She whispered back, something incoherent, something that expressed her wonder, her greed for him. He pushed her back against the straw then came over her, looking down, and she looked up at his eyes, his wide shoulders, and thought she'd never seen anything so large and dark and powerful. And he was hers. And she wanted him.

She cried out as he penetrated, arching her hips to take him as deep as she could. And then she had to hold on, because the wild, impossible ride had begun. He came hard, again and again, and she clung to him, taking every drop of pleasure she could, riding on and on, like a princess on a stallion, holding him with her legs, her arms, her body.

Despite his desperate need, he held off until he was sure she was well on her way, and then he let himself find the incredible release that he needed so badly.

And when it was over, he thought he might have died. It had never been so intense before. Could a man really live through this and rise to love again?

She lay very still. If she moved, he might move away and leave her. And she couldn't stand to think of that happening.

This had been an insane thing to do, but it had become impossible to avoid. The desire between them had built until it had to be released. Of course, she could have taken care of it by leaving—but, she thought dreamily, a silly smile on her happy face, that wouldn't have been nearly as satisfying. Joe knew how to make love to a woman. She'd never been so fulfilled.

Her fingers played with his dark, curly hair. He opened his eyes and looked at her.

"You can't leave," he said softly, reaching to touch her cheek with his knuckles.

She raised her head and looked at him. Who was talking here, the real Joe, or the love-starved man who had drawn a wondrous response from her just now? "I thought you wanted me to leave."

He groaned. "I haven't wanted you to leave. Not ever. You know that." His hand stroked her throat.

She sank back down. She knew what he was saying—that a part of him didn't want her to leave, even though he knew it was inevitable. "I'll have to go eventually."

"I know. But in the meantime..." He reached for her with both hands.

"In the meantime." She turned so that her naked body was pressed against the length of his.

He began to kiss her again, her lips, her chin, the line of her neck. He touched her, letting his fingers trace her nipples, test the depth of her navel, slide down between her legs to gather up her warmth, and she arched into his touch, filling his hand with her secrets, filling his mind with wonder at her.

Brief thoughts of Ellen surfaced for a moment. Carly was so different, so warm, so responsive. To Ellen, sex was something to be endured. To Carly...

"Joe," she was whispering, her hand skimming down across his body, reaching for him. Her eyes widened as his mouth closed on her breast, teasing the nipple hard and high. She moaned his name and he knew she was already eager for him again. But it was all right. His arousal was just as swift, and he wanted her again just as wildly as he had wanted her only moments before.

She was so sweet, so hot, so incredibly good, he was almost afraid he might not be able to stop for air. God, but he felt good with her. If only it could last. But he knew better than to hope for miracles.

There was one thing that was nagging at him. She deserved to know the truth about her father. But not right now. He couldn't face doing anything to kill the mood they'd established between them. He'd tell her tomorrow.

Tomorrow, for sure.

CHAPTER FIFTEEN

CARLY LAY IN HER BED and stared into the darkness. She was completely, dizzyingly, insanely, in love with Joe. She'd never been so happy and so miserable at the same time before in her life. This was it. The real thing. There was no need to go off and think things over, to be alone to work things out, to get her head together, or a thousand other excuses she'd made for putting off making the decision about Mark. In this case, the decision had been made for her. She was in love.

Love hurts. For the first time in her life she understood that old refrain. Because this wasn't an easy love, where they both agreed and wedding bells were being polished. She knew without being told the Joe wasn't about to ask her to marry him. He'd tried that before and it had gone so stunningly badly for him that he was determined never to let himself be that vulnerable to a woman again.

He'd never said all this in so many words, but she knew it as surely as she knew he was the only man she would ever feel this way about. Ellen had dealt him a wound he would never recover from.

He wanted her. She knew that. He made love to her like a man possessed by a demon. And it seemed, at least, that he enjoyed having her around. But he would get over it when she left. And he assumed she would leave pretty soon.

Leaving was the last thing she wanted to do. But how long could she stay, knowing there was no future for her here? She would have to leave. She would have to leave before they all got too dependent on her, just as Joe had said.

It made her ache to think of leaving Beth and Jeremy. How could she be sure they would be all right? She couldn't count on Phyllis. She had her own agenda, and the children didn't seem to have a very big part in it. Joe would do the best he could, but he was a father. They needed a mother, too. And if he wasn't going to consider marrying again, they would never have one.

The least she could do was go to see the teachers and find out if there was anything she could do to help there. She would do that first thing the next morning, she decided as sleep began to drag her under. The very first thing.

OF COURSE, THERE WERE about ten other things she had to get out of the way before she could think about going to see the teachers, things like breakfast and taking some supplies up to Phyllis and finding Beth's lost hair ribbon. Joe was up and out early, checking on the avocado crop that was about to be harvested, and he came back in while the children were eating.

Looking up quickly from the toast she was buttering, she met his gaze, her heart standing still.

He glanced at her as though nothing had happened the night before. "Good morning," he said, but his greeting was directed mainly at his children. He bent to kiss them each and give them a hug. "You two be good today."

"We will, Daddy," Beth chirped. "Carly's going to come in and see us at school."

"What?" He rose and turned to look at her questioningly.

She gave him a nervous smile. "I'm going in to see the teachers this morning," she said. "Is that all right with you?"

She knew her look was probably challenging, but he didn't test it. A few minutes later, he did draw her aside so that they could talk without the children hearing. When he looked down at her, his eyes were cool, emotionless, and she couldn't tell what he was thinking.

"I've got to take some samples in to the testing lab in Bakersfield today and see a few other people," he said. "I've got appointments with my lawyer and my banker, so it could take a while. I probably won't be back until late tonight." He hesitated. "Go see the teachers if you want to," he added quietly. "You can take the car, I'm using the truck." He paused, looked at her with a frown. "Just don't go signing my kids up for some rehabilitation program or something."

Carly felt cold, unappreciated. He could have been talking to a hired housekeeper. But that was just about what she was, wasn't it? Did he remember what had happened the night before? Or had it all been a dream on her part?

"Don't worry," she said a bit resentfully. "I'm not going to do anything like that. I couldn't do that without your authorization anyway. They're not my children."

"No." His face hardened. "Remember that. They're not your children."

She felt properly rebuffed but that wasn't going to stop her. If he wanted to pretend there was nothing between them, that was his business. She wasn't going to whine and whimper about it. At least, not where he could see her.

He came down a little later, after the children had gone, dressed in a white shirt, tie and business suit. Carly stared. She'd never seen him like this before, and he looked darned good. Just before he went out the door, he turned and looked at her.

"Drive carefully," she said, wishing they could get back the free and easy feeling they sometimes had between them.

"I will." He hesitated, then erased the distance between them and kissed her, hard. "The only thing I'm reckless about is you," he said. And then he was gone.

She touched her fingertips to her lips, holding the feel of him for as long as she could. If this was reckless, she'd throw her lot in with the daredevils any day.

THE SCHOOL WAS NEW and modern, the colors bright and inviting. Beth turned and waved at Carly as she slipped into the back of the classroom, her face radiant. Every time she got a chance, she turned in her seat and grinned. Carly's heart was warmed, but she felt a sense of pain as well. *This poor little girl. How she must long for a real mother.*

A few minutes later, the teacher let the children leave for recess and came over to sit by Carly.

"Beth is a dear," said Mrs. Green, her young, enthusiastic face beaming. "I love having her. The only

problem—and I think I wrote to her father about it—
is the daydreaming. There are times when I think it's
going to take a nuclear blast to get her attention.''

''But her schoolwork is good?''

''Oh yes. She does her work and gets things in on
time. It's just the dreaming that bothers me. I believe
in confronting reality without the crutch of make-
believe. Do you know what I mean? I like to get the
children to engage life, take it on, make things happen.''

All in all, the teacher seemed to be committed and
determined to get the best out of the children. Carly
promised to talk with Beth about the daydreaming. She
thanked the teacher and went out into the play yard to
get a look at Beth and her friends. What she saw immediately disturbed her.

Beth was walking with Sunny, but there was a group
of girls following them, calling out something. As
Carly got closer, she realized they were yelling insults
at Beth.

''Where did you get your shoes, Beth? The five-and-
dime?''

''No, Beth knows a little cobbler who lives in the
woods.''

The girls all giggled.

''That's probably the same old man who made her
dress. He made it for a giant, didn't he, Beth? And
then he gave it to you instead.''

Carly's first impulse was to stride out and yell at the
miserable little snobs. They were hurting Beth, and that
was insufferable. But she held herself back. She remembered enough from childhood to know that hav-

ing a grown-up run in to the rescue could make things even worse for Beth.

But what was wrong with those girls? Why were they being so cruel? She'd heard kids nowadays were much more concerned with fashion and wearing the right thing than they had ever been before, but this was ridiculous.

And then she began to look at Beth, and it dawned on her why they were doing this to her. Her clothes really were terrible.

How could she have lived with the girl for over a week and not thought to remedy the situation? The dress was a size too big, the shoes looked like they might have belonged to Little Orphan Annie. Beth was a neglected child as far as style went. She did look like a waif from the woods.

Carly gritted her teeth, castigating herself as an insensitive lout. How could she have let Beth go off to school looking like that? It was all very well to say the other girls shouldn't be so concerned with outward appearances and surely shouldn't make fun of someone who seemed to be less fortunate than themselves, but that was the way things were. And Beth had been set up to be an outcast.

She turned away quickly before Beth could see that she'd witnessed the scene, and glanced at her watch. She and Beth had a shopping trip coming up. She'd just decided. But first, she had one more appointment to take care of.

Jeremy was watching for her, and when she came into the room he got up from his desk, despite a sharp command from the teacher, and ran to her. She gave him a warm hug and sent him back to his seat and then sat down to watch Mrs. Emind, Jeremy's teacher. What she saw was not reassuring.

Mrs. Emind gave the class some busywork and came back to talk to Carly. Sallow and pinched-looking, with the face of a woman who has known bitter defeat, she read off a list of Jeremy's transgressions.

"He never pays attention. His homework is fine, but his class work is often wrong. He's sullen and refuses to respond to questions during oral recitation. He plays by himself on the playground."

It went on and on, and Carly had to restrain herself from beginning to challenge the charges the teacher was making. This was not the Jeremy she knew. She had to think that there was something very wrong in the chemistry between Jeremy and this woman. That, compounded by the hearing problem, could be the entire ball game as far as success in school went.

She brought up her hearing theory to Mrs. Emind, who dismissed it out of hand.

"He's been tested. I can show you his folder. He's had all the tests and there is nothing wrong with his hearing. He's just an uncooperative child."

And you, Carly thought as she said goodbye, *are just a stupid woman.* There was no give, no sense of any sort of appreciation for who Jeremy was. Luckily, Jeremy had only a few weeks left before summer.

I hope you can hold out, baby, she thought as she hugged him goodbye. *I wish I could just whisk you away.*

And she did whisk Beth away. She told Mrs. Green exactly what she was doing, and the teacher beamed, agreeing that it was for the best.

"Where are we going?" Beth asked as they left the school hand in hand.

"It's a surprise," Carly told her mysteriously. "You just wait and see."

She'd paid attention at the school and she thought she had a pretty good idea of what was currently cool for little girls. They found the mall and stormed the clothing stores, buying T-shirts and lace shorts, a peasant blouse with an elastic midriff, leggings and name-brand skirts and jumpers and canvas shoes and little ruffled socks, and an organdy dress to die for.

Beth was wonderful to buy for. Her eyes were as round as saucers and she oohed and aahed over everything. Carly felt like Santa Claus. It was so much fun to make someone so happy. And it was so amazingly easy to accomplish.

Once they'd filled the car with bags of clothing, they went to lunch in a little tearoom, ordering watercress and cucumber sandwiches and finger food. They drank tea from porcelain cups and crooked their little fingers, just for fun. They talked and laughed, and on the way home Beth fell asleep in the car. Carly looked at her, love swelling inside her. It was going to break her heart to leave this little one behind.

They unpacked the car and Carly left Beth to look over her purchases. She had another project to complete before she left the valley. She and Millie had to have one last talk.

She drove Joe's car over to Millie's, pulling up next to the corral when she noticed the horses out. Millie took one look at who was driving and Carly could see the panic on her face. Somehow, she knew what Carly had come for. She knew, and she couldn't face it.

Swinging up on a big palomino, she reined the horse through the gate and took off for the hills.

"Millie!" Carly got out of the car and stared after her, shading her eyes. This was ridiculous. They had to get this over with. It was a little late in the day for hide-and-seek.

She looked at the other horses. There were two, a solemn gray mare and a skittish brown gelding named Skippy. She hadn't ridden a horse since she'd been a child, but there had been a time when she had ridden all over these hills. She looked out again at where Millie was disappearing through the trees. She was pretty sure she knew where she was going. With a sigh, she stuck her car keys in the pocket of her slacks and reached for a saddle. If she was going to do this thing, she might as well get going.

Just like riding a bike, a person never forgets how to ride a horse. Adjusting a saddle was another matter— that took her a while. But finally she was up on Skippy's back, heading him toward the lake where Millie had told her she went when she was troubled. And sure enough, as they came over the rise, there she was, standing near her tethered horse, gazing out at the water.

"There's no point in running, Millie," she called out as she approached. "I think I've got the picture pretty well filled in by now."

Millie stood frozen, staring at the lake. She didn't turn around as Carly swung down from the horse and came toward her.

"Tell me if I'm off the mark," she said softly, standing just behind Millie. "You were the reason my mother left my father, weren't you? The man who fathered Trevor was the same man who fathered me. Am I right?''

Millie sank to the ground. "Oh God," she moaned, burying her head in her arms. "I didn't want you to know."

"I can understand why," Carly went on, unable to keep the bitterness out of her voice. She lowered herself carefully to sit beside Millie on the rocky ground, then went on.

"You had an affair with the preacher at the church where you were a singer in the choir. Am I still warm? A married preacher. A married preacher with a child. You, Millie, of all people."

Millie looked up, tears in her eyes, her voice shaking. "I tried to explain to you how it happened. But I have no excuses. It was wrong, and I know it. I've paid for what I did. My mother paid. Trevor has paid."

Carly nodded slowly. "I imagine even my father has paid. Where is he, by the way?"

She shook her head, a picture of abject misery. "I have no idea."

Carly sat beside her silently for a moment, thinking that over. Her father. Instead of coming in clearer, he was becoming more of a shadow figure to her all the time. "How much did he know?"

"You mean, about Trevor?" She shook her head. "He didn't know a thing. I never told him."

There was that saving grace at least. If he had known about her pregnancy and abandoned her, there would be no way Carly could ever forgive him. Still, there were other things left to hold against him. Not the least of which was betraying his family the way he did.

"Well, tell me, Millie," she said, forcing herself to remain calm and logical. "How did the two of you get discovered? How did my mother find out?"

Millie's eyes, when she turned them toward Carly, were haunted, but Carly wasn't in the mood to feel much pity right now. What pity she did feel was for her mother, and for the little girl who lost a father over this.

"She...she walked in on us." Millie dabbed at her nose. "We were in his office."

"His office at church?" She tried to keep the revulsion out of her voice, but she wasn't entirely successful.

Millie nodded miserably. "Yes. It was the most awful day of my life." She turned, trying to explain. "It had all seemed so romantic up to that day. It was exciting, thrilling. His wife...your mother...didn't even seem real to me. And then, there she was, and it all fell apart in an instant. I never knew what shame was until that moment. The shame I felt—"

"The shame you felt was nothing compared to the pain my mother felt." Carly had never hated her father before, but she had a sudden feeling that she might be able to develop a really thriving detestation with a little effort. "It's unbelievable," she said softly.

"Yes." Millie's head came up. "You're right. When I look back at it now, it's unbelievable."

"Did you know my mother at all?"

"No. Not really. She only came to the service on Sunday. She hardly ever showed up for choir practice or Bible study or any of the other functions."

Functions where Millie obviously thrived. Carly closed her eyes for a moment, then turned to look at the woman. "My mother was a really great person—funny, supportive, loving. She was a terrific mother. I think she was probably a pretty good wife, too."

Millie reached toward her, then let her hand drop. "Carly, I'm sure she was."

Carly frowned, searching her own soul, trying to see the father she hardly knew. "But how...how could he do that to her?"

"Please, Carly. Don't blame him." Her voice broke. "Blame me. It was my fault. I tempted him and he couldn't resist. It...we loved each other. I know that's hard for you to accept, but it's true. And it was to save me that he left town. He was everything good, Carly. Please believe that."

They didn't speak for a few moments, each staring out at the sparkling water with her own thoughts. "What are you going to do?" Millie asked at last.

"Do?" Carly turned to look at her.

Millie's face was filled with dread. "Are you going to tell Trevor?"

"It's not my place to tell Trevor. Although he is my brother." That was a soaring thought amid all this sordidness. She had a brother.

She rose slowly to her feet and looked toward where she'd left the horse. He was still there. Funny. The way her life was going, she'd half expected him to have run off on her.

"I think you ought to let Trevor know that Joe isn't his father," she said shortly. "Other than that, it's up to you what you tell him and what you leave out. As far as I'm concerned, I've finally found out what I wanted to know."

She turned without another word and went to the horse. A part of her felt pity for Millie, but she wasn't ready to express it yet. That would have to wait for another day.

CHAPTER SIXTEEN

"GOOD NIGHT, CARLY." Beth scrunched down under her covers and smiled. In what had become a nightly ritual, her little arms shot out and captured Carly around the neck. "I love you, Carly," she said softly, giggling at the same time.

"I love you, too, darling." She gave the little girl a kiss and turned off her light. "Sleep tight."

Jeremy was already asleep. She watched him for a moment, then leaned down to kiss his cheek, and he surprised her, turning with his eyes wide open.

"'Night," he said.

"Good night, sweetheart." She went through with the kiss and was surprised when she felt his arms come around her, just as Beth's did every night. He only held her for a few seconds, but it was enough to bring tears to her eyes.

"Love you, Jeremy," she whispered. She wanted to take him up and hold him, but she knew that would be too much at this point.

And yet, for the first time, he answered her.

"Love you, Carly," he whispered back.

Smiling through tears, she turned off his light and went out, closing his door. And then she let the tears fall. How was she going to leave these children?

Phyllis had already gone up to her room, so she was alone, waiting for Joe to come back from Bakersfield. She had a few things she wanted to say to him. Turning off all the lights but one, she sank onto the couch and began her vigil. She could wait all night if she had to.

Sitting in the semi-darkness, staring into the void, her mind kept going over the same things again and again, like replaying a movie, a movie she hated, a movie she had never wanted to see in the first place. She thought she was hardened to it, but little by little her shell began to crack and then tears were coming again, until she was shaking and great, gulping sobs of grief were wracking her body. Grief for her mother, grief for her father, grief for Trevor...and grief for herself.

It took awhile before she could calm herself. She heard Joe's truck drive up and she closed her eyes. She had no idea what she was going to say to him. There was anger inside her. Was it really directed at him? Yes. Why hadn't he told her the truth?

Joe walked in, threw down his briefcase and sample bag, and looked at her. One glance at her face told him the story, even in the gloom. He loosened his tie and pulled it off, unbuttoning the shirt halfway down his chest, before he said a word to her.

"So...what now, fair lady? Have you uncovered all the secrets that you came to find?" He came into the room and sat on the couch beside her. "Have you found yourself? Do you know who you are and where you're going?"

She looked at him without smiling. "Do you know that about yourself?" she asked softly.

"Yes. Yes, I do. I'm staying right here and raising lemons and avocados and two children. And that's my life."

"That's all you want?"

He shrugged and met her crystal eyes with his own dark gaze. They both knew what else he wanted.

She moved impatiently. "I wish you'd told me from the beginning. About my father, I mean. I could have saved myself a little time."

"And gotten back to Mark sooner?" He said it with suppressed bitterness that made it sound colder than he had meant.

She looked up, surprised. "Mark? No. I called Mark the other day and told him it was over."

He didn't say anything for a long moment. It shocked him how much he cared. It made him angry, too. He shouldn't care this much, not about her, not about whether or not she ended up with Mark or anyone else.

"I see," he said at last. "Is that the way you usually get rid of old lovers? Just a phone call?"

She raised both eyebrows, accepting his lunge and offering a parry of her own. "At least I tell the truth as soon as I know it."

He winced. She had reason to be angry at him and he knew it. "Carly, I didn't really know anything until several days after you got here." That was true, as far as it went. But he had known things he should have told her. And now he was sorry he'd remained silent. "I've told you again and again, they weren't my secrets and I didn't feel like I could tell you."

She stared at him and he had the feeling she wasn't buying his excuses. Well, he deserved that. He hadn't done anything much to inspire confidence.

"Millie told me that you helped her back when the others wanted her to get an abortion," she said carefully. "That sounds like you knew quite a bit, quite early, to me."

He frowned, thinking back. "Oh sure, I remember that. She was pregnant, but I didn't know who the father was. I assumed it was some jerk from school or something. I didn't really want to know. It was none of my business." He moved uncomfortably. "I mean, if she'd been raped or mistreated or anything like that, I would have found the guy and beat him up or something. But she made it very clear, as I remember, that it was nothing like that. So... well, she was a friend, and she was in trouble, so I helped her. Simple as that. I stood behind her."

Carly's gaze didn't falter. She sat, waiting for him to go on, and he found himself spilling his guts like he hadn't thought he was capable of.

"A fat lot of good that did, when you come right down to it," he admitted candidly. "I stood behind her and then waved bye-bye as I took off for college. I hardly ever thought about her again until I moved back here with Ellen. By then Trevor was—what?—about five years old. And I just ignored the background he'd come out of."

Carly nodded, but she had another question. "Didn't you ever wonder who the father was?"

He shook his head. "Tell you the truth, Carly, I never really gave it a whole lot of thought. What difference did it make? She didn't marry the guy, so who cared?''

Carly gazed at him in astonishment. Men. They could be so practical, so down-to-earth...and so bloody thickheaded. She closed her eyes and put her head back, trying to accept everything that was being offered her, trying to assimilate it without drowning in unpleasant truths she didn't want to face.

And there were plenty of those. Had it all been worthwhile, coming here and finding out? She wasn't sure. She wasn't sure at all if she would do it all over again, given the chance.

"Joe, I can hardly stand it," she whispered, curling up in her corner of the couch as though that would somehow protect her. "My father had an affair with Millie. She was sixteen years old.''

He nodded, reaching out to put his hand on her shoulder. "Yeah. Pretty heavy stuff, huh?"

She looked small and vulnerable. He wanted to take her up and hold her and not let anything bad happen to her again, ever. He moved closer to her on the couch.

"I'm sorry, Carly," he said softly. "I'm really sorry. But there's nothing you can do about it now."

She nodded. That was true. But she had to work her way through this mess somehow.

"Are you still going to look for him?" Joe asked.

She curled her lip in disgust. "For him? What for? I hate him now."

He reached for her, taking her in his arms. "Don't hate him, Carly."

"How can I not hate him? Look at what he did. He ruined so many lives, just because he couldn't resist a little temptation."

Their eyes met and they both remembered the night before, how temptation had reared up between them, how easily they had succumbed to its tantalizing song.

"But we didn't hurt anybody," Carly protested, as though the thought had been stated aloud.

"You're right," he agreed, tangling his fingers in her hair. "But, Carly, I have to tell you, from what my mother told me, your parents' marriage was pretty rocky before Millie entered the picture. You've got to throw that into the equation."

She shook her head, not accepting that. "They always say that about situations like this. How do you know it's true?"

"Supposedly your mother filed for divorce about a year before this incident, and then withdrew the request a few weeks later. That doesn't sound like wedded bliss to me."

Carly frowned. "How do you know?"

"Phyllis told me. But you could probably check it. It should be a matter of public record."

She nodded. "Phyllis seems to know everything," she said softly.

"From what she told me, she was directly involved in a lot of it. After all, she was the one who urged Millie to join the choir. Then she watched in horror as Millie and your father fell in love."

"Did she tell you that?"

"More or less. She told me taking Millie to church was the worst mistake of her life. And once she realized what was going on, she'd tried everything she

could to put a stop to it. But by then it was too late."
He laughed shortly. "Her last-ditch effort was telling
your mother about it. At the time, she had no idea
Millie was pregnant. By the time the pregnancy was
discovered, both you and your mother and, soon after, your father, had left town."

"Millie said Phyllis and her mother tried to make her
get an abortion."

He nodded. "She was determined to keep the child.
That I remember."

She shivered and he held her closer.

"Come on," he whispered into her hair. "Let's go
to bed."

She looked up into his eyes and he bent to kiss her
softly on the lips. "Your bed or mine?" she asked innocently.

He laughed. "You read my mind. I'm not going to
let you sleep alone tonight."

SHE DIDN'T WANT TO SLEEP alone. It was heaven in his
big, fluffy bed, holding his hard body with her own.
She seemed to be aware of sensations now as she never
had been before—the coolness of the sheets, the scent
of soap from his bath, the scrape of his callused hands
on her skin, the heat that rose from his body. He was
whispering something in her ear. She hardly heard the
words. The tone was enough; caressing, loving, arous-
ing, and she writhed as his hands began to explore her,
looking for something he might have missed before.

His lovemaking was becoming a drug, a need, an
obsession. Her body cried out for more, her mind was
fogged with desire. With him, she felt like a dancer in
a long, filmy dress, all dazzle and flow and leaping and

contact, a smooth, sliding touch, a gasp, a whirl. His palm rubbing her nipple sent electricity quivering through her and she writhed, aching for more. He took her slowly, softly, gently, still whispering magic words that made her feel like an object of solemn, reverent passion at the same time that she felt like a creature of wicked pleasure.

And then he was spreading her legs and rubbing, rubbing, until she thought she would go mad with need for him. He came in just as she cried out, reaching for him with both hands, her eyes open and wild and demanding. The reverence was gone. What they had between them now was hot and erotic, hunger meeting hunger, body feeding body, pure fusion, a merging that sizzled and threatened to melt the two of them together in a bond as old as time itself.

"Joe," she moaned. "Joe, never leave me."

"Never," he declared huskily into her ear. "I'll always be with you, Carly."

Liar, she thought a moment later as she lay beside him, still breathless from their wild flight. But it was a nice thought.

"CAN I SHOW DADDY my new clothes?" Beth's face shone.

Carly smiled at her. "Sure. Why don't you put on a fashion show while he eats breakfast? It's still early enough."

"Okay." She ran off to begin dressing, and Carly went on with the breakfast preparations, humming while she worked. She was up early, earlier even than Joe for once. There was a glow inside her. She could feel it. This, she told herself, was the good side of love.

"Whatcha cooking? Smells great."

Joe came up behind her and, since no one else was in the kitchen, wrapped his arms around her from behind and buried his face in her neck.

"But you smell better," he breathed and began to nibble. "Give me one good reason why I shouldn't eat you up right now."

She laughed, leaning back into him, luxuriating in his strength, his warmth. "You should always save dessert for later," she counseled wisely. "Besides, didn't they ever tell you that you can't have your cake and eat it too?"

She turned to smile at him and see what kind of smart-aleck retort he would make to that, but before he had a chance Beth could be heard clattering down the stairs, and they drew apart quickly.

"Daddy!" She peeked around the doorjamb, not coming all the way into the kitchen. "Sit down and get ready for your big surprise," she commanded. "I'm going to give you a fashion show."

"A fashion show." He looked questioningly at Carly. "What kind of fashion show?"

Beth giggled. "A great fashion show. Sit down and wait."

Carly laughed at her and smiled at Joe. "I'll go see how preparations are coming for the big event. She might need a little help coordinating things. I'll be right back and serve you breakfast."

He looked around the kitchen, all modern male and helpful. "If the food's ready, I can serve my own breakfast," he called after her. "I'm not helpless, you know."

She knew. Did she ever. "I'll be right back."

When she returned, he was sitting down to a plate full of scrambled eggs and sausages. "Ready?" she asked him.

He looked up. "Shoot," he said recklessly.

"Okay." Carly took up a position beside the doorway. "For your viewing entertainment," she intoned in an announcer voice, "Miss Beth Matthews presents—ta da!—the Good..."

Beth appeared in the doorway, as cute as a button in a baby blue smocked dress with a lace collar and an underskirt. She whirled, peeking to see her father's reaction, giggled and fled.

"Now if our audience will be patient," Carly continued, "our model is so fabulously perfect for these clothes, she is the only one we could possibly have modeling them, so it will take her a moment to change."

Joe still looked puzzled. "Where did she get these things?" he asked.

"The Fashion Fairy," Carly told him. "Just sit back and appreciate your daughter. She could use a lot of applause."

"Yeah, I guess we all could," he muttered, but he didn't look pleased.

Beth was back in a flash, coughing decorously outside the door, and Carly announced, "And now we have progressed to the Bad..."

Beth dashed in and pretended to boogie in hot pink, tight lace leggings and a tiny cropped top. Throwing a flirtatious look over her shoulder, she exited again, screaming as she ran for another change.

Carly glanced at Joe to see what he thought of his daughter now, but his face, once Beth had left the room, was impassive, and he didn't meet her gaze. Shrugging, she turned to get ready for the reappearance of the miniature model.

Back in mere moments, Beth whispered loudly, "I'm ready."

And Carly said ponderously, "You've seen the Good. You've experienced the Bad. Now, prepare to endure—the Ugly!"

Beth slunk in wearing sunglasses and designer jeans with factory-made holes burned into the knees, and a huge T-shirt that looked as though someone had taken a blowtorch to the area where hems ought to be.

Carly laughed. The girl looked so cute. She looked to see how Joe was taking it, and to her surprise, his smile looked forced.

"That's great, Beth," he started, but she held up a hand, shaking her head.

"Wait, Daddy. Just one more."

He didn't say anything while she was gone. He went back to eating, but Carly was beginning to get nervous. Something was wrong. She just wished she knew what it was.

"Here I am," Beth announced, and then she walked in, a vision in white organdy, white stockings, and black patent-leather Mary Janes.

"Hey, Beth." Joe put down his fork for this one, his eyes shining with appreciation despite his reservations. "You look beautiful, honey."

Beth's pride radiated from every pore. "Thanks, Daddy," she said proudly, her head high. "Carly bought me all these clothes. Isn't she great?"

She ran to her father and kissed him, then ran out to change into what she was going to wear to school.

Carly turned apprehensively to look at Joe. His face was darkening. A storm cloud was brewing. What now?

His eyes met hers and he frowned. "What the hell is this all about?" he said fiercely.

She blinked. "What do you mean?"

"What are you doing, buying all these clothes? I didn't ask you to give her a fancy wardrobe. That wasn't part of your job."

Overreaction, that was what it was. But she wasn't really sure why. Maybe if she just explained...

"Joe, I went to her school. You should have seen her. The other girls were making fun of her. She looked like a refugee. I could see right away that she needed new clothes in order to fit in."

He threw down his napkin and scraped back his chair, his face hard and angry. "Clothes don't mean a thing. Only shallow people are hung up on fashion. I won't have my daughter thinking things like that are important."

Carly suddenly remembered the beautiful clothes in Ellen's closet. "Oh, Joe, I didn't mean to give her distorted values, believe me. And I don't think this will. The clothes are a present from me. I just wanted to do something for her, help her..."

His face was as cold as she had ever seen it. "You're not staying," he said evenly. "You've made that clear from the first. So don't do things like this. Don't try to make her love you. I don't want you to play at being her mother. She can't lose her mother twice."

Yes, of course, they had been over this before. Didn't he get it yet? It was too late to stop love. She already loved these kids. She would never do anything to hurt them. But she wasn't going to hold back, either. She was an affectionate person who had to express her love. She couldn't live any other way. If he couldn't understand that it was because he didn't want to.

Her own anger began to surface. "So what do you want me to do? Leave right now? Get out of their lives immediately?"

The tortured look was back in his eyes. "I don't know. I don't know." He reached out almost helplessly, touching her face with the back of his hand. His eyes softened, but only to show the pain. "I don't want you to go. You know damn well I don't want that. But my kids...I have to think about my kids...."

Jeremy was suddenly in the doorway and he drew away from Carly, changing the subject. "Thanks for the food. I'm going out to check on the avocados."

She nodded, glancing at him briefly, then turned to smile a welcome to the boy. His eyes were very big as he watched his father leave, then looked questioningly at Carly. What had he heard? she wondered. But in a moment she was caught up in the rush to make the school bus, and she forgot all about it.

Joe came through the kitchen just as she was handing the children their lunch boxes. He cast her a look as he walked by, and she hurriedly said goodbye to the kids and followed him up the stairs.

"What is it?" she asked him, stopping him with a hand on his arm.

He swung around and stared at her. "I don't know, Carly. It's not right, me keeping you here for my own selfish needs, when it's not good for the kids."

She felt as though ice water had been shot through her veins. "I think you're making too much of this," she protested.

He shook his head slowly, then reached out with both hands and took her face in his grasp. "You're a dream, Carly," he said, his voice low and husky. "You make a perfect lover. And I know you would make a perfect mother. But you're not their mother. And for them to start believing you are..."

She nodded quickly, wanting to get away from him before the tears started. She was crying all the time lately. It probably was time she got herself back to Washington and regained her stable life-style. But if she was going, he was going to have to keep away from her.

She pulled away from his touch, holding her head high, but unable to look him in the eye. "Fine," she said briskly, hurt anger vivid in her tone. "I'll pack up and go."

His arms hung uselessly at his sides, his own anger growing out of frustration more than anything else. "Why don't you just do that?" he said coldly.

They glared at each other, and then a sound made them both turn. There was Jeremy, watching them, wide-eyed.

Carly knew immediately that he had been shocked by what he'd heard. She gasped and reached for him.

"Jeremy, honey..."

He shook his head, rejecting her, rejecting his father. And then he turned and ran, books in his arms, for the school bus.

Carly looked at Joe, her face worried. "That wasn't good, for him to see us quarrel that way."

Joe knew it, too, but he didn't see what they could do about it at this point, so he shrugged it off. "Don't worry, he'll get over it."

"Will he?" She went to the window and watched the two children trudging along the dirt path to where they caught the school bus. She wasn't so sure.

"You really care, don't you?"

She turned to look at him, tears shimmering in her eyes. "I love them, Joe," she said clearly. "I'm going to miss them. They aren't the only ones who are going to be hurt by this."

His face softened and he grimaced. Unable to resist her when she looked so woebegone, he pulled her to him and kissed her firmly, caressing her lips with his, showing her with his touch how much affection he held inside for her. When he drew back, she felt as though she had melted.

"Don't go yet," he said softly, his eyes full of pain.

She forced back the tears. "Maybe I should, Joe. We can't keep going through this..."

He swore and turned, hitting the wall with the flat of his hand. "You're right," he said harshly. "Make plans to go. It's for the best." He turned and looked into her teary eyes, then turned away again quickly.

"I've got to go into town," he said, straightening his shirt. "My mother is sending me on an errand. There's someone at the café she wants me to give a ride to or something. I'm not real clear on what exactly she expects me to do."

She blinked back tears and forced herself to speak normally. "When will you be back?"

"I'll be home for lunch. We'll talk more about this then. Okay?"

She nodded, her gaze moving over him, examining every feature as though she needed to memorize him for a future of loneliness.

CHAPTER SEVENTEEN

"HERE'S A FLASH FOR YOU, honey. Your boyfriend just hit town."

It took Carly a moment to put a name to the voice on the phone.

"Oh, hi Doris," she said as realization struck. "What boyfriend?"

"Mark Something-or-other. He's here at the café and he's asking around about you. Now I know you wanted to stay incognito, honey, but I think he's got your number. He's trying to hire a car right now to get out there to see you."

Carly's heart skipped a beat. Mark Cameron had found her. How could this have happened? Hadn't he gotten her message?

"You're kidding," she blurted out. "How did he find me?"

"Well, honey, that I don't know, but...uh-oh."

There was silence on the other end of the phone.

"Uh-oh what?" Carly demanded. "Doris, speak to me!"

"Carly honey, brace yourself." Doris was now speaking in a heavy whisper. "Joe just walked in."

"What?" Carly's life flashed before her eyes.

"They've seen each other. Joe is walking toward him. What do you think? Pistols at twenty paces?"

Carly's heart was running ragged, forgetting all about things like rhythm and timing.

"Doris, don't kid around," she said breathlessly. "Tell me what's happening."

"Ohmigod, you won't believe this! This looks very odd. They're shaking hands."

"Doris! Stop them."

"I can't, honey. It's too late. They're leaving together."

Her voice returned to its normal tone. "It's my bet you're about to have company for lunch, honey. Hope you're prepared."

Prepared? How did one prepare for a natural disaster? Carly stood with the phone in her hand, paralyzed, for a good five minutes, thinking hard. It had to be Phyllis, she decided at last. It was Phyllis who had let that Washington reference slip. She'd probably seen the item on television and jotted down Mark's name. Sure, that was it. Phyllis had contacted Mark, sent for him, sent Joe to pick him up.

Phyllis. If she had time, she would go up and challenge *her* to a duel. But she had no time.

The place was a mess. The breakfast dishes were still in the sink and morning papers were all over the den. Beth's ribbon collection had fallen out on the stairs and Jeremy had forgotten to clean up his matchbox cars from the hallway where he'd been racing them. This would never do. So she ran around like crazy, straightening things up.

"Wait a minute. What am I doing?" she asked herself at last. "I don't want to see Mark. I didn't invite him here. I don't want him here. I've got to get out of here. I'll hide in the orchards."

She was actually halfway out the door when the truck came cruising up the driveway. There was no escape now. She stood on the porch and tried to smile, pretending she was just there to greet them both.

"Carly, darling!" The passenger door flew open and a man in an expensive Italian suit stepped out.

Yes, it was Mark, the same old handsome, debonair Mark. She walked out to greet him, trying to smile. But it was Joe's eyes she was searching for, Joe's mind she wished she could read. Did he realize who this was? What on earth was he thinking? There was no way to tell.

Mark caught hold of her and kissed her on both cheeks. "I'm so glad I finally found you, you little devil. I've been going crazy wondering where you were."

She looked into his eyes and saw a man she hardly recognized.

"Hello, Mark," she said coolly. "I hope you had a nice trip out."

She refused to apologize. She'd done that already, on the answering machine, and she wasn't feeling very apologetic anyway. What right did Mark have to come here this way?

"How are you, Mark?" she asked, her smile chilly.

"Fine, darling. A bit lonely, of course. But otherwise, quite well."

He didn't seem to notice that his reception was not the warmest. But then, Mark was a politician. He didn't live his life according to what was real. He made things up and pretended they were real. It was second nature to him.

He stood back and looked at the ramshackle house. "So you gave up your lovely apartment in the Melbourne Building for this, did you?"

His smile was supposed to be affectionate, but for once, she saw it rather as cloying and a bit condescending. Had it always been that way and she just hadn't noticed? Or was it that others were usually the recipients of his sarcasm, so it hadn't really mattered to her before?

"What is this?" he was saying slyly. "One of those campaigns to get back to the old roots? Go out and kick the dirt with the country crowd?"

That hardly deserved an answer. She looked at Joe, trying to read his eyes, but they were blank, no emotion showing whatsoever.

"Come on in, Mark," he was saying. "I'll fix you a drink. You must be thirsty. You've come a long way."

"That sounds good. I appreciate it."

Carly was numb. What the heck was going on here? Why the friendly attitude? What was with the buddy-buddy routine?

The two of them together. She couldn't help looking from Mark's perfect hair and impeccable suit to Joe's faded jeans and hole-studded sneakers. They were so different. Mark was the better groomed, but next to Joe he looked superficial, insubstantial. Joe had a solid look. The salt of the earth—with a little bit of pepper thrown in. Mark looked like an upper-crust used-car salesman.

They settled Mark in the living room and she followed Joe back to the kitchen where he had gone to set up drinks.

"So, you're really a high-powered administrative assistant for a United States congressman," Joe said, his voice as unemotional as his face. "Funny. You had me fooled."

"That seems like a very long time ago," she said lamely, her heart falling. She hated him to think she might feel the pull of her old life, because it wasn't true. She hadn't really missed it yet, and she didn't foresee a time when she would.

"But it isn't a long time ago," he said dryly, pouring the liquid into glasses. "It's now, Carly. Or should I call you Carolyn?"

"Call me Carly. That's me. That's who I am."

His eyes met hers, but glanced away quickly. "Think you can rustle up a quick lunch for us?" he asked her. "I told him he was invited."

"I didn't invite him," she said shortly, glaring at him.

His eyes were impenetrable. "Didn't you?"

"No. Your mother invited him. Let her fix him lunch."

He picked up two glasses and turned to go. "Just a little salad or something. Take your time. Mark and I have a lot to talk about."

She watched him leave, seething. What was this, some sort of male conspiracy against her? But no. Old Ma Phyllis was the ringleader, wasn't she? So she guessed she couldn't really blame it on sex discrimination. But she would have to think this over, because she definitely wanted to blame it on something.

There were plenty of fixings to make a nice salad, and she had fresh rolls. Lunch was no real problem. She fixed it quickly, then set the table in the dining room and put everything out, along with tall, icy glasses of lemonade.

They came to eat when she called them, but they continued their conversation almost as though she weren't in the room. They went on and on about California citrus as opposed to the crops from Florida, about water rights and the drought, and how best to market avocados to Eastern consumers—and she sat looking from one to the other, wondering why she was even there.

"Mark," she broke in at last, unable to stand it any longer. "Are you going to tell me why you came?"

He looked at her as though she were being unbelievably rude, then seemed to forgive her and patted her hand. "I came to get you, Carly. It's time you went home."

She yanked her hand out from under his and glared at him, but before she could express her indignation, he went on.

"I understand that you came looking for your past, that your father's missing or something, and you wanted to try finding him...."

"Who told you that?" she demanded, eyes flashing fire.

"The woman who called me. Her name was Matthews. Your mother, I believe, Joe?"

Carly groaned. "I might have known."

"She told me how lost and confused you've been since you came. Darling, I knew right away that you needed me. That's why I dropped everything—and we have a very important highway-spending bill pending before the committee right now—and came as quickly as I could."

He tried to cover her hand with his again, but she deftly avoided contact. "Mark, I hate to disillusion you, but this is home to me. I grew up in this valley."

"We all came from little hick towns, darling. We go to the big city and we grow. You outgrew this place before you turned twenty-one, I'm sure of it."

She shook her head, liking him less and less. Why hadn't she ever noticed before what a snob he was?

"You shouldn't have come."

"I had to come, of course."

"Didn't you get my message on your answering machine?"

"I heard it, darling, but I understand. You've been under a lot of stress..."

She turned to Joe, hoping for something close to a rescue, but she might as well have saved herself the bother. He wasn't going to help, she could see that.

"It might be best," he told her softly, "if you go on back with Mark."

Her heart fell. What was this, the old brush-off? Was Joe really in on this too? Had they all gotten together and decided what would be the best way to dispose of her inconvenient presence?

Well, Joe could kick her out if he wanted to. But that didn't mean she was going back to Washington.

"I don't want to go back," she said, her chin out at a stubborn angle.

"Oh come now, darling. I know you don't mean that. You must miss it—the crowds, the restaurants, the theater. Your job."

Did she miss it? A little, perhaps. But she'd found so much more here. She'd learned what a family could really be. A family was a wonderful thing, strong and resilient and yet terribly fragile at the same time. Building a family could be one of the most important and rewarding things a woman could do with her life.

She couldn't even imagine building a family with Mark. But Joe had a ready-made one—a family kit, so to speak. All it needed was a mother. Funny. For the first time in her life, she realized she could be one of those. She realized that she wanted to be one of those.

"There's more to life, Mark," she said stoutly.

"What?" He was beginning to get annoyed with her. "What else could there be?"

She threw down her napkin and glared at him. "Love," she said loud and clear. "A concept neither one of you seems to know anything about."

She thrust back her chair and got up. "I'll bring in dessert," she said lightly. "You two just go ahead and chat. You obviously have so much in common."

She charged out of the room without looking at Joe. She was hurt and furious. But before she'd had time to develop a really good rage, the telephone rang and she had to stop to answer it.

"Hello?"

The voice on the other end was high with anxiety and at first she had trouble understanding what the woman was saying. But finally the words began to sink in. She felt as though all the blood had drained out of her.

"All right," she said quietly. "We'll be there right away."

Running quickly to the dining room, she went straight to Joe. He looked up the moment she entered the room, knowing instinctively that something was wrong.

"That was the school. Something's happened ... there's something about Jeremy on a roof about to fall ... I'm not sure what. I said we'd be there right away."

Joe was up and out of his seat before she'd finished speaking. "Let's go," he said with quiet authority.

They ran out behind him, Mark included. No one invited him along, but when they piled into the bench seat of the truck Carly found herself sitting between the two men. Joe gunned the engine and they were off, barreling along the dusty road as though it were a racetrack.

"What exactly did they say?" Joe asked as they sped along.

"The woman was sort of incoherent at first. Jeremy seems to be on the roof of the school. She didn't say how he got there. They're afraid he'll fall or something."

"Have they got the paramedics there? The fire department?"

"I'm sure they've called everyone. Let's just get there in one piece, okay?"

The school loomed before them. The paramedics were there, all right. And so were three fire trucks and four squad cars. The three of them jumped out of the truck and ran toward where the crowd was gathering. Carly hardly dared to look up, and when she did, she gasped and felt as though she were about to faint. There was Jeremy, sitting on the edge of the high, flat roof of the two-story building. He looked very small, very young and very vulnerable.

Her heart flip-flopped in her chest and she closed her eyes for a moment. "Oh God," she began to pray. "Please, God..."

"How did he get up there?" Joe was demanding to know. "What happened?"

The principal fluttered nervously. "He climbed up there on his own. The children were at recess, and Mrs. Emind noticed he was missing when they came back in. We instituted a search, and there he was."

Joe shaded his eyes, looking up. "Has he said anything?"

"No. Nothing. The police have tried to get him to talk, but so far..."

Joe looked around for Carly. Grabbing her hand, he looked into her eyes. "Ready?" he asked her.

She nodded. She was ready for anything he wanted to try.

Moving too quickly to be challenged, Joe started through the crowd with Carly in tow. He walked right through the police lines. No one said a word. They got into the building and ran for the stairs, taking them two at a time. Guessing at which room they wanted, they tried three before they found the right one—the one that had a window facing right where Jeremy sat. They ran inside and shoved open the window.

"Jeremy!" Joe called to him. "We're here, kiddo. Why don't you get on down from there now?"

Jeremy looked at his father and shook his head. From where she was standing, Carly could see the tendons in Joe's neck tighten.

"What is it?" Joe asked Jeremy. "What are you upset about?"

He shook his head again, not speaking.

"Can you tell me why you're doing this?"

Jeremy just stared.

"You've got to put your face where he can read your lips," Carly urged Joe.

"What?" He looked at her as though she were crazy.

"Do it, Joe. I swear to you, he can't hear very well sometimes."

"Carly, not now..."

There was no time to argue. She squeezed out next to Joe, making sure her face was fully visible to the boy.

"Jeremy, hi. I'm here too. What's the matter, honey?"

Jeremy looked up and stared at her.

"Can you tell us what it is, darling?"

He stared longer, then finally spoke. "Is Carly staying for my birthday?"

Joe turned and looked at her. She stared back. What could she say? The birthday. It was still about a month away, if she remembered right. And Joe had been acting like he wanted her out by nightfall.

"We can't lie to him," she said urgently to Joe, plucking at his shirtsleeve. "That would only make things worse farther down the road."

He nodded, but his gaze kept flickering back out the window. "What do you say, Carly?" he asked, desperation just below the cool tone of his voice. "Think you could stand to stay with us a while longer?"

"Oh, Joe." She stared at him. What a question. Did he have any idea what he was asking of her?

"Of course. I'll stay as long as Jeremy needs me. Tell him..." She blinked and started for the window. "I'll tell him—"

"No." He held her back. "I'm going out there. I want to tell him in a way he'll believe it. No more chances."

She nodded, backing away. "Yes. Of course. Only…Joe…" She touched him, her hand to his cheek. "Please be careful," she whispered.

He kissed her quick and hard and turned, swinging up onto the window ledge. "Hey, Jeremy!" he called out. "You got room for two people up there?"

She watched him disappear, her heart in her throat, and then she went to the window and watched him inch his way nearer to Jeremy. The boy began to move away. Carly gasped, her hand to her mouth. But Joe said something to him and he stopped. Joe came to rest a few feet away from Jeremy, and he began to talk. They were too far away for Carly to hear what he was saying. But after a few minutes of restlessness, Jeremy began to watch him closely.

He's reading his lips, she thought. "Oh Jeremy, Jeremy."

It seemed like forever. At times she thought she couldn't stand it any longer. But finally, Jeremy was moving toward Joe, and Joe's arms were around the boy, and the two of them were making their way back toward the window Jeremy had originally climbed out of.

Carly could almost breathe again. She raced downstairs. She had to be there when they arrived, safe and sound.

The principal, the teachers, Beth and Mark, everyone gathered around her, hungry for news.

"They're coming down," she cried, laughing and crying at the same time. "They should be down any second."

And then, there they were. Joe came out through the doorway with Jeremy in his arms and Carly and Beth flew to them.

"Oh, Jeremy, are you all right? We love you, baby. Oh, Joe!"

Arms, faces and tears blended into a mass of confused relief and affection. The four of them hugged, a tiny knot of family against a cold, cruel world.

Watching, Mark Cameron shook his head, a rueful smile on his face. Like any good politician, he knew when the votes were in. Today, he was the loser. But there would always be another day.

"Are you staying?" Jeremy looked earnestly into her face, needing confirmation.

She smiled and hugged him close. "Yes, Jeremy. I'm staying. For a long, long time."

His face relaxed. "I didn't know," he said softly, just to her. "When you and Daddy were yelling, I couldn't tell what the words were..."

Carly looked up at Joe. He'd heard it, too. She stepped back while Jeremy was getting his books from his teacher. He and Beth were going home for the day. When attention was focused elsewhere, Carly made her case to Joe.

"I'm taking him for testing," she announced firmly. "I don't care what you say, Joe. If he can be helped—"

His arm came around her shoulders. "Calm down," he said dryly. "I agree with you. We'll take him together."

The sense of relief in having him on her side was incalculable.

"Let's go home," Joe said. His gaze found Carly's, even as he held his son in his arms. "You ready?"

She nodded, her heart full with happiness for Jeremy's safety and a sense of wonder at being included as part of the family, if only for a little while.

They climbed into the truck and were rolling toward the highway when Carly remembered something.

"Wait! We forgot Mark."

Joe looked at her over the heads of his children. "Don't worry about Mark. I'll go back for him after I get you home."

There was something about his diabolical grin....

"What are you going to do with him?" she asked suspiciously.

"Take him back into town. Hell, I might drive him all the way to the airport, if that will get him out of here faster."

His eyes met hers again and despite herself, she laughed.

They got the children home and settled, and when they had a moment alone, Joe pulled her behind the kitchen door and kissed her soundly, his hands spreading across her back as though he could capture all of her and hold her there.

Drawing back, he looked down and searched her eyes. "You don't mind staying awhile longer, do you?" he asked.

"I told you, Joe. I'll stay as long as Jeremy needs me." *And as long as you need me.* Couldn't he see that yet? Didn't he understand?

But no, it really seemed that he didn't. They went on with their day and every time they spoke, she realized more and more that he assumed she would be leaving as soon as she could—in fact, that she could hardly wait to get out of there.

"Joe," she said at one point, "haven't you caught on yet? I like it on your citrus ranch. In fact, I love it here."

He nodded as though he'd heard that one before, but he looked at her oddly, as though it had finally occurred to him that she might be serious.

Later that evening, when the kids were in bed and Phyllis had finished ranting on about how no one ever told her anything and why had they left her in the dark when her own grandson was stranded on a rooftop, his life hanging in the balance, Carly and Joe sat together on the couch and tried to unwind from their hectic day.

"I should have listened to you about Jeremy," he told her, looking down the couch at where she sat, just out of reach.

"We'll find out if I was right or wrong when we take him to the specialist."

He nodded. "I guess it sometimes takes an outsider to see what's wrong."

She stiffened. An outsider. Was that what she still was? An outsider, like Ellen had been. When was he going to face the fact that she wasn't Ellen?

The telephone rang before she had a chance to protest. She sat staring at the wallpaper while he answered it, talking in low, urgent tones. She couldn't make out the words, but she knew something was going on. There was always something. One thing about this place, she never got bored here.

Joe put down the telephone and came back into the room, frowning.

"That was Jake. Trevor didn't show up for avocado-grove patrol. I'm going to have to go take his place." He grabbed his jacket and started toward the door. "I don't know what's got into Trevor lately. He's screwing up all over the place. If you hear from that kid, tell him I'm this close to firing his ass and getting somebody to replace him. You tell him that." He disappeared out the door with a bang.

"Sure," Carly murmured after him. "That'll be the day." She grinned, but her grin faded. It was disturbing that there was something wrong with Trevor.

It was almost an hour later that she heard a car in the drive and found Millie at her door.

"Carly." Millie's eyes looked puffy and red. "Where's Joe?"

"Gone. The question is, where's Trevor? Joe had to go cover for him on avocado patrol."

"Oh." Millie put a hand to her face, her expression harried. "I forgot all about that. And we were out in the corral, so we couldn't hear the phone..."

"Millie, what is it?" Carly took her by the shoulders and led her to a chair, concerned. The woman looked like death. "Let me get you some tea."

"No." Millie sat but she held Carly's hand and wouldn't let her go. "I don't know what to do, Carly. I told him the truth. Everything. He...he..." Her eyes filled with tears and her voice choked. "He hates me now."

"Oh no, Millie." Carly reached down and gave her a shoulder to lean on. "He doesn't hate you. He's just upset—"

"He's leaving. He's packing a bag right now." She started to get up, distraught. "I've got to find Joe. Maybe he can talk to him—"

"Sit down, Millie. You've got to get hold of yourself. I don't know exactly where Joe went. You could ride around for hours looking for him." She turned toward the door, reaching for her keys. "I'll go. I'll talk to him."

"You?" Millie looked confused. "But you're—"

She came back and took Millie's hand, looking down at her earnestly. "I'm the perfect one, Millie. In a lot of ways, he and I are in the same boat. And I've already worked through a lot of my anger. I can talk to him." She went to the door and looked back. "You stay here with Beth and Jeremy. I'll be back as soon as I can."

It took only moments to get to the house. Turning off the engine, she ran right in without knocking. Trevor was on the stairs, his bag in his hand.

He saw her and raised his hand, pointing at her like a curse. "You—stay away from me. You're the one. You're the reason all this came out."

"Where are you going?" she asked him calmly, ignoring the accusations.

"I'm getting out of here. I'm old enough." His eyes were bright with anger, his face twisted with pain. "I can go on the road, find something better—people that don't lie to you."

He came down the stairs, about to brush past her. She reached out and got a grip on his arm.

"Trevor, no," she said firmly. "You've got to stay."

He looked at her hand on his arm, then into her eyes. "Why? Why should I stay? Joe's not my father. There's nothing to keep me here."

She shook her head. "You have Millie. She's your mother."

"Yeah? She's been my mother for seventeen years. I guess that's long enough. I'm out of here."

He broke free of her grip and started for the front door with her coming right behind him.

"Trevor, you're all she has," she called out to him. "You can't do this to her."

He whirled and faced her. "Why not? I didn't ask to be born. I especially didn't ask to be born a bastard. I especially didn't ask to have to grow up without a father. I don't owe her a damn thing." He turned toward the door again.

"Trevor," she said softly, appealing to him. "You may be all she has, but right now, she's all you have, too."

He froze, his back to her. "That's what you think," he said, but he didn't keep going.

"What are you going to do, go grab your girlfriend and go running off into the sunset like Bonnie and Clyde?"

"Maybe."

She caught up with him and turned him so that he would have to look in her face. "Oh Trevor. Don't you see? This isn't the end of something. It's the beginning."

His face was so full of hurt. But she knew exactly how he felt. She'd felt the same way only a day or so before.

"It's definitely the beginning of something for you and me," she explained to him, gently touching his arm. "We're brother and sister."

His eyes widened. Obviously, he hadn't thought of it in those terms.

"I never had a brother before, Trevor. And you never had a sister. How can you leave now, before we've had a chance to sort through what all this means to us?"

His eyes were hooded and resentful. "I didn't ask for this either," he grumbled, but he put his bag down.

She smiled at him. "Hey, neither did I."

Anger contorted his face again. "She did it. She's the one who made the mistake."

"Was having you a mistake?"

"It was for everybody else involved."

"Everybody but her. You've been the light of her life ever since you were born and you know it. How can you treat her this way now when she needs you the most?"

He turned, restless, angry, frustrated because he didn't know what he could do to change things, to make himself feel better.

"She doesn't need me. Why doesn't she go find *him* somewhere? Your father."

She smiled at him. "Our father," she said softly. "Nobody knows where he went, Trevor, and he never knew that you existed, or he surely would have come to see you. You can't blame him for not being there for you when he didn't even know about you."

"She should have told him." He looked young for a moment, like a boy about to cry. "Why didn't she tell him?'' His bright eyes appealed to her for answers, things he needed to know to settle this in his mind.

This was something Millie would have to explain to him as best she could, but for now, Carly could only give him her interpretation of what had happened.

"She was sixteen and sick with shame for what she'd done. She went through hell.'' She shook her head, looking at him. "And now you want her to go through that all over again.''

He let out a long, painful breath and his shoulders sagged.

"Give her another chance, Trevor. Give yourself another chance. Give us a chance.''

He stared into her eyes for a long, long moment. Then he shook his head and started to back toward the door. "I'm going to go see Tracy,'' he told her defiantly.

"Okay. Go see Tracy. But leave your stuff here.''

He left the bag right where it was. She waited, standing in the middle of the living room, and listened to him leave. He revved his hot car and took off in a swirl of dust. But she knew he was coming back. His first burst of anger and hurt was over. He was a strong kid. He could handle it.

CHAPTER EIGHTEEN

THE LONG WHITE HALLS of the hospital echoed with the sounds of steel pans and rubber tires and heels clicking along the tiled floor.

Carly and Joe walked down the hall with Jeremy between them, each holding one of his hands.

"We're going to be with you, Jeremy," Joe promised. Since the episode at the school the week earlier, Joe was being careful to look directly down at him. "We'll stay with you through the whole thing. It won't be like the last time."

They went into Dr. Kenton's office and sat in big heavy chairs facing the doctor's desk.

"So, this is Jeremy, is it?" The doctor shook his hand and smiled at him. "And you suspect he may have a hearing problem?"

"Yes." Joe leaned forward. "We suspected it before, Jeremy's mother and I, and he was tested. But I've recently found out that the testing was done by a health clerk at his school. She did the best she could with the training and equipment she had, but ... we're afraid she might have missed the problem."

Dr. Kenton nodded. "I see. This is not unusual. A bright boy like Jeremy has very little trouble fooling the ordinary tests and an inexperienced tester. And the people he lives with in some cases."

Joe nodded. "I'm afraid we haven't been as vigilant as we might have been," he admitted.

"Well, he's here now, and we'll find out what's what. We have the very latest in methods and equipment here." He smiled at Jeremy. "So we'll take a look in those ears and see what we can see, shall we?"

Jeremy leaned toward Carly. "Will it hurt?" he asked softly, his eyes huge.

"Hurt?" The doctor had overheard him. "Good heavens, no."

Carly smiled in relief. "We did promise that we would stay with him the entire time. He had rather a bad experience with the last testing."

The doctor waved a hand in the air. "No problem. Shall we begin?" He rose and ushered them from his office into the examining room.

An hour later they were back in the office, sitting just as they had sat before. Dr. Kenton cleared his throat and shuffled papers before looking across his desk and smiling.

"From the preliminary tests, I think I can state with some confidence that Jeremy does indeed have damage to his hearing."

Carly found Jeremy's hand curling into hers and she held it very tightly and reached over to pull him closer.

"Tell us the truth, Doctor," Joe said. "Don't hold back. We want to know everything so we will know what we can do to deal with it."

He nodded and took off his glasses. "There are obstructions in the middle-ear canals in both of Jeremy's ears. This looks like a congenital defect to me, though further tests may prove me wrong. I'm sure this has caused him much trouble hearing. Although his hearing isn't totally gone, evidence suggests that it varies according to the time of day, the temperature, his mood, etcetera.''

"Yes," said Carly, nodding. "That was what it seemed like to me."

Joe shrugged and put out his hands, palms up. "What can we do?"

Dr. Kenton leaned forward. "There is a delicate surgical operation that may help restore his hearing to seventy-five or eighty percent of normal. There is some risk involved. I'll go over the details with you at our next meeting, when we have all the results in and can talk more confidently. For now, let me just say I think we can do something to help Jeremy. In fact, I'm sure of it."

Carly hugged Jeremy to her, looking over his head into Joe's eyes. They smiled at one another, and Jeremy's arms came around her neck. Tears threatened. She had to blink fast.

"Thank you, Doctor," she said shakily. "Thank you very much."

SURGERY WAS SCHEDULED for the week after Jeremy's birthday. Carly knew she would be staying at least that long. But staying for what? Sometimes she wondered. There were days when Joe was the lover most women could only dream of—gentle, kind, loving and passionate. And then there were days when his eyes were distant and he answered questions with grunts or shrugs. When he was like that, she had no idea what he was thinking.

She loved him with a depth and a conviction that she hadn't known was possible. There were times when she was sure he loved her too, though he never said it in so many words. The strange thing was, though she was closer than ever to the children, Joe seemed to be receding from her more and more some days.

He brought in his avocado crop with no real problems and it did beautifully on the market. He was gone for a few days, setting up the sales, and when he came back, he seemed distracted. She began to notice frequent absences. She couldn't understand it. They were so happy together when they were together. But so often he was gone, and he didn't seem to have any good explanation for where he had been or what he was doing. Where was he going?

She had no idea. But now and then she would catch him looking at her with a strange, questioning look. If he would just go ahead and ask her the question that was bothering him, she would have tried her damnedest to answer it. But he never came right out and said what he had to say.

As Jeremy's birthday moved closer, a feeling of dread began to build in the pit of her stomach. How much longer could she stay? How much longer would he want her?

JOE WAS CLEANING OUT his closet. He pulled each one of Ellen's dresses off its hanger and stuffed it unceremoniously into a big plastic bag. The Goodwill had been called. These last remnants of Ellen and her reign of terror were about to be tossed out on their collective ear.

Once these rags were gone there would be very little left to remind him of Ellen. When you came right down to it, she hadn't exactly put her stamp on this place, or their lives in it.

He turned and looked at the big double bed where Carly often met him late at night when they were sure the children were asleep. Things happened in that bed now that he had never dreamt of when Ellen was sharing it with him. Having Carly made him feel whole again. She'd changed his life.

But if she left... The thought brought on pains in his chest so severe that he sometimes wondered if he were having a heart attack. He couldn't lose her. She couldn't leave.

She was proving to him by the day that she wasn't like Ellen, that she could stick it out here. In fact, she claimed she loved this life, and he almost believed her. If only he could just let go of that last bit of distrust.

He wanted to tell her that he loved her, but every time he got ready to say the words, they stuck in his throat. He couldn't just tell her. Words meant nothing. Ellen had taught him that. Words were cheap. He had to do something to prove it to her, to show her—to make him worthy of having her stay. He'd made a bargain with himself. If he couldn't do it, he wouldn't ask her. It was as simple as that.

CHAPTER NINETEEN

"OKAY, HERE'S THE DEAL," Millie announced as she barged into the kitchen, her arms full of a beautifully decorated sheet cake. "This is the third cake I've baked for this boy. I am not baking another one, no matter what happens to it."

Carly helped her put it down on the kitchen table. "What happened to the others?" she asked.

"The first one I set down on the kitchen counter to cool. Before I'd even iced it, Trevor's pet raccoon found it. Little paw prints everywhere. You should have seen my kitchen." She shook her head in sad remembrance.

"I went right to the store and bought more eggs and flour, went home and started on another one. This time I locked up the raccoon. I frosted the whole thing, wrote 'Happy Birthday' and everything, and was carrying it out to the car about ten this morning to bring it over. I had to put it down on the ground while I cleared some stuff off the back seat, where I was going to carry it. And Skippy, that damn horse, backed right into it. Squashed it flat."

"Oh no!"

"You wouldn't believe what it looked like! I left it right there in the middle of the driveway and went back into the house and started again. But Carly..." She gripped her arm. "This is it. There won't be any-more."

Carly laughed and turned to help Trevor who was bringing presents in from the car. She loved to watch him, the way he walked, the way he talked, the way he flipped his hair back off his face. He was a part of her in a way no other human being would ever be. She found him utterly fascinating.

He'd calmed down a lot, though there were still times when he was moody and she was sure the roots of the emotion lay with the new things he had learned about his mother and father.

"I want to find our dad," he'd told her one day. "I don't know where to start looking, though. Do you have any ideas?"

Carly had recoiled from the very thought. "I don't want to find him," she'd told her brother. "I figure if he wanted to find me, he would have done it by now. And after all I've learned about him, I'm not sure he would be someone I would want to know."

She could see that he wasn't convinced, and she didn't try to argue any further. After all, she of all people should know that you had to do what you had to do about your background. If he had to search, he would.

Millie was outside stringing Chinese lanterns and balloons. Carly smiled. The two of them were almost back on the friendly footing they had enjoyed from the first. There were things Carly would probably never understand. But she wasn't about to let them stand in the way of a friendship with her brother's mother.

"CARLY, DEAR, could you please get this necklace? The clasp is too delicate for these old fingers."

Carly turned obligingly. She was "dear" to Phyllis these days. She suspected it was more a case of "if you can't beat them . . ." than anything else, but she appreciated it. As long as she was here in this house, she knew there would always be something of a tug-of-war between her and Phyllis for Joe's attention. But the animosity was gone. And that was a relief.

"Beth is going to sing," Phyllis told her confidentially once her clasp had been fastened. "It's a surprise she and I cooked up. A little program."

Carly held back a full expression of her gratified response. This was just what she had been hoping for, that Phyllis would give Beth the benefit of her experience. "Great," she said, forcing herself to answer casually. "She's got such a good voice."

"Of course," Phyllis replied. "She has my blood in her veins."

Funny how Phyllis could turn good feelings around in an instant. But Carly didn't care. Beth was happy, and that was all that was important.

"We're about to start," Millie called in. "Where's Joe anyway?"

Where was Joe? Carly frowned and looked toward the driveway again, wondering that very thing. He'd gone out mysteriously the night before, but he'd promised to be back in time for Jeremy's party.

Jeremy and what seemed like a couple hundred friends were shrieking and dashing through the yard, making sorties past Beth and Sunny who disdained them with all their might. They were ready for games and ice cream and cake and the opening of the presents. But nothing could begin until Joe got home.

She sighed and walked out into the front yard, looking at the flowers. There were rows and rows of them now. The yard looked quite presentable. And there was a painter hired to begin doing the house next week. Things were changing. Things were getting better.

All except her relationship with Joe. They seemed so near—and yet so far. She loved him so. What was she going to do if it all fell to ashes?

The sound of wheels on gravel brought her head up. Joe's car was barreling up the drive. She watched it come with her hands on her hips, ready to read him the riot act for this crazy performance.

But there was someone in the car with him, so she knew she was going to have to hold back most of her choicer comments until they were alone. The car came to a stop and Joe got out. He smiled at her, then said something to the man in the passenger's seat. The passenger door opened and a tall, distinguished-looking gentleman with silver hair got out. But he didn't come toward her. He stood very still, staring at her, and slowly, she began to realize who this was.

Her hands went up and covered her mouth and she stood as though she were frozen, staring at him. He finally left the protection of the car and walked closer, stopping before her.

"Hello, Carly," he said in a rich, low voice that triggered a thousand memories from her past. "How are you?"

She looked at him with wonder—his eyes, his ears, the square cut of his fingers, it was all so familiar. And yet it had been so very long since she'd seen him. But there it was—the quirky smile... Trevor had a smile just like that. The way his eyes squinted a little just before he said something—she did that herself. Friends were always commenting on it.

No matter how much she wanted to hate this man, she couldn't do it.

"Daddy?" she asked softly, her voice trembling, her eyes filling with tears. "Daddy? Is it you?"

His arms came around her and she closed her eyes waiting for heaven to envelop her. How many times had she dreamed of seeing him like this? She'd wanted her daddy's arms around her, protecting her, loving her. She needed it. Oh, how she needed it.

Great, wracking sobs shook her, and she wasn't sure why. She was happy. Why was she crying like this? But cry she did, on and on, with the one man in the world who knew how to give her the comfort a little girl needed patting her, holding her, giving her all he had.

"Oh, Daddy." It was all she could say.

He was crying too. When she finally drew back she could see the wetness on his face, and that made her laugh through her own tears.

"Carly, honey, I never thought I would be able to see you again."

"Why didn't you ever try to find me?" she asked, feeling like a little girl, but needing an answer.

His blue eyes clouded. "I didn't have the right, Carly. After what I did to you and your mother. I moved out to Cambria and started a little newspaper. That's where I've been living ever since, helping run a local church and putting out a hometown newspaper."

She wiped her eyes. "You never remarried?"

He shook his head. "There were things that happened when I lived here that I couldn't put out of my mind, Carly. I wasn't able to work through them well enough to leave them behind. They still haunt me."

She nodded. She liked him. She understood him. "Millie is here," she told him.

His face clouded. "She won't want to see me. I have no right to make her see me. I'll go soon. I don't want to bring back painful memories. But I would like to see..." His voice trailed off and he looked at Carly expectantly.

"Did Joe tell you about... Trevor?" she asked.

His eyes seemed to shine. "Yes, he did. Is the boy here right now?"

She nodded.

"I'd like to see him. You don't have to tell him who I am. I'm pretty sure his mother would just as soon he didn't know. But if I could just see him..." He touched Carly's cheek, his eyes soft with unshed tears, his voice breaking. "That, along with seeing you, would surely make me a happy man. Happier than I deserve to be."

She shivered. She did like him. There was no point in trying to fight it. "Come along," she told him, leading him to the corner of the house, facing the backyard. "There he is, playing catch with that little boy. Why don't you go on in and say hi?"

He started walking casually toward Trevor and Joe came up beside Carly, putting an arm around her shoulders and drawing her near. "Did I do good?" he asked softly.

Her smile was joyful as she turned to him. "You did good. But how did you find him?"

He shook his head with a rueful grin. "My mother actually found him for me. You know her and all her contacts."

"Phyllis? But...does that mean she's finally accepted that you and Millie will never marry?"

"I couldn't venture a guess. But she did help me. I got his address and tried to call him, but he didn't respond. So I took a few trips over to the coast to visit with him." He sighed. "It took long enough to talk him into coming."

"Why did he hesitate?"

Joe shrugged. "He didn't think you would be able to forgive him, and he didn't really know if you should."

"I do," she said promptly, surprised herself, but glowing. "He can forget all this guilt. We'll start over again. I've got my father back, and that's all I care about."

Joe nodded. "I told him you would feel that way. But he was...afraid, I guess you could say."

She nodded, watching her father as he moved slowly across the yard, taking in every detail. "He doesn't want to see Millie?"

"No. He was adamant about that. He says she deserves to live her life without having to think about him ever again. He thinks she won't want to see him anyway. What do you think?"

Carly shrugged. "I don't know. In some ways, I think she would just as soon never see him again. There's just too much she's kept secret for too long. But Trevor is another story...look."

They watched as Trevor spoke to Howard, friendly at first, then suspicious. He turned and looked at Carly's face, then looked at the tall man again, and realization broke across his expression like the sun clearing away a cloudy day. Howard put out a hand, and Trevor stared at it. Slowly, hesitantly, he accepted it with his own, then looked up into Howard's eyes, wary, but somehow eager. Carly felt tears stinging, threatening again.

A startled gasp drew the attention of everyone within earshot. Carly turned and saw Millie, standing on the porch, her face as white as a sheet.

She was going to run. Carly could see it in her face. She looked quickly at Howard. He'd seen it, too, and since he'd said he didn't want to face her, Carly was afraid he would turn back toward the car. She took a step forward, ready to try and stop him. But she needn't have bothered.

Seeing Millie seemed to give Howard a surge of youthful power he hadn't exhibited up to that moment. As Millie turned to escape back into the house, Howard strode quickly toward the porch, taking the steps in two bounds, and stopped her, hands on her shoulders. "Millie," he said. "Millie, I'm sorry. I didn't want to hurt you again. But I just had to see Carly, and see . . . him . . ."

She stared up at him, her face mirroring her distress.

"Millie," he said brokenly, his hands sliding down her arms as he began to back away. "Oh Millie, you're so beautiful, just like you look in my dreams."

His hands fell away from her and they stared at one another for a long moment.

"I'll go," he said softly. "I'm sorry. I'll get out of here, and I won't bother you again."

He turned blindly, lurching away, but Millie reached out, moving like a sleepwalker, and took hold of his arm.

"Don't go," she whispered, her eyes full of tears.

He turned and looked down at her, his expression becoming reluctantly hopeful. "Do you mean it?"

She nodded, tears streaming down her cheeks. "Don't leave me again, Howard," she sobbed, and then she was in his arms, and they were both crying.

Carly reached for Joe. His arms came around her and held her tightly. She looked at Trevor, barely making him out through the dampness in her eyes. But she could see that he was grinning. It was going to be all right. They were all going to be all right.

Millie pulled away from Howard, called to Trevor, and the three of them disappeared into the house. Carly sighed and tilted her head back, looking into Joe's face.

"Why did you do this?" she asked softly.

His arms tightened around her. "Because I love you, pretty lady, and I wanted to do something to prove it."

She searched his face. "You really love me?" she asked breathlessly. "You're not just saying that?"

"I don't just say things like that," he reminded her, stroking her hair. "I love you, Carly Stevens. And I want to marry you."

He kissed her softly on the lips.

She laughed low in her throat, raising her arms to envelop him. "And all this time I thought you were just waiting for me to get on out of here," she teased, her eyes shining with love for him.

"Don't be crazy," he said softly, between kisses. "I needed a miracle, and you dropped into my lap. I'd be a fool to let you go."

"Ah, I see." She turned her head a little so his kisses could proceed down her neck. Her eyes were half-closed with pleasure. "You realized you were going to have to start giving me a salary if I stayed around any longer. Is that it? And you thought it would be cheaper to get married."

He drew back and laughed at her. "Believe me, dar-lin', it's never cheaper to get married." His eyes sobered, darkening. "But it's going to be better," he told her softly, taking her face between his hands. "Oh God, Carly, this is going to be so much better."

She nodded, biting her lower lip, her eyes full of tears. She knew it, too. Nothing could stop them now. But she was just too full of emotion to say so.

EPILOGUE

"SHH." Beth put her finger to her lips and motioned to her brother. "Quiet. They'll hear us."

Jeremy nodded and slunk in behind her as she led the way to the doorway at the end of the hall. Beth reached for the doorknob and slowly opened it. They scampered inside.

The room was dark, the shade drawn, but they could make out a crib on the other side of the room.

"Shh," Beth said again, unnecessarily. "He's asleep."

They tiptoed up to the edge of the baby bed and looked over the side at the infant sleeping on a little blue mattress inside it. His black hair was stiff as straw, his tiny little nose a round button in the middle of his little red face. The legs gave a feeble kick and his arms waved for a moment, but the eyes didn't open.

"Happy birthday, Stephen Jacob Matthews," Beth whispered, gazing down at her precious little brother.

"How can it be his birthday, he just got borned," Jeremy protested sensibly.

"It's his one-week birthday."

Jeremy made a face. "That's dumb."

"It's not dumb. I have a one-week birthday present for him."

"What is it?" Jeremy asked suspiciously.

She reached into the pocket of her dress and pulled out a crushed carnation. "It's a flower."

Jeremy made a sound of disgust. "Boys don't want flowers," he informed his ignorant sister.

"Stephen Jacob Matthews likes flowers," Beth corrected him primly. She laid it down on the table beside his little bed.

"Better not put it where he can get it or Carly will get really mad."

"Carly doesn't get mad at me," Beth one-upped him. "She gets mad at you when you do bad things or forget your chores. But I always do the right thing."

Jeremy didn't bother to contradict that. "Carly will get mad if you touch her baby."

Beth turned her nose in the air and reached down to put a finger on the tiny hand. "This is *our* baby," she told him. "I can touch him if I want."

Jeremy frowned, looking down at the monkeylike figure. "Carly is his mom, right?"

"Right," Beth agreed.

His brow furrowed even further. "Then, is he going to call her Carly, like we do?"

"Of course not, silly. He's going to call her Mom."

"Oh." This was a concept that he was having trouble with.

"That doesn't mean she will love him any better than she loves us," Beth informed him.

He gave her a glance of pure disgust. "I know that."

"She loves us just as much. But we already have a mom, even though she's far away and doesn't want us."

"I don't care about that mom," Jeremy said.

A tremendous crash from the yard sent them flying to the window. Pushing aside the shade, they looked down.

"Look," Beth said, excitement lighting her eyes. "They're starting."

The yard had been converted into a wonderland of flowers and lanterns and ribbons everywhere. Baskets of pansies lined the fence. Sprays of lemon branches filled the air with sweet scent. White lace covered small tables and a huge wedding cake sat in the center of the main table.

"Look," Beth said, pointing down. "There's Carly's dad."

Jeremy looked, frowning again. "What are we going to call *him?*"

"Carly said we could start to call him Grandpa, if we want."

Jeremy nodded solemnly. "But today he's gonna marry Millie. So, are we supposed to call her Grandma?"

Beth sighed with exasperation. "No. Millie's Millie. Besides, we already have a Grandma. Phyllis Matthews is our Grandma. There she is, by the fountain." She smiled. "She's leaving for Florida tomorrow. On an airplane."

Jeremy shrugged. Phyllis was always leaving on airplanes these days. He didn't pay much attention.

"There's Doris, Carly's cousin. Carly told me she's the one who got her and Daddy together. Did you know that?"

Jeremy didn't know, and neither did he care. But he did like Brian, Doris's husband. "Brian has a coo car," he told Beth. "He said he would take me for a ride sometime."

Beth rolled her eyes. "In your dreams," she muttered, still searching the growing crowd for familiar faces. "There's Trevor and his new girlfriend."

Jeremy perked up. "The one with the sexy clothes?" he said straining to look down again. But all he could see was the awning stretched over the main seating for the ceremony. "How come there are so many chairs?"

"Lots and lots of people are invited to this wedding. People from all over the place."

Jeremy stirred, getting restless. "It wasn't like this when Carly married Dad."

"I know. Then it was just you and me and Carly and Daddy and Millie and Trevor and Grandma and Mr. Stevens."

"I thought you said we're supposed to call him Grandpa now."

Beth gave him a look. "I forgot."

Jeremy looked back down at the preparations. "I liked that wedding better," he said softly, almost to himself.

"Oh, no. This is going to be the most beautiful wedding." Her eyes took on a dreamy quality. "But mine is going to be even better."

A sound from the hallway brought both their heads around. "Come on," Beth whispered. "We better get out of here."

She slipped out into the hallway, but Jeremy went by the crib for one last look at his new brother. The baby moved, scrunching up its little face, and Jeremy laughed.

"Hey little buddy," he whispered. "I'm going to be your friend. I'm going to teach you how to sail boats in the irrigation canals and where the best rabbits are hiding on Stouter Hill and where Grandma hides her candy and what to do if a rattlesnake tries to getcha'." He grinned, thinking of happy days ahead. "Stick with me Stevie. I'll take care of ya'."

Sliding back down, he slipped out, too, and took the stairs on a run that launched him out the door and into the crowd. He searched through a forest of long legs and billowing skirts, trying to find some sign of Carly or his dad. No luck out on the driveway or in under the awning, although he heard, more than once, someone say, "Isn't that the boy? Jeremy isn't it?" He just ignored it and went on. He paused to look at the wedding cake. It was very tall. Would anyone notice if he just tasted the icing? Just a little dab, right here, behind the...

"Jeremy! You get away from there."

Oops. Oh well, there would be time for that later when everyone had their attention on the bride and groom. He went into the house, walking right into the kitchen. It was full of strangers, ladies with aprons, fixing food. The food smelled good, but the ladies didn't look friendly. He went on through.

Where were Carly and Dad? He looked in the living room, the den, the dining room, then went back upstairs. He heard voices. They were in their bedroom.

"Don't forget to knock, Jeremy." Carly was always saying that. But Jeremy forgot. He pushed open the door and there they were, standing at the foot of the bed, in each other's arms. His dad was holding Carly real tight and she had her head back, like they did in the movies.

"*How* many more weeks?" Joe was saying, aghast.

Carly was laughing, but she saw Jeremy and shushed Joe.

"Here's our *big* boy," she said, disentangling herself from Joe's embrace. "Hello, sweetie." She bent down to align his tie. "You look so handsome in your suit."

He straightened his shoulders, proud to please her.

She tousled his hair and rose. "I'm going to check on the baby," she said. "You can stay here and help your dad pick a tie for himself. Okay?"

Jeremy nodded solemnly, watching her leave in a whirl of cool silk. As soon as she was out of sight, he turned and tugged on his father's pant leg.

"Dad, what are we going to call the baby?"

"Hmm?" Joe set out a stack of ties and began to go through them. "I don't know. Steve I guess."

"I want to call him Stevie."

"Okay, big guy. You can call him what you want. He's your brother."

He looked down at the carpet and kicked his foot against it. "What are we going to call Mr. Stevens now?"

Joe pulled out a bright red tie, looked it over critically, and shook his head. "I don't know. Oh, I suppose you could call him Grandpa if you want. Why don't you talk it over with him?"

"But Millie is still Millie?"

"Yes." He grinned for a moment, thinking of how she would respond to Grandma. "Yes, Millie is definitely still Millie."

He nodded. "So...what is Stevie going to call Carly?"

Joe stopped and looked at him, beginning to get where this was headed. "Mommy. She's his mommy."

Jeremy was silent for a long moment, and when he spoke again, his lower lip was trembling. "But I knew her first," he said.

"Jeremy." Reaching out, he took the little boy into his arms and sat down on the bed. "Jeremy, you already have another mom."

Jeremy was fighting hard against tears. "But she's not like a real mom."

Joe's heart ached. "I know, Jeremy. You never see her. She's...sort of in another world. But legally, biologically, she's your mother."

Jeremy looked up into his father's face, every bit of his soul in his huge eyes. "She's my mother. But she's not a mom. Carly is my mom." He blinked rapidly, trying to get his point across. "I could call that mother my mother. And I could call Carly my mom. Okay?"

Joe stared at him. "Gee, Jeremy, I don't know...." A grin began to develop along the lines of his wide mouth.

"What would Carly say?" Jeremy asked anxiously.

"What would Carly say?" He laughed softly, leaning down to kiss his son's head. He thought he knew her well enough to have a pretty good idea of what Carly would say. "Come on," he said to his son, getting up and swinging the boy to the floor before taking his hand. "Let's go find out."

They went into the hall and started into the baby's room. Carly had the baby in her arms and she turned, smiling, to greet them.

"Hey, Carly," Joe sang out as they entered the room. "Have you got a minute?" He grinned and gave his oldest son a wink. "I think I've got a present for you."

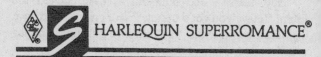

HARLEQUIN SUPERROMANCE®

COMING NEXT MONTH

#546 AFTER THE PROMISE • Debbi Bedford
Despite all his knowledge and training, Dr. Michael Stratton could
only stand by helplessly as his small son, Cody, battled for his life.
But something good might come of this—Cody's illness had
thrown Michael and his ex-wife, Jennie, together. While others
worked to heal his child, Michael could heal his marriage.

#547 SHENANIGANS • Casey Roberts
Paul Sherwood was a man with a mission: to take over ailing
cosmetics giant Cheri Lee. Lauren Afton was a woman with a
goal: to save her mother's self-made empire. Lauren knew she was
a match for Paul in the boardroom, and she had a sneaking
suspicion they'd also be a pretty good match in the bedroom....

#548 THE MODEL BRIDE • Pamela Bauer
Model Jessie Paulson had been on the jury that convicted
Aidan McCullough's father of murder, yet now the verdict was
beginning to haunt her. Aidan, too, was haunted by his father's
conviction. Not only had it uncovered a past best left buried, it
was standing in the way of his future with Jessie.

#549 PARADOX • Lynn Erickson
Women Who Dare, Book 5
Emily got more than she bargained for when she decided to start a
new life in Seattle. Her train crashed and she woke up to find
herself in the year 1893, at the home of rancher Will Dutcher.
Trapped in time, Emily had to discover a way to return home. But
how could she abandon the man she loved?

AVAILABLE THIS MONTH:

#542 WORTH THE WAIT
Risa Kirk

#543 BUILT TO LAST
Leigh Roberts

#544 JOE'S MIRACLE
Helen Conrad

#545 SNAP JUDGEMENT
Sandra Canfield

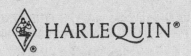

THE TAGGARTS OF TEXAS!

Harlequin's Ruth Jean Dale brings you
THE TAGGARTS OF TEXAS!

Those Taggart men—strong, sexy and hard to resist...

You've met Jesse James Taggart in FIREWORKS!
Harlequin Romance #3205 (July 1992)

And Trey Smith—he's THE RED-BLOODED YANKEE!
Harlequin Temptation #413 (October 1992)

And the unforgettable Daniel Boone Taggart in SHOWDOWN!
Harlequin Romance #3242 (January 1993)

Now meet Boone Smith and the Taggarts who started it all—
in LEGEND!
Harlequin Historical #168 (April 1993)

Read all the Taggart romances!
Meet all the Taggart men!

Available wherever Harlequin Books are sold.

Following the success of WITH THIS RING and
TO HAVE AND TO HOLD, Harlequin brings you

JUST MARRIED

SANDRA CANFIELD
MURIEL JENSEN
ELISE TITLE
REBECCA WINTERS

just in time for the 1993 wedding season!

Written by four of Harlequin's most popular authors, this
four-story collection celebrates the joy, excitement and
adjustment that comes with being "just married."

You won't want to miss this spring tradition, whether
you're just married or not!

**AVAILABLE IN APRIL WHEREVER HARLEQUIN
BOOKS ARE SOLD**

JM93